Unearthing the Past

by

W. L. Brooks

The McKay Series, Book 3

Unearthing the Past

Cover Art by *The Wild Rose Press, Inc.*

The Wild Rose Press, Inc.
PO Box 708
Adams Basin, NY 14410-0708
Visit us at www.thewildrosepress.com

Publishing History
First Crimson Rose Edition, 2020
Print ISBN 978-1-5092-2953-6
Digital ISBN 978-1-5092-2954-3

The McKay Series, Book 3
Published in the United States of America

Twenty minutes later, she put the finishing touches on her meatloaf. She cranked the timer for another fifteen minutes and went to set the table. She had just put out the forks when she remembered the box. Maybe one of her sisters had sent them something.

Out on the porch, Charlie took a few minutes trying to figure out how to get the thing inside—it weighed a ton. Finally, she decided to open the package right where it was. From the smell, something had gone bad. There was no way she was bringing it inside her house, much less her kitchen. Maybe if she hadn't forgotten about the darn thing, it wouldn't have had a chance to spoil.

"It's freezing out here, so it isn't my fault," she told the box. Shaking her head, Charlie used a paring knife to cut the tape. She opened the flaps, wincing at the stench, and looked inside.

Charlie rushed to the porch railing and emptied her stomach. She closed the box, her hands shaking. It couldn't be! Oh, God.

Dedication

To Emilie Marie:
Thank you for being my shotgun rider, partner in crime,
and best friend for the last twenty years.
"Now I'm real thirsty!"

Chapter One

Someone was in his bedroom.

Craig Sutton feigned sleep, even though the hairs on the back of his neck stood on end. He rolled over, slid one hand beneath his pillow, grasped cold steel, and opened his eyes. He didn't know whether to laugh or curse. Standing on the bed next to him was four-and-a-half-year-old Mackenzie McKay. Her big black eyes were wide and unblinking.

He released his weapon and sat up. "Uh...hi."

"Hi." She twirled one of her white-blonde pigtails.

Craig had come across Mack, the niece of his landlady, on a number of occasions. But... "How'd you get in here, sweetheart?"

She pouted. "I'm allowed."

"Well...I don't think anyone told you, but because I'm staying here, you need to knock first." Craig didn't want to scare her or, God forbid, make her cry. He'd never been able to handle female tears, especially the tiny variety.

She crossed her arms. "Auntie Alex shoulda said."

"I'm sure she meant to...How about you go in the other room while I change, and then I'll take you to find your aunt."

"Ohskay." She jumped down and closed the door behind her.

Craig went to the bathroom, brushed his teeth, and

1

changed his clothes in record time. When he came out, he was surprised to find her sitting at the kitchen table, humming and swinging her legs. Craig shook his head and smiled; the kid was adorable.

"Ready, sweets?"

"Yep!" She hopped off the seat and took Craig's hand.

He shivered the moment he stepped outside; he should have grabbed a jacket. It was freezing, and Mack didn't have a coat on. He swung her up in his arms, she giggled, and his heart warmed.

She pressed her cold nose into the crook of his neck. "Grandpops does that too."

"He's a nice guy then."

"Uh-huh. You smell pretty. Kinda like my Uncle Ryan but with more pepper," she said with a small nod, then her mouth pinched. "But you don't itch my nose."

Craig laughed. "Is that so?"

"Uh-huh."

They walked across the gravel parking lot toward the bed and breakfast Alexandra McKay owned and operated. It was called Granny Vaughn's, and the place was both massive and impressive, if one was into that kind of thing. There was a closed-in porch leading to the kitchen, which was off limits to B and B guests, but whose entrance he was told he was welcome to use if he needed anything—like paying his rent or chatting up his landlady.

Craig had expected to come across Alexandra but found her sister Charlie, Mack's mother, instead. It was a pleasant surprise. He enjoyed this particular McKay, with her short blonde curls, big brown eyes, and supple pink lips—kissable lips. Almost every time he was in her company, he'd been drawn to her mouth, not that she noticed. It was for the best; he had his own agenda here in Blue Creek, and he needed to keep his priorities straight.

Charlie put her hands on her jean-clad hips. "Mackenzie Annie McKay, where have you been? I've been looking everywhere for you!"

"Uh-oh, kid." Craig put Mack down. "She used your full name; looks like you're in trouble."

Mack's gaze darted between the adults. "I went to the playhouse."

"Do we need to talk again about going somewhere without telling me, or going into places without being asked?"

The child looked down and shuffled her feet.

Charlie offered him a small smile. "I'm sorry, Craig."

"It was a shock to the system, but what the hell, it woke me up," he said looking around the room. "Is Alexandra here?"

"She's running errands, but she'll be back soon." She turned to Mack. "Do you want to help me or play with your doll babies?"

It only took a second for the child to dash out of the room.

Craig eyed the pot of coffee sitting on the counter. "Are there any guests?"

Charlie, the consummate hostess, poured him a cup. "This is the slowest time of year for Alex, but there was a sweet older couple staying here last night; they left a bit ago. I was helping them load their luggage into their car, hence my daughter slipping away."

"Don't worry about it." He took the offered mug, then sipped. "You do make the best coffee."

She gave him a shy smile. "There are muffins too, if you're interested?"

He homed in on the basket of baked goods, sat down at the table, and helped himself. "Keep me company?"

Charlie shot a quick glance in the direction her daughter went. "Okay, but just for a bit." She poured herself a cup of coffee, then took the seat across from him. "How's Blue Creek treating you, so far?"

He shrugged. "I can't complain, but let's not talk about me; tell me about *you*." He eyed her over the rim of his mug. Was she debating what to divulge? How stimulating!

"Well...I—"

"I didn't see your ride in the parking lot."

"No, my sister Casey took it for an oil change."

"She's the mechanic, right?"

Charlie nodded.

"It's an interesting choice," he said around a mouthful of muffin.

Her brow pinched. "Sorry?"

He swallowed both his food and his grin. "Your SUV—not your sister's career. A female mechanic is pretty badass, but so is your ride. It's vintage, isn't it?"

Her lips quirked upward. "Yes. I saw one like it in a movie once. I've never really been into cars, but I wanted *that* Blazer! I asked Ward Jessup, who was the town mechanic at the time, how hard it would be to get one, and he said he'd look into it. It took him years, and I'd actually forgotten about the entire thing, but after I had Mackenzie, it showed up in my driveway."

Craig's eyebrows rose. "He gave it to you?"

A fine sheen glazed her eyes. "Yes, Ward was very special to my family—to me. He died over a year ago."

And now he was a dick. "I'm sorry."

"It's okay." She shrugged. "You didn't know."

He shifted in his chair. "What about your family?"

"What about yours?" A blush swept up her cheeks. "I didn't mean to sound—"

He waved a hand. "Don't mention it. My mother died when I was a kid. It was just me and my dad until college—two men trying not to let life knock them down, or so he always said. He owned a bar, so I'm continuing the tradition. I'm on my own now." Sort of.

"Oh, I'm—"

"What about Mackenzie's father?"

She flinched.

Damn. "Sorry if that's too forward."

"He's dead."

Craig sat back. "I see…sorry."

Charlie stood, dumped her coffee in the sink, and started loading the dishwasher.

He drummed his fingers against the table. "So, tell me about my landlady."

She glanced over her shoulder. "Alexandra?"

"Yes, is she as—I don't know—cold as she seems?"

"Alex isn't cold; she's shrewd—there's a difference."

"Yeah?" He smirked and stood. "She seems a bit stuck-up to me."

"I wouldn't say 'stuck-up.' " She closed the dishwasher and smiled at him. "We've always described her as prissy, and that's Alexandra to the core. She's always been like that—she's a trip. You seem to have a lot of opinions about my sister."

Craig cocked his head to the side. Was Charlie jealous? "I'm the curious sort, but if you're wondering if I'm interested in her, then the answer is no. She's not my type."

"And what is your type?" Her face went red.

"Why? Are you interested?" Wouldn't *that* be stimulating?

Her brow pinched. "I…"

She was a picture with big doe eyes, apple cheeks, and pink, kissable lips. He downed his coffee and walked over to her. Priorities be damned. "Well, Charlie, are you?"

"I have a four-and-a-half-year-old and own a diner. I don't have time to be interested."

Craig leaned down and breathed her in. She smelled like cookies. Delicious. "Pity that."

Her gaze searched his, and, God help him, she licked her lips.

"Good morning."

And there went all the heat. Craig winked at Charlie, then turned. Even with the cold stare in her dark blue eyes, Alexandra was breathtaking. "Good morning, Landlady."

She put her shopping bags down on the table and eyed him. "Was there something you needed, Mr. Sutton?"

"Nope, and it's Craig, remember?" He turned to Charlie. "Thanks for the coffee and conversation."

Charlie's cheeks were still flushed, but she smiled. "You're welcome."

He gave a curt bow to Alexandra, then headed out

the door. Despite the dismissal, Craig smiled. Things were shaping up his way.

****

Craig Sutton...holy moly, but the man caused Charlie to pulse in places best not thought about. From the moment he walked into her diner, she had been taken by the sight of him. And today was no different; his tawny hair had been tousled by the wind, and his dark blue eyes were the perfect mixture of mischief and sincerity. Not to mention how his tight jeans fit his backside oh-so-snugly. Even a ratty sweatshirt couldn't diminish the drool-worthy factor.

Charlie shook her head and turned to her sister. "Do you want to tell me what all that was about?"

Alex paused from putting away groceries. "What all *what* was about?"

Charlie rolled her eyes. "Oh, you know very well what I mean."

"I thought you'd sworn off men?"

She could only stare at her sister. A few years ago, Charlie's choice in the opposite sex had sent her reeling into a black pit of shame and despair. She had promised herself she wouldn't go down that particular rabbit hole ever again, but it didn't mean she couldn't enjoy the scenery. And she missed being in a man's arms, not to mention kissing. Goodness, she loved kissing. If Alex hadn't come in, Craig may have...*Don't even go there, Charlie girl!*

"Cat—or something else—got your tongue?"

Charlie gaped. "What in the world has gotten in to you today?"

Her sister sighed. "Sorry, I'm not trying to be a bitch—"

"You could have fooled me!" She shook her head. Alexandra was more than a sister, she was Charlie's best friend, and…and… "Do *you* like him?"

"Who?"

"Seriously!" She huffed and snatched a package of coffee filters out of her sister's hands. "Do you like Craig?"

"We don't know enough about him." Alex held out her hand.

Charlie gave the filters back. "That doesn't answer my question."

Most men fell over themselves when they first met Alex, and Craig was no exception. Charlie couldn't blame him; her sister was like a goddess with her crown of fiery locks and unrelenting confidence. And Charlie wasn't jealous, but this particular man's reaction to Alex, and her sister's odd behavior, did prickle under her skin.

"Are *you* interested in him?"

Charlie shrugged. "I can't afford to get in a tizzy over any man."

"Exactly! Men make a mess of things, and that's all we need to say on the subject."

"Fine." Charlie began to help unload the groceries, knowing full well her sister hadn't answered the question.

****

"Did you get me a surprise?" Mack asked.

"Yes, baby, but you have to wait till we get home," Charlie said for the third time since they'd left her parents' house. It was her own fault for mentioning she'd gone shopping after she'd picked their SUV up from the garage.

She pulled into the driveway, enjoying how the moonlight haloed their little house, a small white-sided ranch with navy-blue shutters and a wraparound porch. It was the house she'd always pictured having—a home of their own.

Putting the vehicle in park, Charlie squinted at the package on the front porch. She didn't remember ordering anything. She got Mack out of her car seat and hurried up the steps after her.

"Look, Mama!" Mack clapped. "It's a present for us."

"Let's go inside first, then I'll come and get it." Charlie unlocked the door and urged Mack in. She waited a beat, then went back to get things she'd picked up at the store. She glanced at the box and rolled her eyes. It looked heavy.

Mack tried to take the bags out of Charlie's hands the minute she walked into the kitchen. "Can I have my surprise now?"

Charlie handed her daughter the new coloring book. "Here, sweetheart. Now go to the playroom, and I'll come in there in a minute."

Mack shouted her thanks and skipped away.

Charlie hated admitting it, but she couldn't wait for preschool to start again. She understood the teaching staff had the flu, but how long did it really take to get better? *Take a chill pill, Charlie girl!*

Twenty minutes later, she put the finishing touches on her meatloaf. She cranked the timer for another fifteen minutes and went to set the table. She had just put out the forks when she remembered the box. Maybe one of her sisters had sent them something.

Out on the porch, Charlie took a few minutes

trying to figure out how to get the thing inside—it weighed a ton. Finally, she decided to open the package right where it was. From the smell, something had gone bad. There was no way she was bringing it inside her house, much less her kitchen. Maybe if she hadn't forgotten about the darn thing, it wouldn't have had a chance to spoil.

"It's freezing out here, so it isn't my fault," she told the box. Shaking her head, Charlie used a paring knife to cut the tape. She opened the flaps, wincing at the stench, and looked inside.

Charlie rushed to the porch railing and emptied her stomach. She closed the box, her hands shaking. It couldn't be! Oh, God.

"Mama, what—"

"Go to your room, Mackenzie, and don't come out until I get you."

Mack hesitated.

Charlie shouted, "Now!"

Her daughter ran back inside.

Charlie rubbed her face. "Holy shit," she whispered; she choked out a sob, then took a couple of deep breaths. She could handle this; she had to calm down. She pulled out her cell phone and dialed.

"McKay."

"Fletcher, someone sent me a package." She gulped for air. *Do not fall apart, do not fall apart.*

"Hells bells, just spit it out! I got a grave robbed out here, and you won't believe whose it is neither."

"Rick's?"

"How the hell did you know that? Shit—"

"That's what I've been trying to say. He's here…someone put him on my porch."

"Holy fuck! Don't touch anything! Jasper and I'll be there in a few minutes."

Charlie shoved her cellphone in her back pocket. Not only did someone out there know her secret, but they'd dug it out of its grave, chopped it into pieces, and left it at her door.

Chapter Two

Rick Randle. Charlie's lips quivered. The last time they'd been face-to-face she had told him she was pregnant; that was also the first time she saw him for who he truly was. His words were vicious, accusing her of lying and whoring herself out. Like she'd ever been with anyone else!

Before they first started seeing each other, he had secretly ended his marriage to Marylou Thomas, and having been a victim of Marylou's hatefulness, Charlie felt an instant camaraderie with him. Boy, was she wrong. Like Dorian Grey, the true picture of Rick's character was revealed; she was disgusted with him—and herself.

All Rick cared about was getting his hands on the Thomases' money. He said he would never admit to being the bastard's father, and, as it worked out, he never had to. He died nearly a year after Mack was born—murdered during a robbery in his home. Charlie was ashamed to admit that news of his death had offered her nothing but relief; poetic justice, some said.

Now here he lay, her biggest regret, ugliest secret, and deepest shame—rotting. Lights flashed across the lawn breaking into the darkness of her thoughts. Charlie took a step back when Fletcher and the sheriff got out of the sheriff's SUV.

Her sister looked official in her tan uniform: a gun

at her hip, deputy's badge on her chest, and her long brown hair in a tight braided bun at the back of her head. Concern showed in Fletcher's blue-green gaze, but her gait was all business. As was the sheriff's.

Sheriff Jasper Hart had been the law in Blue Creek for thirty-plus years. He was considered an honorary member of Charlie's family, though it would embarrass him if she said so. He was nosy by nature, which meant there wasn't much the old sheriff didn't know, and it would do them well not to forget it.

Jasper's hair had gone completely white in the last few months, and there was talk around town about him retiring soon. It was hard to imagine; the man was practically an institution unto himself. Charlie didn't think she'd ever been so relieved to see him.

Jasper eyed the box, then glanced at her. "Pretty shook up there, are you, Charlie?"

"Hard not to be, Jasper."

"Reckon so." With the tip of his pen, he lifted one of the flaps aside.

Charlie turned away.

"Oh, fuck," Fletcher hissed.

"That's Rick Randle, no doubt about it." Jasper shook his head. "I didn't think the day could get any weirder. We've never had a grave robbing before. Made me edgy when we found out it whose it was."

Fletcher knocked her elbow into Jasper's arm. "I told you your instincts are as sharp as ever. I'll call the crime scene techs."

He held up a hand. "Get the Guthrie brothers. They're the only ones know how to keep their traps shut for any length of time. And we need to keep this quiet for as long as we can."

Relief washed over Charlie. "Thank you!" She knew the news wouldn't hold for long—not in Blue Creek—but she appreciated the effort.

Jasper nodded.

Fletcher pulled out her cell phone and stepped away.

Charlie eyed the box. "I never thought I'd see his face again—heck, I thought he'd be bones by now."

"It's only been about three years give or take; he was embalmed and in one of those fancy coffins." Jasper shrugged. "It could take a good long while for a body to decompose in those conditions."

Charlie rubbed her hands up and down her arms. She didn't want to think about it.

Fletcher pocketed her phone and came over to Charlie. "You're as pale as I've ever seen you." She hugged her. "Where's Mack?"

Finding comfort in her sister's embrace, Charlie closed her eyes. "She's in her room watching a movie. I told her not to come out until I said it was okay."

Fletcher stepped back. "Good thinking."

"Maybe you should call your parents to come get her. This is going to take a while. There now," Jasper said and gave Charlie a brief hug. "I'm the sheriff. I can hug ya if I want."

Charlie smiled when he let her go. "Thanks, Jasper. As far as my parents are concerned, I would say let's not tell them, but I know you'll talk to Pops anyway."

"As well he should." They all jumped when Pops walked up the porch steps. A baseball cap covered his salt and pepper hair while his blue-gray gaze was apprehensive.

"Dagnabbit, McKay," Jasper hollered. "I swear,

you got eyes all over the damn place."

Charlie sighed. This was one of the problems with having a house on McKay land; nothing got by her father.

"I was on our porch and saw the lights," Pops said. He took the pen from Jasper's hand and looked in the box. Closing his eyes, he shook his head.

"Pops, you're not an agent anymore." Fletcher took the pen and handed it to Jasper. "You can't go around interfering with a police investigation."

Charlie could only stare when her father swung around to glare at Fletcher. Her sister had never spoken to Pops like that before.

Jasper's mouth moved, but nothing came out.

"What did you just say to me, young lady?" Pops shouted.

"You heard me!" Fletcher shifted on her feet. "Now, I'm going to go check on my niece."

They all stared after her.

Jasper scratched his head. "What in tarnation was that about?"

"I haven't the slightest." Charlie turned to her father. "Pops?"

"We haven't been seeing eye to eye lately, is all."

Jasper huffed. "She's been acting strange all damn day!"

Charlie swallowed. The last time Fletcher had acted "strange," someone had been drugging her. No! That train of thought did no one any good.

"Could be that man," Jasper mumbled.

"Let's not even—"

"What man?" Charlie wanted to know. Craig Sutton? *And why was he your first thought, Charlie girl?*

Jasper cleared his throat. "Nothing for you to worry about."

Charlie was about to comment when her father said, "Jasper, I have to know if you agree with Fletcher about my involvement."

Her gaze swung to the sheriff. All of a sudden, she was a kid again, listening in on a grown-up conversation she didn't understand. What *was* going on?

"Hell, McKay, I've known you since you were in diapers. I trust your opinion, and I always appreciate another trained eye."

"Well, that's a relief," Pops said, then looked at Charlie. "Are you all right, sweetheart?"

"Oh, sure. Someone sent me a dead body, but yeah, I'm as fine as a fiddle." She winced. "Sorry. I'm not having the best night." She welcomed her father's hug. Pops' arms were always the safest place to be.

They waited together inside while the Guthrie brothers processed the scene and took away what was left of Rick Randle. Charlie sipped her tea and sighed. Her meatloaf was ruined, but at least Mack had fallen asleep. She didn't know how she could have explained all this to her daughter. Now she wouldn't have to.

Jasper stood next to the front door whispering to Fletcher, who kept jerking her head.

Charlie turned to her father, who was drinking the cup of coffee she'd made him. "I'm sure Fletcher didn't mean what she said."

"She and I've been having a rough time of it, but that's not for you to worry about."

Charlie nodded and glanced back to the two

arguing.

"Now," Jasper shouted, "go make yourself useful!"

Fletcher said something unintelligible and slammed the door shut.

The sheriff shook his head and took a seat.

"What was all that about?" Pops wanted to know.

"Nothing to worry about, McKay. Charlie, let's get—"

"*Jasper*, what is it?" Charlie asked. Something was going on; Jasper's color was up, and he kept fiddling with his badge.

"Did she talk to either of y'all about what happened this morning?"

"I spoke to her earlier," Charlie said. "But she didn't mention anything. She was headed to the gym before her shift."

Jasper huffed. "Well, that's where we had a bit of trouble."

"What kind of trouble?" Charlie glanced between the two men.

Jasper stared at her father. "Did she say anything to you?"

"No, but if there's something you think we need to know—" Pops motioned with his hand for the other man to talk.

"It ain't my place."

"Jasper, you asked if she'd told us anything, which suggests you think she *should* have talked to one of us," Charlie prompted.

"I think I have a right to know if my daughter's going through something and needs help."

Jasper winced. "Fine. But when Fletch finds out she ain't gonna be happy 'bout me telling y'all. Hell, she'll probably throw a fit so big that…well, you know how she is."

Charlie sat back while Jasper told them what he knew. She winced when Pops slammed out of the house. If he woke Mack up…

Jasper cleared his throat. "Now that that's done, I'll take your statement, Charlie, from the beginning."

****

Craig was behind the bar, on his back, looking at the pipes under the sink. All he had meant to do was empty the P-trap, but he'd sprung a leak instead. After hours of tinkering and online tutorials, he knew what need to be done. With a grunt and a wrench, he went to work fixing the issue.

Twenty minutes later, boots crunched against the floor, and he glanced up. "We aren't open and even if we were, you"—he pointed to the girl with his wrench—"aren't welcome. No minors allowed." He got out from under the sink when she didn't scurry away. The girl was a cutie for sure in her ripped jeans and sweatshirt, but a kid was a kid.

"Did you hear me, young lady? Go on now," Craig said with a bit of force. Still she stood. "Look, I don't want to call the police."

She snorted. "Go ahead. Jasper would get a kick outta this."

"Who?"

"Jasper Hart. He's the sheriff in Blue Creek." She waited a beat, then smirked. "He's also my boss."

"What do you mean, your boss? Just who the hell are you?"

"Deputy Fletcher J. McKay at your service. Wanna see my badge?"

He stood and walked across the scarred linoleum with an open hand.

She narrowed her eyes and pulled out her badge.

He studied it, then handed it back. "I'll be damned."

"Happy now?" She shoved it in her pocket.

"You look sixteen, seventeen at the most." Craig shook his head. She was a cop *and* the youngest McKay sister. Unbelievable. He had heard about her, of course, but seeing her in person was something else entirely.

"Believe it, Mr. Sutton. Glad you don't serve to minors though. Nasty trouble that," Fletcher said with a sniff. "And, trust me, I'm all grown up."

"Sorry," he said and hopped up on the bar. He liked this kid. She had spunk. "What are you doing here, Deputy?"

"Wanted to get a look at you, is all."

"And what do you think?" Craig couldn't help himself; now that he knew she wasn't jailbait, he felt free to tease.

Fletcher cocked her head to the side. "About what?"

"About me, of course."

"Oh, well." Fletcher shrugged. "I don't know you yet."

"Are you serious?" His brows bunched. "I'm flirting with you."

She snorted. "That's the stupidest fucking thing I've ever heard."

"I didn't mean to offend—"

Her cell phone rang, and she held up a finger. "What now? Yes, it's me, Jasper. Who the fuck else would be answering my phone? No, nothing's wrong.

I'm *making myself useful*, as per request. No. Damn it, you're pissing me off. Oh, all right. Bye."

"You always talk to your boss like that?" Craig grabbed a beer out of the cooler and offered her one.

She hesitated.

"It's not a bribe, and I take it you're not on duty."

"My shift ended about an hour ago." She rolled her eyes and snatched the bottle out of his hand. "And if you must know, Jasper and I have an understanding."

He nodded. "I'm renting the apartment at the B and B. I'll presume you're one of Alexandra and Charlie's sisters."

"Can't go too far 'round here without running into one of us."

"I'm finding that out."

She smirked. "Were you fixing a leak or something?"

"Or something."

"By the looks of things…" She pointed to the mess he'd made by the sink. "You've been at it for a while."

He grunted. "All damn night, if you want the truth."

She rocked back on her heels. "Truth is best."

"Agreed." He toasted her with his bottle, took a long pull, then glanced at his watch. Damn, it was almost midnight. Where had the evening gone?

"I can take a hint…I'm going."

"There's no hurry, honey."

"Okay, you's need to understand a few things. You's can't go flashing endearments at me; you's can't be…be—"

"Flirting," Craig supplied.

"Yes. I's mean, no! I's mean, *yes*." She growled.

Craig laughed. "Did you know that your speech changes when you're upset?"

She closed her eyes and took a couple deep breaths. "Yes, I am perfectly aware of how my speech degrades during times of duress."

"Well put." This one was sharp, and it would do Craig well to remember it.

"You should also know—since we're being so honest—as a deputy of the law, I'm *always* armed. Always."

He stared at her for a minute. "Understood."

They eyed each other over their beers; then she handed him her empty bottle and turned to leave.

"I'll be seeing you around then."

She snorted. "You bet your ass."

Craig let out a breath after the door clicked shut. Well, that was something. Shaking his head, he looked around and decided to call it a night.

Chapter Three

Charlie's nerves were close to shot. She had made it through the breakfast rush without any issues, but that all changed by noon. News of the grave robbery broke out in time for lunch. The entire town was pulsing with the gossip of *who* had been unlawfully exhumed.

Rick's name hovered around each table she served; everywhere she turned there he was. She couldn't escape it—couldn't escape him…again. Fear crept up her spine and settled into her shoulders; it was only a matter of time before her secret would be out. Before everyone knew.

She carried the tray of discarded dishes into the back of the kitchen and set them up for the dishwasher. She dabbed sweat from her brow; now she knew how the women of the night felt at Sunday service. She said a silent prayer for strength and slapped another smile on her face.

A big hand squeezed her shoulder. "You're doing great, shug."

Charlie turned to her cook, often time co-conspirator, and all-around best buddy, and gave him a genuine smile. "Thanks, Tiny."

Tiny Wellington, standing a foot taller than her five-foot-four frame, was anything but. Tattoos, remnants from his days in the marines, played across his dark skin; the gold front tooth and bump in his nose were from his days as a semiprofessional boxer. And the man was a master in the kitchen. Skills, he said, he picked up from his mother and grandmother. To her, he was the perfect combination of sweet and spice.

He had come in early this morning, so she could tell him everything. It was only a matter of time before people found out that Rick's body had been put on her porch, and she wanted Tiny to hear the truth from her. The whole lurid affair. She owed him that much.

The big man had dried her tears and hugged her right off her feet. "You don't need to worry yourself one bit. I got your back. Always."

She was surprised how much it meant to her—healed her—to hear him say that. Then and now, Tiny's words gave her the courage she needed to straighten her shoulders and go back through the swinging door.

But strength failed her when she walked up front to find Noah Reed coming through the entrance. Charlie's stomach dropped, and sweat broke out on her forehead. Noah was a homicide detective for the city. Was he here because of her? Because of Rick? Oh, God...

"Good morning, Charlie." He took a seat on one of the red-vinyl topped stools lining the stainless-steel counter.

Noah was one of the most eligible bachelors, if not *the* most eligible, in Blue Creek. The women, both single and married, drooled over him. He was a large man—massive even—in the muscle department, with jet-black hair and silver eyes. But it wasn't any of those things that were making her nervous right now.

"Hi there, Noah. Long time no see," she said, despite having no moisture in her mouth whatsoever.

He eyed her. "Are you all right? You seem a little

on edge."

She handed him a menu and smiled. "Nope, just tired. You know, life with a four-year-old."

He gave her his order, then asked how Mack was doing.

She poured him a glass of iced tea and said, "She's doing well, thanks."

"I heard the preschool was closed."

"Yes! Some sort of stomach bug. I'm lucky though. Mama is taking care of Mack while I'm here." She rushed into the kitchen to give Tiny the order, not waiting for Noah's response. She handed over the ticket and let out a pent-up breath. Noah didn't seem to know anything about the Rick situation, thank goodness. The man had come in for lunch, not an inquisition.

Relieved, Charlie went back out front and helped other customers. She proceeded down the line of people at the counter until she reached Noah again. She topped off his tea and asked how he was; knowing he wasn't here because of Rick put her at ease. The big detective did look ruffled, now that she could look at him without being blinded by nerves.

"I'm well, thanks. I've been busy finishing up a bunch of my old cases."

"Oh." She set a roll of silverware down for him. "Are you planning a vacation?"

A look Charlie didn't recognize played across his features, then it was gone. Noah sipped from his glass, then said, "Something like that."

She was about to ask what he meant, but Tiny called out that Noah's order was ready. She fetched his plate, set it in front of him, then left him to his meal. Charlie refilled drinks, cashed out checks, and bussed a couple of tables before Noah had finished.

When he looked to be done, she went to clear his plate. "Would you like a slice of pie? We have a nice custard," she offered. It was his favorite.

"I'll tell you what…give me two slices and a cup of coffee to go."

Charlie smiled. "Sure thing!" She had the pie boxed up and the coffee ready in a matter of minutes. She handed the items over to Noah, who gave her cash for his bill.

"No change," he said with a nod and headed for the exit.

Her words of gratitude died on her lips when another customer opened the door. Bile rose in Charlie's throat, and her hands shook as she put Noah's payment in the register. The McKay girls' archnemesis and the bane of Charlie's existence, Marylou Thomas—in all her bleached-blonde glory—hovered by the diner's entrance and flirted with the big detective.

Charlie's fingers turned white as she gripped the register like a lifeline. Marylou couldn't know, right? She couldn't possibly know where Rick's body had ended up—not yet. No, she would have made a beeline for the counter. She would have started raging from the moment the door opened. No one loved to make a scene like this viper.

Charlie nibbled her lip, unable to look away, as Marylou patted Noah's shoulder, gave a haughty laugh, and said her goodbyes. The other woman headed toward the counter, and Charlie steeled herself. No one brought out the worst in her like this woman.

"Hello, Charlie, *dear*," she said in her saccharine southern drawl.

"Good afternoon, Marylou. What can I get for you today?" *Bowl of rat poison? Glass of antifreeze?*

She narrowed her ice-blue eyes. "Oh, I just wanted to stop in and say hello to Detective Reed. Such a nice man, don't you think?"

"Yes," Charlie said with hesitation. She never knew when this one was springing a trap.

Marylou turned and waved to a couple other customers, who nodded in return. She leaned over the counter. "I'm sure everyone is talking about what happened in the graveyard last night."

Charlie swallowed. "You know how news travels in Blue Creek."

Her mouth pinched. "Yes, well—"

"Can I get you anything, Marylou?" *Please leave, please leave...*

She huffed. "I'll take an iced tea—to go, Charlie. I have more important things to do than stand around your dinky diner all day."

"Coming right up." Charlie didn't think she'd ever poured a glass of tea so fast in her life. She handed Marylou the cup and looked up when the bell chimed over the door.

"Afternoon, ladies." Alex breezed in and leaned over the counter to kiss Charlie on the cheek.

"Alexandra, what a pleasant surprise."

Charlie blinked. No one could change Marylou's demeanor like Alex. The bimbo went total fangirl—it was a sight to see.

"Oh, Marylou, I didn't realize that was *you*. I thought you were out of town, New York or something." She took a seat and sipped the iced tea Charlie set in front of her.

Marylou rushed to take the seat next to Alex. "No, I went to New Orleans. Mother and I got back not two minutes ago."

"I hear New Orleans is fantastic. But, goodness, that means you haven't been to the Villa yet," Alex began. "They just released the spring line, and it's to die for. I think the sale ends today though."

"Will you look at the time?" Marylou said, making a big production. "What do I owe you, Charlie?"

"I'll be happy to cover your tea," Alex offered.

The halfwit smiled and made a hasty retreat.

Charlie giggled. "You're so bad. You know she's going straight to that store."

"It got her out of here, didn't it?"

"Yes, thank you." Charlie went to refill drinks and cash out a couple customers. When she came back to Alex, she asked, "What brought you in?"

Alex's eyes widened. "You're kidding, right? I came to check on you."

Reality crashed back. "Oh."

"Yes, 'oh.' Listen, why don't you and Mack come stay at the B and B for a few days?"

A weight lifted off Charlie's chest. "Really?"

"Of course! Winter is my slowest season, so there's plenty of room."

"Thank you. Mack will be excited too."

Alexandra smiled. "It'll be like the sleepovers we used to have with Granny Vaughn."

Charlie laughed. "Those were the best!" Thinking of her sisters reminded her of what Jasper had said last night. "Invite Casey over for dinner too."

"Why?"

"Jasper shared something about Fletch, and I want

to talk to you guys about it."

Alex raised a brow. "*And* you can tell us everything that happened last night."

Charlie stared for a moment. Then the bell chimed over the door, and she was granted another reprieve.

****

Charlie blew a goodnight kiss to Mack and shut the door. She was grateful to Alex for letting them stay here. She knew she would sleep well tonight; of course, any sleep was better than none. Bad enough last year's ordeal still had her sleeping with the lights on, but last night every time she closed her eyes, she saw Rick's decomposing face resting upon his severed limbs. Whoever had dug Rick up had had to fit his entire body into one box. It was like a jigsaw puzzle with body parts, gross. What kind of person could do such a thing?

She had discussed the entire scene with her sisters while Mack played in another room. Now, she could move on to a less disturbing topic—Fletcher.

Her sisters were still sitting at the kitchen table. Charlie grinned at the sight of them. She loved them so much and had since the moment she'd set eyes on them all those years ago. By the time Pops adopted Charlie, the others had already been McKays for five years. And that first night...

"Why the funny grin?" Casey asked. Her long black hair was up in its usual sloppy bun, and mischief danced in her violet gaze.

Charlie sat down next to Alex. "I was thinking about our first night together."

"What a night that was!" Casey snorted. "You called me and Fletch the ugly stepsisters and Alexandra here Cinderella. Like she didn't have a big enough head."

"As I recall, and I recall correctly, you didn't take much offense. In fact, Fletcher initiated a game of tag," Alex said.

"And that brings us to why I wanted to talk to you guys."

"So you said when you called. My husband, on the other hand, said whatever it is, we should wait for Fletcher to tell us herself...when she's ready." Casey shook her head, making her bun bob. "Ryan said to give her time, but I hate waiting."

Charlie smirked. "Yes, we know."

"We *all* know," Alex added.

"As I said on the phone, Jasper uncovered something about Fletcher yesterday."

"It's funny how Jasper conveniently finds things out," Alex said, then sighed. "What did he say?"

"He said—"

"Fuck Jasper. It ain't nobody's damn business," Fletcher said from the doorway. She shrugged out of her jacket and poured a cup of coffee.

"How'd you know we were here talking about you?"

"Wouldn't you like to know, *Mrs. Keller*."

It only took a moment for Casey's eyes to narrow. "Ryan called you, didn't he?"

Fletcher snorted. "Whatever you said to him got him worried, so he had to check up on me. Then he got chatty."

"Ha!" Casey said with a satisfied smile. "Seems I'm not the only one who couldn't wait."

"No changing the subject, Fletcher. You may as well come clean, because I will if you won't."

Fletcher rolled her eyes and took a seat next to Casey. "Did you tell them about last night?"

Charlie nodded.

Casey pointed to Charlie. "It's only a matter of time before the good people of Blue Creek figure out what your relationship was to Rick."

"They already figured it out."

The sisters turned when Craig walked inside. Charlie closed her eyes and wished him away. Great, now he thought she was an adulteress. She cringed. Who was she kidding anyway?

"He wasn't married at the time. Nobody knows that," Fletcher huffed out.

"I figured that out for myself, thanks. What?" he asked when the room glared at him. "If people don't know Charlie isn't the type of woman who would sleep with a married man, then they don't know her."

"You met me all of what—" She looked at her watch. "—two seconds ago, and you think you know me?"

"What can I say? I can read people pretty well. Comes with the job," Craig said and took a sip of the coffee he'd poured. He groaned. "You make the best coffee."

"Thank you," Alex murmured.

Charlie looked at Alex with a furrowed brow. She didn't understand Alexandra's tone. Charlie shook her head and glanced at Fletcher. What was that look?

Casey nodded. "I can see that working in a bar."

"Yeah." Craig grinned. "Something like that."

"Thank you." Charlie didn't want to think about why she was relieved he knew the truth, but she was all the same.

"You're welcome, honey." He winked at her.

"I'm Casey McK—Keller, by the way." She stuck out her hand.

Craig gave it a shake and stepped back. "Craig."

"Was there something you needed?"

"No, Landlady. I saw all the vehicles and figured there was a meeting of the minds taking place." He shrugged. "If you ladies need anything, let me know." He lifted Charlie's chin and looked into her eyes. "I know a little something about security and can get you hooked up with a great system. I'll make some calls."

They all stared at the man as he left.

"What was that all about?" Casey asked.

"I'm not sure. He's trying to be helpful, I guess," Charlie mumbled, heat creeping up her neck.

"Sounds like he wants to get into your panties to me," Alex said. "Sorry, I didn't mean—"

"It's okay," Charlie said, but it wasn't. She didn't understand Alexandra's contempt. She turned to Fletcher and decided to get back to the subject at hand. "Are you going to tell them or not?"

Fletcher shifted in her seat and stared into her coffee cup.

"Fine, I'll start for you," Charlie began. "Yesterday, while at the gym, one of the other deputies noticed a mark on Fletcher's back."

Casey released her hair from its bun and put it back up again. "So what?"

"It's not like the others," Charlie murmured. She had a hard time getting the words past her throat. Fletcher's body was scarred from an incident last year, and her flesh was a testament to the hell their sister had gone through.

"You're talking about her birthmark," Casey said, her tone a mix of relief and annoyance.

Fletcher's cheeks flushed, but she remained silent.

Charlie sighed. In for a penny... "That's the thing, Jasper said Deputy Hewitt knew it wasn't a birthmark right away—"

"*Good* little girls do not talk back, and when they do dare to speak, they speak proper. Good little girls use the powder room and *do not* get dirty."

Casey's hands tightened around her mug. "What the hell is that supposed to mean, Fletch?"

"I had a bad habit of getting dirty, and the woman who birthed me wasn't pleased. She had this silver ring she always wore. One day she held it to a flame for a long, long time...do I need to finish?" Fletcher stood.

"She burnt you?" Casey whispered.

"No, she branded me. 'Let's see if this keeps the devil out of you, Jamie,' she said."

"You were only, what, two? Three?" Charlie asked. She was younger than Mack is now.

Casey stirred in her chair. "How the hell do you remember?"

Fletcher shrugged. "The nightmares have kept it fresh in my memory."

"Damn it, Fletcher!" Casey pushed her cup away from her, sloshing coffee on the table. "Why didn't you ever say anything?"

"You don't talk about rats, and I don't talk about rings—seems fair." Fletcher turned to Charlie. "Now, let's get back to this body business—"

"Not before you tell us why you told Jasper about the mark and not us," Charlie said.

"Good question," Alex said.

Fletcher huffed. "Deputy Hewitt wrote a paper for some head-shrinking class he took in college about mutilations, branding, and the human condition. He recognized it for what it was and casually mentioned it to the boss—fucking tattletale that he is. Anyway, the only reason I came clean to Jasper was because he threatened to tell Pops *just* how many times I actually broke into the sheriff's station."

Casey dabbed at her spilled coffee with a napkin. "You don't have to look so damn happy about it."

"I can't help thinking those were the days." Fletcher grinned.

A small smile played on Alex's lips. "Ever the delinquent."

Charlie giggled and waved a finger at Fletcher. "You always had a penchant for breaking and entering."

She shrugged. "We all have our talents."

Alex tapped her nails against her cup. "But why was Jasper in such a snit about you talking to one of us about it?"

Charlie glanced at her sister; Alex was right. There had to be more. Jasper must not have told them everything—go figure.

Fletcher sighed. "Because he thought it was time I told you guys what I remember about her."

Charlie sat up. "About your birth mother?"

"Yes, and I told Jasper that the past is as dead as she is—let the dead fucking lie."

"Your birth mother's dead?" Casey asked.

"She died, and social services put me in the home. Best thing that ever happened to me." Fletcher picked up her jacket and went out the front door before anyone could respond.

"You don't think she ki—I mean, she was only two?" Charlie squeezed Alex's hand.

"She's a genius, remember," Alex said.

"Think of how many grades she skipped to go to college with us. And I remember, she could hold a conversation pretty well when I met her. She was two then." Casey shrugged. "It's more than possible."

"I keep forgetting how much Fletcher and I have in common," Alex said.

Charlie turned toward Alex. "Do you want to talk about it?"

"What's there to talk about? I've killed in self-defense and so has Fletcher; there's nothing else to say."

"You protected yourself and us," Charlie began. "That's nothing to be ashamed of. And you got justice for Uncle—"

"*Uncle*," Alex said under her breath.

Casey gripped the edge of the table. "We agreed not to go down that particular rabbit hole again, Alexandra."

Alex fiddled with the centerpiece. "As you wish."

"I—"

"Let's talk about something else," Charlie suggested.

"Okay," Casey agreed. "Why don't we talk about how what's happening now might be related to what happened last year?"

"Works for me." Charlie shuddered. "I no longer like surprises."

****

Outside the kitchen door, Craig closed his gaping

mouth, then jogged to his apartment. He hadn't expected to overhear all that. His landlady had killed someone in self-defense, and it looked as if the youngest McKay may have killed her birth mother. Craig decided it was time he did some more research, maybe go to the town library. He had a lot of questions, but first things first. Taking out his cell phone, he made a call.

"Reed."

"Noah, it's Craig. I just overheard some crazy shit—you got time for an old friend?"

Chapter Four

Craig sat in one of the overstuffed chairs in Noah's den. He waited for the other man to finish his phone call. Sipping his water, Craig looked around the room.

Noah grabbed his own bottle of water and sat down across from him. "Sorry about that."

"Not a problem. You've done well for yourself. Definitely beats our apartment in college."

He snorted. "Not hard to beat that dump. And as for this place, Emmit McKay gave me a good deal."

"Emmit McKay?" Craig asked, though he knew already. Truth be told, it had been Noah who had led him to Blue Creek in the first place. It gave new meaning to the idea of a small world, but Craig rarely looked a gift horse in the mouth.

Noah shrugged. "This house belonged to Judge J. T. Vaughn originally. The Judge was Emmit's father-in-law by his first wife, and he left the place to Emmit."

"Seems most things in this town revolve around the McKay family."

"It doesn't just *seem* that way. Now, what did you find out? You don't do or ask anything without a reason, and I'm curious."

"Alexandra McKay killed someone in self-defense."

"Yeah, I read the police report."

"I heard a little about what happened last year."

Actually, he'd *heard* a lot about it from the little old lady who ran the library. Yep, Millie Mitchell had not only let him stay past closing time, but also told him the entire story, as far as she—and the people of Blue Creek—were concerned, anyway.

"People around here can't stop talking about it." Noah shook his head. "And poor Charlie, it brought up all the old whispers. Now this."

"What 'old whispers'?"

"Not long after I moved here, Charlie got pregnant, and it had the gossip mill churning. Everyone talking about who the father might be, and when I say everyone, I mean it. Hell, I think even my name was tossed around for a time. But she never said a word; until last night, no one in their right mind would have guessed."

"Did you know Rick Randle?"

"I met him once, and trust me, that was enough." Noah narrowed his eyes. "There's more to this conversation than idle curiosity, and I'd like to know why you're so interested. And what in the hell did you come here to tell me other than about Alexandra?"

"I wanted to know what you knew about the youngest McKay—" Craig smacked Noah on the back after his friend choked on his water. He took his seat and grinned.

Noah stood to pace. "What did that bitch do now?"

"I don't think I've ever heard you refer to a female with that term." Reading people was in Noah's blood, but on this Craig had to disagree.

The big man prowled around the room. "You've only been here for a few weeks; I've been here for a few years. That *girl* may look sweet and innocent, but she isn't. In fact, she's pretty callous."

"I didn't get that impression. I think she's misunderstood, and she might have low self-esteem." She was a pearl in a basket full of gems, and no one seemed to notice.

Noah guffawed. "Low self-esteem, my ass. That girl's ego is twice her size, and her mouth's bigger than that. I don't know how the hell Jasper puts up with her. Her sisters actually condone her behavior, which I could understand after meeting Casey and knowing Alexandra."

Craig shifted in his seat. "I might agree with you on the oldest, but Alexandra?"

"You've been around her enough to know. Your damn testosterone blinds you. Alexandra McKay is a ruthless and dangerous woman. Hell, they all are, except Charlie; she's a sweetheart. Wait a minute...this isn't about—"

"Charlie is a sweet woman," Craig cut in. "Too trusting if you ask me, but genuine. What about the others?"

Noah eyed Craig and took a long sip of his water. "Okay, old friend, I'll play...I met Casey last year, and she's a piece of work. Tough as nails and about as giving as a brick wall, but she's softened a bit since she married. Her husband's a good guy, one I happen to like. Ryan Keller's his name. He's a private investigator; pretty good one too. He's got a twin brother—but he doesn't live here."

"Good to know."

They eyed each other for a minute, then Noah glanced at his watch and winced.

"Hot date?" Craig stood up at the other man's half

smile.

"Something like that. I'm sure you'll hear about it if you haven't already."

"All right, have fun." Craig gave a mock salute before he shut the door. He would think over Noah's opinions but hold off his own judgments until he had more information.

****

A truck door slammed, and Charlie winced. "Uh-oh."

"What?" Alex sighed when Fletcher came into view. "She's back."

Casey shook her head. "Looks like something's got her riled up."

"If she wakes up Mackenzie, I'll kill her." Charlie looked up at the ceiling to where her daughter slept.

Alex went over to the coffee pot. "Do you think it's too late for coffee?"

"Make decaf. By the looks of things, Fletcher doesn't need any more caffeine," Casey suggested.

"Yeah, she won't know the difference." Thank God for her sister's antics, or Charlie might have to think about boxes with rotting Ricks inside.

"You guys won't *believe* what I just found out."

"Shhh!" Charlie pointed to the ceiling. "Don't forget Mack's asleep upstairs."

Fletcher winced. "Sorry."

"It's okay." Charlie patted her sister's cold hand. Where were her gloves?

"So, what won't we believe?" Alex asked from her position at the counter.

"Sweet, you're making coffee!"

"Yes, Alex is wonderful!" Casey said. "Back to the

breaking news."

Fletcher nodded. "Noah Reed—"

"Not this again, Fletch. Could you let the poor man alone? Jeez." Charlie shook her head.

"Oh, he's so nice?" Fletcher shrugged out of her jacket and sat down with a thud. "Do you know who he's dating, perchance?"

"No, and I don't care." Charlie didn't like her sister's sly smile.

Alex put cream and sugar on the table. "I do."

Fletcher rolled her eyes. "Course you do, Alexandra."

"Fine." She shrugged. "Don't tell me."

Casey rocked back in her chair. "Just spit it out, Fletch."

"Marylou Thomas."

Charlie blinked. "What about her?"

"That's who Reed's dating. Apparently, they've been seeing each other for a while."

Casey hit her fist against the table, shaking the centerpiece. "That rat bastard! You were right, Fletch. There's something off about that man."

"No way!" Alex shook her head. "I can't see it. I mean, Marylou is…is…I obviously gave Noah too much credit."

Fletcher snorted. "*Obviously*. Charlie? What's wrong?"

"She has to know by now, doesn't she? Marylou, I mean. She has to have heard…" Charlie covered her eyes. Her chest hurt.

"Oh, honey, they were divorced already—"

She rubbed a hand over her face and glanced at Alex. "People don't know that."

"They do now." Fletcher shrugged. "I couldn't have people thinking you committed adultery, or saying shit about my niece, now could I?"

Alex set a cup of coffee in front of Fletcher. "What did you do?"

"I called Mildred and told her the facts. It was the safest bet."

Mildred Lawrence was in her midsixties and had been the secretary of the Blue Creek Elementary and Middle School. She was a close family friend and a person whose opinion meant a great deal in this town. When Mildred said something, people listened—her word was law.

"I didn't realize Mildred was back in town," Casey said with a grin. "I can't wait to see the old battle ax!"

"Really, Casey," Alex began, "a little respect."

"She got back last week," Fletcher informed them.

Casey took the mug Alex offered her. "She was touring the world, wasn't she?"

"Yes, that's why she wasn't here for your wedding," Charlie said. "Remember I told you, after Ward died, she needed a change of scene."

"They'd been seeing each other for years," Alex explained to Casey. "One of the few secrets that everyone knew and no one talked about in Blue Creek. It reminded me of Granny Vaughn; how she and Granddaddy had been having a secret affair…"

They all took a moment to remember their grandparents.

Alex handed Charlie a cup of decaf and sat down next to her. "Mildred will make sure your reputation is taken care of, Charlie. Fletcher was right to go to her."

Charlie nodded. "I guess that was the best way."

Life was getting messy, and she didn't like it. Marylou was the type of person who took information and twisted it to suit herself. The woman was plain mean-spirited and had been since the first day Charlie met her.

"Damn straight, it's the best way," Fletcher said. "Marylou's gonna start something for sure; I can feel it in my bones."

Casey sighed. "Maybe I should call Ryan…"

"I'm one step ahead of you." Fletcher gestured to the headlights pulling around back. "That should be him now."

"You know, I'm getting tired of everyone trying to handle my life for me. I mean, I'm quite capable of handling myself."

"Hells bells, Charlie, we know that, but—"

"But we're worried about you," Alex said.

Charlie sighed and shot Ryan a smile as he walked in. With his light brown hair and steely green eyes, there was no denying Ryan Keller was a handsome man. And after marrying Casey, he'd added jeans and sweatshirts to his assortment of Armani suits.

"Good evening, ladies," Ryan drawled and took a seat next to his wife.

Alex poured him a cup of coffee, while Casey and Fletcher filled him in.

"I don't think Noah dating Marylou is a declaration of war, Casey," he said.

Charlie glared at Fletcher, who mumbled, "You can't prove it isn't."

Casey tapped the table with her index finger. "The Thomases have been the McKays' worst enemy for decades, and everyone knows it. Marylou tried to make life hell for us at school, and she still enjoys needling Charlie any chance she gets. And now that I think about it, Marylou could be behind digging up Rick's body!"

"No!" Charlie screeched. "Marylou didn't know about my relationship with Rick."

"I wouldn't put it past her. We still don't know who was consorting with our would-be killer last time," Alex offered.

"Sorry to burst your bubble, but it wasn't Marylou," Ryan said.

"Unfortunately, he's right."

"How do you know, Fletcher?" Casey asked.

"Marylou was out of town."

"Alex, we knew that. Remember? She told us yesterday she'd just gotten back from New Orleans. Darn. That's why she was speaking to Noah; she wanted to talk to her boyfriend." Charlie's stomach dipped. Part of her wished the blonde bimbo was doing this. Charlie would like nothing more than for Marylou to get what was coming to her. It shamed her to feel that way because, in a sense, the other woman had been taken for all she was worth. Which, speaking in terms of personality, wasn't much.

"What about his family? His sister or brother?"

"No, Ryan. Dana and Daemon wouldn't have done it. Dana worshiped Rick. I can't see her"—Alexandra waved her hand in the air—"digging him up. Is the woman a gossip? Yes. A grave-robbing lunatic? I highly doubt it."

Fletcher shifted in her seat. "As far as Daemon is concerned, I—"

Charlie stood and gripped the back of the chair. "Oh, God! They're going to know Mackenzie's their niece. What if they try to get visitation or worse, custody? Could they do that? Could they take her away from me?" She would not lose her daughter. *She would not!*

"No," Fletcher said. "You didn't put Rick's name on the birth certificate, and he didn't object."

"But they could fight for custody or visitation with a DNA test or…" Charlie swallowed.

Fletcher shook her head. "It's taken care of."

Charlie spun around. "What did *you* do?"

"*I* ain't done a damn thing!"

Alex's eyes narrowed. "What did Jasper do?"

Charlie squatted in front of Fletcher and took her hands. Her sister would bristle at an inquisition. "What did Jasper do?"

"I don't know exactly." She shrugged. "He said you didn't have to worry about custody; he'd taken care of things. And, well, Jasper doesn't tell me everything."

Casey snorted. "Raise your hand if you believe that bullshit!"

"He doesn't!"

"It's okay, Fletcher. I'll talk to him." Charlie patted Fletcher's arm and took her seat. She'd see him in the morning anyway. The sheriff was her first customer most days. She always liked chatting with him, but right now she felt more like giving him a good talking to.

"All right, Charlie will speak with Jasper. Now, did y'all find any fingerprints or anything?" Alexandra wanted to know.

"I can't tell you the details of an ongoing investigation, Alex."

Casey sat up straighter. "Since when?"

Charlie was baffled. "What's gotten into you, Fletcher? Yesterday you told Pops to butt out, and now you won't even tell me what's going on in an investigation that concerns me? What the heck is wrong with you?"

"Fletcher probably has her reasons," Ryan said looking at his sister-in-law. "And I'm sure she'll tell us what they are."

"Oh, you're so sure."

"Fletcher Jamie McKay, why in the world are you acting like this?" Charlie used her mom voice. She only hoped it worked as well on Fletcher as it did on Mack.

"If you don't tell us what's going on, you'll leave me no choice but to tell them about Daemon Randle and what he is to you," Ryan warned.

Casey turned to glare at him. "What the hell are you talking about?"

"You're bluffing," Fletcher accused.

Ryan shrugged. "We'll see."

"Fine! No, there weren't any fingerprints, not one. And there was a note…" Fletcher pinched the bridge of her nose. "Whoever dug Rick up and severed his limbs stuck a note in his mouth. It was addressed to Charlie."

"Dear God." Charlie choked.

Alex took Charlie's hand. "What did it say?"

"It said that the past has a way of being unearthed, no matter how deep you bury it. *And* that it was time Charlie was held accountable for her crimes."

Ryan shifted in his seat. "Jesus."

"So this wasn't some kind of sick joke?" Charlie said to no one in particular. She knew it wasn't a joke, but she'd been hoping. What crimes had she committed? Sins, she could understand, but crimes?

"It's no joke," Casey said. "I think you should take that Craig Sutton up on his offer to put in a security system for you."

"*Craig* Sutton?" Ryan asked.

"The guy who bought Shmittie's," Fletcher said. "You know, the one who's renting the place over Alex's garage."

Casey stared at her husband. "I told you about him, remember?"

"You didn't tell me his first name."

"What difference does it make?" Alex wanted to know.

"Craig Sutton, if it's the guy I'm thinking of, was a securities expert. And when I say expert, I mean it. The guy was renowned."

"So…if it's the same guy, then what the hell's he doing in Blue Creek?"

"Exactly!" Ryan got up and pulled out his cell phone. "Excuse me."

"Tell Jake we said hi," Charlie said, and Ryan smiled.

Casey cleared her throat. "Am I the only one here thinking whoever dug up Rick is the same person who was corresponding with the nutjob who came after us last time? That this isn't over?"

"Did you really think it was?" Fletcher wanted to know.

Charlie shivered. "I'd hoped…I'd really, really hoped it was. I don't know if I can handle someone coming after us again."

"I don't think it will come to that," Alex said, but her tone said she didn't really believe that.

Chapter Five

Charlie yawned into the crook of her arm and turned on the three coffee pots. Much to her chagrin, sleep had avoided her last night. She would have to face the town today, and it wasn't an appealing prospect.

"Tiny, I think I'll make the farmer's breakfast the special this morning."

"That sounds nice on this cold morning, shug. Yep, real nice." Tiny slung a towel over his massive shoulder. "You're worried about today?"

Her eyes stung. "Yes."

"Don't be. There are a lot of people in your corner, and that counts for something."

"You're right! Thanks," Charlie said.

"Julia said she could recommend someone if you needed to talk."

Charlie was caught off guard. Julia, Tiny's wife, was somewhat of a local legend. Not only did she come from a long line of healers, but she was a well-respected psychologist. Whenever she stopped by to see Tiny, she drew a crowd. She had a strict rule about her neighbors not being her patients, and for that reason her practice was not within the city limits. Of course, Julia had an even stricter rule about the McKays. Charlie suspected it had more to do with Fletcher's incessant questioning of "head doctors" than the fact that most of the McKays had worked with Tiny at some point and in some fashion.

Charlie swallowed. "Thank Julia for me, but I think I'm all right at the moment."

He nodded. "If that changes…"

"I'll let you know."

"All right. And don't worry about today." Tiny's gold tooth flashed. "We'll kill 'em with cooking!" He pushed through the swinging door.

She grinned, then glanced at her watch as the front door swung open and Jasper came in, right on time. She gave him a tight-lipped smile.

"How are you, Charlie?" Jasper took a seat at the counter and sighed when Charlie set a cup of coffee in front of him.

She leaned against the counter. "I was hoping you could tell me how I am; it seems you know more than I do."

"What's that supposed to mean?"

"Fletcher said you'd 'taken care' of certain things involving my daughter, and I'd like to know what they are."

He choked on his coffee, and she handed him a napkin.

"Dagnabbit, Fletcher," he hissed and dabbed at his mouth. "I knew Rick Randle was Mackenzie's father from the word go—"

"How could you possibly have known when I didn't tell anyone? And I'm pretty darn sure Rick wouldn't've offered up that kind of information."

"I saw you meeting him at that fancy apartment of his. Now, I ain't proud of it, so don't be glaring at me like that. I already got one of you McKay girls giving me that ass-kicking leer. I don't need another!"

Charlie's mouth pinched. She reached behind her and picked up a blue mason jar whose label read "Pay for Profanity." "That's a dollar."

Jasper grumbled under his breath but did as he was told.

She thanked him and put the jar back. "Were you following me to Rick's?"

Something unreadable flashed across his face. "I was looking into him was all."

"Okay. Why?" Charlie could admit she had been blind to Rick's darker side, but so had most people. It made her feel stupid that she hadn't seen it before it was too late, and she hated feeling stupid.

"I was doing a favor for"—Jasper stretched his neck—"the Thomas family."

Charlie sucked in a breath. "Did they know about me?" Oh, how humiliating.

Jasper patted her hand. "I never said a word. Not one blessed word. The Thomases had asked me to look into what Randle was doing. If I hadn't owed Ian Thomas a favor, I probably wouldn't have been there."

"You owed him a favor?"

"Still burns my britches ever having owed that man anything, but sometimes you have to pay the piper. Even if the piper works for the devil."

Charlie was going to ask him to explain, but the bell above the door rang and her father walked in. She understood the hurt in his eyes. None of his daughters had been keeping him up to speed on what was going on. In fact, they'd been neglecting their parents, which was unacceptable to Charlie.

"Morning, Dad." Charlie leaned across the counter and kissed his cheek.

"Morning, sweetheart," Pops said. "Jasper."

"McKay."

Charlie handed him a cup of coffee. "I should probably apologize; we've been so caught up in everything that...we haven't had a chance to talk things out with you or Mama, and I'm sorry."

"I don't blame you," he reassured her. "You've got too much on your plate to worry about me."

"I'll apologize anyway." She filled him in on everything they'd found out last night.

Pops turned toward Jasper. "So, what is it you did exactly?"

"Fletcher said she *may* have mentioned my involvement, so I brought this with me." He pulled an envelope out of his pocket and handed it to Charlie. "When you got pregnant and refused to tell anyone who the father was, I figured it out and had a little visit with Randle. I'll spare you the details of that particular argument; it wasn't pretty."

She opened the document, and tears filled her eyes. She looked up at Jasper. "Rick signed it," Charlie began, and handed the papers to her father. "He gave up all parental rights to Mackenzie. How did you do it, Jasper?"

"He failed to claim Mack, his child born out of wedlock, or provide for her in any way the first year of her life, and I used that as cause. Had anything happened, all you would have had to do was sign it; I had already spoken with a judge, who owed me a favor. I told Rick if he put his John Hancock on the agreement, I wouldn't tell the Thomases what he'd been up to. Greed's like a second skin to some; he didn't even blink."

Pops nodded and handed the papers back to Charlie. "With DNA testing, I don't believe leaving his name off Mackenzie's birth certificate would have protected you, but this document will stand up in court if the Randles even think of wanting visitation."

Jasper agreed. "I wouldn't have put it past that boy to come after the child for revenge of some sort—or monetary gain. And that's the truth if I ever spoke it."

"I don't know if I can thank you enough. I...I don't know what to say." Charlie smiled through her tears. No one could legally try to take Mack away.

"You could get me some breakfast before you go making me blubber like an old woman," Jasper said gruffly.

"You got it! And it's on the house. Dad, do you want something too?" Charlie asked, headed for the kitchen.

He smiled. "I wouldn't say no."

Her heart was lighter. She had just reached the swinging doors when her father said, "Now, Jasper, tell me what in the hell is going on."

****

Craig decided whoever had put linoleum on top of wood flooring should be shot. He'd started tearing the ugly mess out this morning and was amazed to find the oak floor underneath. Now that it was late afternoon, he was tired and hungry. He also figured the stench wafting up to his nose was coming from him.

"Definitely need a shower."

"Ah, is it you I smell?"

Craig jumped up and quickly covered his naked torso with his T-shirt.

Alexandra wrinkled her nose.

"What are you doing here, Landlady?" Craig glanced around the place. It was trashed. He didn't want anyone to see it like this.

"I was going to ask you the same thing, *Mr. Sutton.*"

"Oh?" Craig shifted from foot to foot. Alex had on a dark skirt and a matching sweater. Compared to his torn jeans and the all-over shabbiness of the place, she looked like a flower in a junkyard. Damn.

"Yes, I usually do background checks on my tenants, and I was quite puzzled when neither I nor my brother-in-law, who's a private investigator, could find anything on you. There was this horrid little fiasco not too long ago, and I learned no matter how sure I am I have someone pegged, checking them out is a must. You no doubt understand."

"I'll tell you what you want to know. All you had to do was ask."

"Good to know. Are you the same Craig Sutton who ran a security company—"

"Yes, I was founder of Sutton Security and CEO until four months ago when I sold it. I was tired of the long hours and stuffy clients. I grew up in my father's bar, so I thought I'd carry on the family tradition."

"Fascinating. But why Blue Creek—"

"My college roommate lives here," he began, aware she was annoyed he'd cut her off again. "When he talked about the place, I figured why the hell not and moved down." That was partly true. He grabbed a beer and offered her one; he wasn't surprised when she declined.

"Who's your friend? I'm sure I'll know him. Don't be shy. It's Blue Creek, for heaven's sake! If he lives here, I know him and his life story."

"Noah Reed."

"Damn it," came a voice behind Alex.

"Fletcher," Alex hissed. "You are, without a doubt, the nosiest creature on this planet! Did you follow me?"

Fletcher rocked back on her heels. "Ryan said you were coming out here, and I thought I'd tag along."

"Good to see you again, Deputy," Craig said, grinning when the girl's cheeks flushed.

She narrowed her eyes. "Drop the shit. Any friend of Reed's is an enemy of mine. You stay the fuck away from my sisters, or I'll shoot you," Fletcher threatened. She opened her mouth to say something else, but her cell phone rang. "McKay. Oh, hi…" Her voice trailed off as she left.

"What was that about?" he asked after the door slammed shut.

"Don't mind Fletcher. She's touchy about certain things, and she has an intense dislike for your friend."

"Yeah, I'm pretty sure the feeling's mutual." Craig rubbed his forehead. This was not good. In order for everything to work out, he needed to have an in with the sisters. Damn, Noah.

"So…why didn't you stay with Noah, if you're such good friends?"

Craig shrugged. "I've lived with him before—"

"And staying in the apartment over my garage was a better option?"

He grinned. "Much."

Alex pursed her lips. "Are you going to put in the alarm for Charlie?"

"Sure," he said, relieved by the change of subject. "The system should be here tomorrow. And I can install it whenever it's convenient for her."

"Tomorrow would be good," Alex said and handed him a key and slip of paper. "This is Charlie's address and the spare key to her house. Thank you, and goodnight."

"No problem," he began when she walked away. "I didn't have plans or anything."

"No, I didn't think you would," she said over her shoulder before she went out the door.

Craig laughed. He threw the key in the air and caught it. Things were looking up again.

****

"Are you sure I can't get you anything to drink, Craig?" Charlie asked for the thousandth time the next evening. She'd been surprised when Craig showed up at her door an hour ago with a security system in hand. Well, in a large box, at least. She had been home for five minutes when he pulled up. Apparently, Alexandra had given him the go-ahead. It would have been nice if her sister had asked, but Charlie couldn't complain. She hadn't told Alex that she was going to be coming back home tonight.

He looked up from the wiring. "Do you have any beer?"

"Yes!" Charlie hurried to the fridge. She didn't often drink, but her father and her sisters—Alex not included—enjoyed a beer once in a while. She popped the top and handed it to him.

"Thanks. I'm almost finished here; then I'll be out of your hair." He took a long swallow and closed the panel.

"Oh, I don't mind." She needed to control herself. She was acting like she'd never seen a man before. But, in her defense, Craig was so…male. And his backside was not one to ignore.

"That should do it." He turned to her. "Now you have the codes you want to use, and the hand alarms are placed where you can access them easily."

"Check and check. I really appreciate this, Craig."

"No problem. I used to do this for a living."

"That's what Fletcher said." Something he conveniently left out of every conversation they'd had. She would have to be careful. Charlie walked into her kitchen and started getting out what she'd need to make dinner. She looked up to find him staring at her. "What?"

"You don't share your little sister's opinion of Noah?"

She snorted. "Noah's always been nice to me. I like him fine." Even though he was dating Marylou—*don't even think the name, Charlie girl!* The woman hadn't shown up at the diner yet, but it was only a matter of time; why jinx it?

"That's good then." He finished his beer and found the recycle bin to dispose of it. "I guess that's it."

"Do you want to stay for dinner?" She didn't sound desperate. Did she?

Craig scratched his chin. "You're cooking after you cooked all day?"

"When Tiny's working, he does most of the cooking, but I love to help out in the kitchen whenever possible. Or when he lets me." She pulled on her apron and washed her hands. "When I was a little girl, before my parents got married, I did all the cooking at the house. Even after the I-do's, I prepared most of the meals. I think they liked to indulge me." She smiled.

Some of Charlie's favorite memories were in the kitchen with her father stealing a taste of whatever she was making.

"Mama, what's for supper? My tummy's singing something awful," Mack announced coming out of her room. Her eyes darted to the man in the house. She made a production of looking up, then smiled and said, "Hi, Pepper."

"Pepper?" Craig and Charlie said in unison.

"Yep, but not like from *Annie,* Mama. He ain't a girl," Mack said with a snort. "Ya see, he smells like Uncle Ryan but with more pepper." Mack rolled her eyes. "Grownups is strange."

"Are strange," Charlie corrected, blushing when Craig laughed.

"That makes sense, I guess." Craig shook his head. "I'd love to stay for supper."

"Great. Mackenzie, why don't you set the table for three, sugar," Charlie said.

Mack pulled on Craig's sweatshirt. "You can help."

****

Charlie turned off the overhead light in Mackenzie's room and eased the door shut. It had taken her twenty minutes longer than usual to get Mack to bed. Her daughter had shown Craig all of her dolls and all of her books. Then the little tyrant had instructed "Pepper" to read to her. Craig had sat right down on the floor and read her daughter *The Princess and the Pea.* If it wouldn't have been so obvious, she would have taken a picture.

Dinner had gone over wonderfully. It worried her that he had put her at ease, making her feel like they had known each other for years. He'd told stories of growing up with his father and learning the ins and outs of the bar business. Charlie hadn't laughed so much in a long time.

Then there was the fact that he fit; like all this time there had been an ingredient missing and Craig was it— all they'd needed was a dash of pepper. Again, not a good sign! Especially when all he wanted to hear were stories about her sisters. Charlie sighed; it was probably for the best.

She found him in the kitchen drinking his after-dinner coffee and looking at the pictures on her fridge.

"See anything interesting?" she asked, smiling when he looked guilty.

"Yeah. You were a cute kid too." Craig pointed to an old photo of the McKay sisters in front of a farmhouse.

"Thank you. That picture was taken in front of the Judge's home in Virginia. My sisters and I used to spend breaks from school there. It was wonderful."

"The Judge was your grandfather, right?" He hopped up on the counter when she took a seat on a stool.

"Yes, on Pop's first wife's side. The Judge later married the Widow Madison, as she liked to be called then," Charlie said with a touch of whimsy. Her grandmother had been a wonderful woman and a delightful cook.

Craig smiled. "The Widow Madison, huh?"

"Umm. Sadie Madison was her name; then she married the Judge and demanded everyone call her Granny Vaughn. That's who Alexandra named the B and B after. They died a year apart. It was heartbreaking."

"I'm sorry. My mother died when I was a kid, so I understand."

"I remember you telling me. You said you lived with your father afterward, right?"

"Good memory."

She gave him a small smile and stopped herself from reaching out to touch him.

"I don't know if it's my place," he said, looking sheepish, "but is it true you and your sisters were adopted? I've heard it around town."

"Yes, it's true. Casey, Alexandra, and Fletcher were all together in the same orphanage, and Pops adopted them as a unit. I came along five years later."

"Did you know your biological parents?"

"My birth mother died when I was born, and I was put in the system. I was with one woman for a few years—"

"Years?" His eyebrows rose. "Sorry, do you not talk about it?"

"Not usually, no. It always feels like it happened to someone else...another life."

"I get it; that's how I was after Mom died. It's like there's who you were before and who you are after, but no in between."

Charlie stared at him. Her heart dipped. "Yes, exactly."

"What was her name?"

She smiled. "Anita, Anita Harmon, and she was wonderful. She took me to the movies almost every weekend, or we'd have a movie marathon and make popcorn at home. She taught me how to paint, sew, and how to cook—she was a wonderful cook."

He laughed. "So that's where your love of the culinary arts came from?"

She nodded. "Yep. Most of my recipes belonged to her. See, she was going to adopt me, but she got diagnosed with cancer and she couldn't…"

"I'm sorry, Charlie."

Tears glazed her eyes. "I don't know whose heart it broke more, hers or mine. She died not long after I was sent back."

"What do your sisters say?"

"I don't talk about Anita with them; not because they wouldn't understand—they would, but I suppose I wanted to keep her memory for myself, like a treasure. But I do talk to Tiny about her."

"Sharing tips of the trade, no doubt."

She laughed. "Yes."

"Was it long before you were adopted?"

"Not too long, no. The social worker had to put me back in the system, and I was shuffled around a bit until I landed in the home where my father found me. Then I was a McKay, and there was no looking back."

A nice silence fell between them, and Craig finished his coffee.

"I'd better get going." He jumped down and reached for his jacket. Charlie followed him out.

"Thank you again for putting in the alarm," Charlie said, rubbing her arms. She stepped out on the porch and wondered if it would be a bad idea to replace the whole thing. She stifled a gasp when Craig tilted her chin up. The porch light made his eyes a midnight blue.

"I didn't mind. Thank you for dinner." And then he kissed her.

Charlie opened her mouth to his, relishing the feel

of his firm lips. Oh, God, she hadn't kissed anyone in ages. His tongue caressed hers, and she wrapped her arms around his waist. He pressed his hard body against her, and her heart sped up.

He stiffened and backed away. Her hands fell into the emptiness.

"What…" was all Charlie could get out until she looked behind Craig. "Fletcher, what are you doing?" Charlie couldn't believe it. The nerve! Here she was enjoying the first kiss she'd had in years, and her sister was holding a gun to Craig's head. "Put that thing away."

"Ah, Fletcher? Can we talk about this?" Craig asked.

"I told you if you came near my sisters, I'd shoot you. Did you think I was lying?" Fletcher sniffed, but after one look at Charlie's face, she holstered her weapon.

"I think you should go, Craig. I'm so sorry, I…" What could she say? My sister has lost her ever-loving mind?

Craig surprised her by grinning. "Don't worry about it, honey, really. I'll see you tomorrow."

A small hysterical giggle slipped from Charlie's lips. "Umm, okay." Craig got into his truck. She couldn't believe he wanted to see her again. He wanted…She turned to her sister. "What in the world is wrong with you?"

Tears spilled down Fletcher's cheeks in torrents.

Charlie swallowed. "Oh, Lordy, what now?"

Chapter Six

"Okay, what's happened?" Charlie asked once they were inside. She couldn't believe what Fletcher had done to Craig, but that could wait.

Her sister's gaze darted around the room, then she blubbered, "I've got good news, and I've got bad news."

Charlie's scalp prickled. "All right, honey. Do you want me to call..." Charlie looked up as Alex and Casey came in. She'd forgotten to lock the door. "Hello."

"Fletcher called us and said to get our asses here. Ryan's out with Jebb, so I didn't call him," Casey said. She looked Fletcher up and down. Casey no doubt had homed in on the tears and blotchy cheeks staining their sister's face—it didn't take a genius.

"There's coffee," Charlie said, pointing to the pot.

Casey nodded and poured a cup.

"What's going on here? Is Mack asleep?" Alex asked taking a seat at Charlie's table.

"I don't know what's going on. Other than the fact that Fletcher threatened to blow Craig's brains out. But yes, Mackenzie's down for the count." Charlie huffed, then refilled her own cup.

"What do you mean she almost blew Craig's— damn it, Fletcher, is someone drugging you again?" Casey asked.

Charlie hoped not. She didn't think she could go through that again. None of them could.

"No," Fletcher whispered.

Charlie rubbed her sister's hair. "Honey, tell me what's happened."

"Well, the good news is that we know for a fact that Daemon Randle isn't involved."

"That's good then." Had they suspected him? Charlie looked at her other sisters; they were confused too.

"How do we know he's not involved?" Casey asked.

"He was murdered tonight," Fletcher said.

Charlie covered her mouth with her hand. "Oh, God." She'd liked Daemon; unlike his brother, he was a good man. "What about his wife?"

"They've been separated for over a year, and I do believe the divorce was finalized four or five months ago. Didn't you know?" Alex asked.

Charlie shook her head. "No, I didn't. Poor Daemon. How did it happen?"

"They're calling it a suicide—"

"Fletch," Casey began, "if the police are calling it a suicide…"

Fletcher jumped to her feet. "He wouldn't kill himself!"

"Okay…but if he just got divorced—"

"No, if I know anything, it was that his wife was a witch and anyone would be happy to be rid of her," Charlie said.

"Exactly! I saw him this afternoon; he was so happy…and…and…"

"And what, Fletcher?" Casey prompted.

"We'd been seeing each other and…and he asked me to marry him," Fletcher said and everything stopped.

They all stared at Fletcher so long that she broke into tears and collapsed on the floor. No one moved until someone knocked on the door.

Charlie went to answer it, shaken by the bombshell her sister had dropped. She looked through the peephole to see their parents standing with Jasper.

"She here?" Jasper asked. He looked like hell warmed over.

Charlie stepped to the side to let them in.

"Where's Mack, sweetheart?" her mother asked.

"She's sleeping," Charlie said. "If she hadn't been so worn out, I'd be worried she'd wake up."

Like bystanders at a train wreck, she and her sisters stood to the side while her father lifted Fletcher in his arms and carried her out of the house. Their mother was hot on his heels. Jasper stayed behind and fixed himself a cup of coffee. His hand shook.

Charlie looked away.

Casey pointed a finger at Jasper. "Did you know about this?"

The old sheriff nodded.

Casey ran out the door.

"Jasper, please sit down and tell us what's going on." Charlie wiped her eyes on her sweatshirt and sat next to Alexandra.

"Yes, please enlighten us," Alex said in her haughtiest tone.

Jasper's deep sigh was heart-wrenching. "Your sister's been seeing that boy for a few months now. She kept it real quiet on account of his pending divorce and all. Not to mention past history." He gave Charlie a sad smile.

"Because of me? Is that what you mean, Jasper? She kept it to herself because of me?"

"No, not exactly. Now don't go getting yourself all worked up, Charlie. She was waiting for things to cool off. Fletcher doesn't have much experience with these types of relationships, and she knew I was against it from the beginning."

"Why?"

"You girls know your sister doesn't do anything like a normal body."

"No," Alex said. "She does everything to the extreme. As Mama always says."

"I told her I didn't think it was a good idea to be seeing Daemon Randle. Something 'bout that boy bothered me. God rest his soul."

"What, Jasper?"

"He messed with her head. I know, I know, it don't seem likely, but it's what he did."

"How?" Charlie wanted to know. But she could figure it out. Maybe the Randle brothers were more alike than she thought. "He showered her with attention." It wasn't a question.

"Oh, she thought she was in love something awful. Still does, I reckon. God forgive me, but I'm glad that boy's gone—not that I wanted him dead, just gone."

Charlie squeezed his fingers. "I don't blame you." Poor Fletcher.

"I'll feel sorry for people later," Alex began. "Right now, I'll take the facts and only the facts, please. She said he had asked her to marry him."

Jasper shook his head. "She wouldn't have gone

through with it; she knew what he was deep down—everyone thought it was his wife, but it wasn't."

"I just said the woman was a witch." Fooled again!

"I'm not saying any different, Charlie, but he made her that way or maybe they were made for each other."

"I don't understand any of this," Alex said, standing up and crossing her arms over her chest. "My opinion of Daemon is ambivalent at best, but Fletcher being involved with him? Fletcher involved with anybody seems laughable, but him?"

"The man had asked Fletcher to marry him, and she was thinking about it; then he up and died. She's spent the good part of the last two months hiding the relationship from y'all, and now she's thinking she's lost the love of her life."

"Did our parents know?" Charlie hoped so. It would crush them if Fletcher had kept them in the dark too.

"Yeah, they knew. That's part of what all that blustering was about between your dad and Fletcher the other day. Your parents didn't approve. You'll have to ask them why, but I'm sure our reasons are similar." Jasper finished his coffee. "I've gotta go back to the station and file a couple of reports. I'll see you girls later."

The door closed behind Jasper, and Charlie glanced at Alex, who looked back at her. Charlie started giggling, and then they were both laughing. It was absurd, but it was laugh or cry.

"I can't believe any of this," Alex said once she composed herself.

"You? God, Alexandra, what are we going to do? I mean, I'm sure Jasper's right about Daemon, but we need to prove it. How can we do that without Fletcher hating us?" Rick had practically had to slap her in the face for her to see him for what he really was. People only saw what they wanted to, and Fletcher was more stubborn than most.

"We get Noah to do it."

"What?"

"She already hates the man. Why not ask him as a favor—no, better yet, we'll get Craig to ask him. They're friends, and coming from Craig it won't seem fishy. But how do we go about it?"

"I don't like the idea of using Craig that way."

"What happened?"

A blush stole across Charlie's face. "He kissed me, and goodness, Alex, can the man kiss! I don't know what it is about him, but I can't seem to help myself. You—you don't mind, do you?"

"Of course not! Why would I?"

"If you're sure."

Alexandra nodded.

Charlie didn't know why her sister was lying, but she was going to ignore it. "I'll talk to Craig tomorrow and see what I can do."

****

Craig was getting out of the shower when someone knocked on his door. Grabbing a pair of discarded jeans from the floor, he headed toward the noise. His face split into a wide grin.

"Good morning, sweetheart." He backed up to let a flushed Charlie inside.

She shook her head and took off her jacket, while he shut the door. She headed for the small kitchenette and started making a pot of coffee. He stared at her until she stopped, midscoop.

"Oh, my goodness! I'm sorry. I came right in and took over." She squeezed her eyes shut.

She dropped the scoop, turned toward him, and Craig made his move. He shoved her against the counter and brought his mouth down on hers. It took a moment, but she sighed and ran her hands over his bare chest.

Craig angled his head to deepen the kiss and caressed his tongue against the silkiness of hers. Her kiss was alluring, and he grew hard against his zipper. He brought his hands up to run his fingers through her hair and hold her in place. Kissing Charlie was like eating chocolate chip cookies, and Craig wanted to binge. She moaned, and he made himself stop. He slowed the kiss and let her go.

"I wanted to get that out of the way," he said when she opened her eyes. There were tiny flecks of amber in her irises; he liked that. He hoped she didn't notice the bulge in his pants. He wasn't a teenager, but hell, she turned him on. He smiled and pointed to the canister. "And you're more than welcome to make us coffee anytime."

Charlie cleared her throat. "Umm, thanks." She turned back to the pot and finished what she'd been doing.

"You know I'm probably putting my life in jeopardy being with you. Your little sister *did* hold a gun to my head last night."

She looked confused for a minute, then her face crumpled and she grabbed a paper towel to dab her tears.

Shit! Shit! Shit! He hated tears. Especially the

female kind. But at least it killed his boner.

"I'm sorry. It's not you. My sister..." Charlie shook her head and sat down at the small table; he took the seat next to her. "Fletcher was a mess last night. Daemon Randle died. The police say it was suicide, but Fletcher claims he was murdered."

"Daemon Randle was Rick Randle's brother, correct?" Craig asked relieved when the tears stopped and she nodded. "Okay, why does your sister think it was murder?"

"Unbeknownst to any of us, Fletcher's been seeing Daemon. You see, he recently got a divorce, and he had asked Fletcher to marry him..." The tears started again.

He handed her another paper towel. "None of you knew?"

"Only my parents, and Jasper, of course. We didn't even think Fletcher dated. She was so upset when she told us—she collapsed in tears right on my floor; then Pops came and carried her away."

"So she wasn't in the best mental state last night when she threatened me?"

Charlie gave a small smile, jumping up when the coffee finished, but he motioned for her to sit back down.

"I'll get it." He took his time preparing their mugs. He was enjoying her eyes on him. Hell, he was surprised his skin didn't have scorch marks. Knowing she wanted him...no, down, boy. Serious business at hand.

Charlie took the cup he handed her.

"I feel a bit better knowing her threat wasn't personal." He reclaimed his seat and sipped. Perfect.

"To be honest," she began, "you should know that

Fletcher doesn't make idle threats."

He saluted her with his mug. "Thanks for the tip." Noah had warned him too, but he hadn't wanted to believe it. Still not wanting to think about it, he went on. "So what happened after your father carried her away?"

"We found out the worst of it. Jasper—have you met Sheriff Hart?"

"Not officially, no."

"Well, Jasper told me and Alexandra that Daemon wasn't a good person, and he'd fooled Fletch, which isn't easy to do."

"What did he mean 'fooled' her?" Craig asked.

Charlie fiddled with her coffee mug and wouldn't look at him.

Was she wondering if she could trust him? Okay, he admitted to himself, maybe she shouldn't, but this was different. "You don't have to tell me if you don't want to."

"Oh, it's not that. It's just that I don't know how to"—she waved her hand—"word it. There wasn't much on the up and up with the man, and Jasper knew it, but he couldn't prove it. If we had proof, then Fletcher could see the truth and move on."

Craig snapped his fingers. "Just like that?"

"I know my sister. If she saw she'd been lied to, then she'd get pissed. I'm sorry to say it, but an angry Fletcher is better than a depressed Fletcher any day of the week and twice on Sundays." Charlie rubbed her forehead.

Craig sat back in his chair. "How do we go about finding proof?"

"Oh, I couldn't ask you to do it."

"Why not?"

"Where Fletcher is concerned, the messenger is usually fair game."

"I see." She wanted his help, but she felt guilty asking him. That was pretty sweet. Unlike Fletcher, who wasn't sweet at all; Noah had been right about— that was it. "I'll ask Noah to do it."

"Oh, my goodness, I never would have thought about asking him! Do you think he would?"

"If I asked him to? Sure. I might have to explain to him why though."

"I guess that's okay. If you absolutely have to." She worried her napkin.

He stilled her hands, and she glanced up.

"Only if it's *absolutely* necessary. I promise." He was about to lean forward and seal the deal with a kiss when—was that "Tomorrow" from the movie *Annie*?

"That's my phone," Charlie said, digging her cell from her pocket. "It's Alex. I'm supposed to be helping out at the B and B this morning." She stood to get her jacket.

"How did your sisters handle all of this?"

She gave him a funny look. "McKays are pretty darn resilient."

"I've—ah—heard that."

"You'll ask Noah and let me know?"

"Yes, of course. Charlie?" he said when she opened the door.

She turned. "Yes?"

"I'll call you when I find out anything."

She nodded and shut the door in his face.

The chill he got hadn't been from the cold burst of wind. No, it was from the last look Charlie had given him. "Good going, pal. Real fucking good," he berated himself as he reached for his phone. He wasn't sure what he'd done to put the hurt in her beautiful eyes, but if calling Noah brought him a step closer to fixing it, then that's what he would do.

Chapter Seven

"How did it go?" Alex asked when Charlie came through the porch door.

"I deserve a flipping Oscar or a Golden Globe at the very least," Charlie said, shrugging out of her jacket. Why had he gone and ruined it by asking about her sisters? Because she *knew* he meant Alex. It wasn't as though Charlie thought she was chopped liver, but Alexandra was and had always been bewitchingly beautiful. Ugh, she needed to stop feeling sorry for herself.

Alex filled a vase with water. "What's wrong then?"

"Do you have a thing for Craig? And don't lie to me either, Alexandra McKay."

"I don't know what you're—"

She growled. "Darn it, Alex! Something's up, and I want to know what the heck it is."

"Don't go getting an attitude with me. I haven't even spent a total of two hours in the man's company. And he's kissing you, isn't he? I thought so. Who's lying to whom here?"

"Fine! Forgive me if I don't believe you."

"*Okay*! I don't know what it is about him...oh, I don't know. I'm entirely confused on the matter of Mr. Sutton. All right, happy now?"

Charlie sniffed. "Yes."

"Thank you, God! Men make things messy, always." Alex set the flower arrangement on the kitchen table. "Now...whether or not you deserve an Oscar remains to be seen."

Charlie poured herself a glass of tea. "A better performance I haven't pulled off in years. I did the McKay sisters proud."

"Is Craig going to get Noah to look into Daemon?"

"Yeah, and he came up with the idea all by himself too." They shared a smile. "I do feel guilty for pulling out the tears, but Craig didn't have a clue." Of course, after he asked about her *sisters*, she was a teensy-weensy bit glad she'd deceived him.

Alex smirked. "Honey, he's a man. None of them have a clue unless we give it to them."

****

Charlie had a lot of errands to run before her shift, but she wanted to stop and bring her sister lunch. Casey had bought Ward Jessup's old auto garage when she'd first come back home, but craziness had stepped in and she had had to rebuild it from scratch; it was a beautiful building even if it did smell like oil and musk. Big sister had always been handy with fixing things, especially things with engines.

Charlie found her sister in her small office on the phone. She waved a brown paper bag in front of Casey's face, then sat down. The room was small and painted the same plum color that adorned the walls in the attic at their parent's home. It was Casey's favorite color, and it was just a tad darker than her sister's eyes. The office was well organized; everything had its own compartment, and that made Charlie smile.

Casey hung up the phone and looked in the bag.

"You're my favorite sister."

"Don't worry, I won't tell anyone you can be bought by a PB and J sandwich," she said with a smirk.

Casey grunted, then moaned after taking a bite. "You used strawberry jam too."

"Of course, only the best for *my* big sister." Charlie bit into her own sandwich.

"Where's Mack?"

"Mrs. Williams has finally recuperated and started class again." Thank God!

Casey shook her head. "Poor kid."

"She doesn't feel like you did about school, Casey. She likes it."

"Give her time. So, you close shop tonight, right?"

"Yeah."

Casey nodded, then looked Charlie up and down. "What's up?"

"Just some covert operations," Charlie said with a straight face. If her sister loved anything, it was causing trouble—the good kind, mind you—and covert operations.

"Who exactly is the target?"

"There isn't a direct target, per se…"

Casey's eyes narrowed. "The indirect then?" She sat back while Charlie went over what Jasper had said last night and then what she'd done this morning.

"What do you think?"

"You're a constant amazement. Just when I think I have you in your cute square peg, you up and move on me." Casey shook her head but grinned. "That Sutton doesn't stand a chance against a McKay…or a Keller, for that matter."

"Did Fletcher talk to you about it?"

Casey shook her head. "You know Fletch—"

"You didn't ask the right questions?"

"I asked all that came to mind. Having Noah deliver the bad news is brilliant though. No sense in us getting verbally or, heaven forbid, physically attacked over this."

"I can't take the credit for the bright idea though. It was Alex's."

"Sneaky little bitch—"

"*Casey*!"

"If you had let me finish, you would've heard the 'can't help but admire her' part of my flipping sentence."

"Oh, sorry." Charlie smiled sweetly. A lot of people thought of Alexandra that way, and if she admitted it—though she never would—Charlie would have to agree with Casey. "The McKays don't take crap from anyone. Or the Kellers either."

Casey grinned. "What's up with you and Sutton anyway?"

Heat crept up her neck. "Where'd that come from?"

"I was thinking we don't know much about the man..." She waved a hand when Charlie would have commented. "We know he was a security expert, but what about before that? And what the hell is he doing here? Noah Reed isn't the type of person to bring about warm fuzzy feelings or inspire someone to move to Bum-fuck."

"You're paranoid." But the thought didn't sit well in Charlie's stomach.

"Why the hell shouldn't I be? And you"—Casey waved her finger in Charlie's face—"you should be even more paranoid than me. Hell, you should be shaking in your shoes. It's not every day an ex-lover's dismembered, decomposing body is delivered to your doorstep."

"You don't have to remind me," she snapped. She stood and turned to the door. "You're not the one who someone wants to 'pay for her crimes.' Whatever the heck that means. And need I remind you that I've been both kidnapped and held at gunpoint? So don't start lecturing me." Slamming the door shut was unnecessary, but it felt good.

****

By the time Charlie closed the diner, she was in a horrible mood. "I'm freaking ticked off," she announced to the empty place. After she'd stormed out of her sister's office, she'd come to work and sent her manager home. Not two minutes later, Mrs. Williams had called to tell her that her mother hadn't picked Mack up from school.

Charlie shoved the mop around. It would have helped if she'd remembered to call her mother this morning and let her know Mrs. Williams was back. Both her dad and Casey were at work, so they couldn't get away; she hadn't even bothered calling them. She'd tried calling Alexandra, Fletcher, and her mother.

Heck, she'd even called Jasper. Wasn't a sheriff supposed to answer his phone? What if it had been an emergency? See if she fixed him his favorite cake for his birthday. Ha! If it hadn't been for Ryan coming in for a bite to eat, she would have forgotten all about having a brother-in-law who was always willing to lend a helping hand. He'd picked Mack up and brought her to the diner.

It wasn't really even the fact that she hadn't been able to reach anyone that upset her. It was that she needed their help in the first place. She didn't like having to depend on other people. Sure, she herself was dependable and loved being able to help when needed, but she hated that *she* needed someone to help *her* with her child.

Then the icing on the cake was when Marylou showed up.

"I despise that woman," Charlie told the napkins as she filled the holders.

She'd known it was only a matter of time before Marylou made an appearance. Charlie slammed the salt canister down to add to her dislike of the entire scene. Marylou had come in and started making accusations. Which wouldn't have been so bad if the place hadn't been packed and her daughter hadn't been sitting right at the center of the storm. Charlie squeezed her eyes shut.

Oh, she'd taken a lot of crap from Marylou over the years, she'd admit that. When they were in high school, the viper had purposely tripped Charlie so she couldn't go to the school dance. Of course, Charlie had then snuck purple hair dye into the shampoo in the other girl's gym bag, but that was beside the point.

Tonight was different. Charlie had stood behind the counter turning so many shades of red Crayola would be impressed, while the witch went on and on. Dana Randle had been here too. The woman had just lost another brother, and she had to hear Marylou's horrific accusations. Poor Dana. Her brown hair had been pulled into a tight bun and her blue eyes, so much like Rick's, had been red-rimmed. She'd run out of the diner in a fit of tears. Marylou had no shame.

She'd made a colossal mistake though. The memory was all too vivid in Charlie's mind.

Mackenzie had been sitting on her stool with her little cherub mouth hanging open while the evil witch ranted and raved. Charlie had asked her kindly to leave. Twice. But she wouldn't shut up. Marylou had stopped in front of Mack and said, "How does it feel to be trash, little girl? How does it feel to have a whore for a mommy?"

Needless to say, that was Charlie's breaking point; she'd walked around the counter and slapped Marylou so hard her hand still stung. Charlie had then thrown the woman out and told her she wasn't welcome in this diner, ever. The entire crowd had cheered. But that was a moot point when her daughter started sobbing.

Charlie didn't know how it happened, but apparently not only had most of town been in the diner, but Craig as well. He'd hugged her—in front of everyone—and picked Mack up whispering, Charlie didn't know what, in her ear. And somehow Craig had taken custody of her daughter and took her with him back to her house. He'd be waiting there when she got home.

Since Marylou left, she'd been in a pissy mood, and the more she thought about what the woman had said, the more ticked off Charlie became. She marched over to the counter, dug a five-dollar bill from the pocket of her jeans, and stuck it in the "Pay for Profanity" jar. She took a breath, then shouted the words that had been strangling her. Getting the anger off her chest helped, but the relief was fleeting when she remembered what happened next.

Jasper had come in talking about assault. Charlie had never been accused of assaulting anyone in her entire life. Had she gotten in fights when she was younger? Yes! But she'd never been accused of assaulting someone. She was a McKay, darn it; they were supposed to fight the good fight. Charlie had explained to Jasper that she had been verbally assaulted and harassed. Not to mention the verbal assault on her four-and-a-half-year-old daughter.

Every patron in the diner agreed with and defended her. After all, most people in town had been dumped on by the Thomas family one way or another at some point in their lives. Jasper had agreed, which didn't surprise her, but he could have agreed with her in the first place! He was *so* not getting a birthday cake this year.

Finally finished with the deposits and cleaning up, Charlie headed for the door. She hit the light switch, jumped when the window crashed, and then everything went black.

Chapter Eight

Mack pursed her lips, and Craig grinned. They were playing Clue Jr., and he was pretty sure she had already figured out the who, where, and with what pet. According to Mack, her Auntie Fletcher had taught her to play. "Auntie Fletch is the bestest Clue player in the whole wide world."

Craig couldn't fathom what the hell happened at the diner. One minute he was watching the way Charlie ran around the place chatting with everyone, and the next minute all hell broke loose. He hadn't had the unfortunate pleasure of meeting Marylou Thomas, and he was utterly glad he hadn't. He couldn't believe Noah was dating such a vindictive bitch.

Mack blew a raspberry. "You ain't paying attention."

Craig tweaked Mack's nose. "It's your turn again, sweets."

"Ohskay." She spun the spinner and took her turn. Cocking her head to the side, she gave him the once-over. "You're pretty fun, Pepper. Mrs. Williams would give you four gold stars for sure."

"You think so?" He couldn't recall a teacher ever giving him four stars for anything; his loquaciousness usually got him in trouble.

"Yep!" She stared down at the board. "I wish my mama was here instead of with that mean lady."

"Me too."

"Marywhosits is a very, very bad person. Even worse than Miss Hannigan."

"Who's Miss Hannigan?"

"You know, from *Annie*. Miss Hannigan was in charge of the orphanage and wasn't nice to Annie. That's how I got my middle name."

Craig grinned. "Your middle name?"

"Un-huh, it's Mama's favoritest movie in the whole wide world. You know, cause Mama and Auntie Alex and Auntie Casey and even Auntie Fletcher were orphans."

"Your mama told you that?"

She stuck out her lower lip. "Well…"

"Who told you that, honey?" The kid looked guilty as hell.

"Auntie Fletch doesn't keep secrets from me."

"So your Auntie Fletch told you?" He was walking a fine line, but he wanted details.

"Yep, she tells me lots and lots of things. Like her real name was Jamie, but she didn't like it, so she had Grandpops change it for her. She got her name from a show too." Mack started putting away the pieces even though they hadn't finished.

"What show was that?" he asked, helping her put the game away.

"I don't remember."

He took a seat next to her on the couch, and she hopped up on his lap. She took a small band from around her wrist, handed it to him, then sat patiently waiting. Luckily, Craig's mother had taught him how to braid, so he had the basics down.

He began parting Mack's hair when she said, "I

don't have a daddy…did you know?"

Craig swallowed. "I know, sweets. Does that make you sad?"

She shrugged her shoulders. "Auntie Alex told me that Mama didn't have a daddy until she was eight. I'm not even five yet, so…"

"Your Auntie Alex is one smart lady."

"Oh, she is. A lady, I mean. Not like the dog movie though; Auntie Alex ain't a dog."

Craig burst out laughing.

She smiled and touched her hair. "Thanks for trapping my hair."

"Trapping?"

"That's what Auntie Fletch calls it. She has a potty mouth, you know." A key turned in the lock, and they both looked up. "Mama!" Mack ran to the door and came to a quick halt.

Craig stood. A teenage boy came into the house. Shit! Where the hell was Charlie?

"Jebby!" Mack shouted. "Oh, we're gonna have a party for sure now."

"Hey, squirt. Sorry, no parties tonight." He stuck out his hand. "You must be Mr. Sutton. I'm Jebbediah McKay."

He shook the kid's hand. "Craig."

"Jebb. No one calls me Jebbediah, unless I'm in trouble."

Craig would have guessed who the boy was without the introduction. He was the spitting image of his father, but he had his mother's sapphire eyes.

"I have my learner's permit, and we're on our property, so Pops lets me drive by myself," he explained, then glanced down at Mackenzie. "Go ahead and get your overnight bag, squirt."

With his stomach in his throat, Craig waited until Mack was out of the room to ask what was going on.

Jebb switched from foot to foot. "Someone threw rocks into the windows of the diner—smashed every single one."

"And Charlie?"

"One of the rocks hit her in the head. She's fine. Really," Jebb insisted. "She has a mild concussion, and she's at Alex's. Alexandra loves to hover, especially over Charlie." He grinned. "Women are weird. Or at least the ones in my family are."

"I understand."

"I'm ready! Where am I gonna go?" Mack asked.

"You're staying with me and Grandma and Grandpops tonight. Your mama's having a special sleepover with Auntie Alex."

"Ohskay. Bye, Pepper. Thanks for playing with me." She motioned for Craig to come down to her level, then kissed his cheek and gave him a big hug.

"I'll see you later, sweets," he said, then waved good-bye. He figured he should lock up and go home. It was lucky his place was right next to Alexandra's. "Nifty that."

****

"Alexandra McKay, if you don't stop hovering over me, I'm gonna leave," Charlie said after Alex took her temperature for what had to be the hundredth time.

They were in Charlie's favorite guest room at the B and B. It was decorated in the old farmhouse style, with a lovely cotton-upholstered settee and cast-iron headboard, not to mention the adjoining bathroom. Alex always let Charlie use this room when she stayed over and there weren't any guests. She usually found it relaxing.

Alex checked the thermometer. "Concussions are tricky."

"I'd rather be shot," Fletcher added from where she sat next to the bed.

"Haven't you been shot enough?"

Fletcher twirled her twin braids around her fingers. "Don't get snitty with me, Alexandra. I don't need your damn attitude; I have my own!"

Casey snickered. "And she has the shirt to prove it."

"Ain't you supposed to be a married woman now? Go home."

Charlie squinted. "Fletcher, please, I feel like a train hit me, and you keep whining." God, her head hurt, but she didn't have a fever. She swatted Alexandra's hand away from her forehead.

"Well, excuse the fuck outta me!" Fletcher said and stood. "Since you don't seem to want me here, I'll go bug Jasper."

Charlie waited until Fletcher had left the room. "She seems to be feeling better today. You would never know she'd had a meltdown last night."

"Yeah, that's what worries me. She's too damn collected. Last night she was a wreck."

"Oh, who cares. Charlie's the one with the concussion, for goodness' sake!"

"Alexandra McKay, take that back right now. She's our sister—our *little* sister, for crying out loud. Back me up, Casey."

"What do you want me to say? Face it, Charlie. I may be the oldest, you may be the sweetest, and

Alexandra here may be the bitchiest, but Fletcher's the meanest." Casey grinned when Alex threw a pillow at her.

"She is not mean! How can you say that?" Fletcher didn't have a truly mean bone in her teeny tiny body. She had a quick, forceful temper, and she wasn't the most tamed, but she wasn't mean-spirited.

Casey rubbed her forehead. "Jeez, Charlie, I didn't mean it."

"Feeling guilty now?"

"Yes. Happy?"

"Yep." Charlie settled back against the pillows. "God, what a day. Did Jebb call yet?"

"Yeah, Mackenzie's safe and sound with the parents. Jebb said he hated to take her away from Craig. Apparently"—Casey smirked—"she talked about 'Pepper' the entire time they were in the car."

"That's what she calls him. Something about the way he smells." Charlie turned her smile inward. Craig smelled divine. "When I find out who did this—"

Casey sat up straight. "That bitch Marylou did this!"

"No, she didn't," Alex said. "Jasper said she has an ironclad alibi."

"I figured she would. She was with Noah, wasn't she?" Poor Noah. Charlie liked him and didn't want to see him clawed to shreds by the likes of Marylou.

"Yes, she was with him. I wonder if he's found out anything yet."

Casey grinned. "I've got to hand it to you, Alexandra. Sometimes your mind is truly a beautiful thing."

"Thank you, I couldn't agree more. I only hope he

can dig up information."

"Ryan's looking into it too," Casey said. "You know...I was thinking a minute ago—"

"Oh, wonderful."

"Shut up, Alex. Like I was saying, there's something not sitting right with me about this whole thing. I mean, you saw Fletch tonight. What's up with that?"

"You may be right. Something seems off," Charlie said. The meds were kicking in quite pleasantly. Everything was kind of whooshy.

"Will someone please enlighten me here?"

"Fletcher's acting strange 'sall, Alex."

"She's always been strange, Casey. What else is new?"

Whatever Casey was about to say died on her lips when someone knocked on the door.

****

Craig came in smiling. He'd been standing outside the hall for several minutes. He'd been maneuvered this morning, and if he wasn't so damn impressed with both Alex and Charlie for the effort, he'd be pissed. As always, Alexandra was impeccably dressed in a wool skirt and matching sweater. Casey had on a pair of torn jeans and a sweatshirt that read "My husband's a private dick!"

Craig guffawed. "I like your sweatshirt."

Casey blushed, then got defensive. "It's true. Ryan is a PI."

"What brings you here, Craig?" Alexandra asked with a tone Craig couldn't place.

"Came to check on the patient."

Casey got up and pulled on Alex's arm. "Come on.

I want to show you something."

"It's nothing revolting, is it?" Alexandra asked before she shut the door.

"Hi," Charlie said with a goofy grin.

Craig took a seat on the bed beside her. "Good drugs?"

"The best," she whispered, humming when he pressed a tender kiss to her lips. She smiled. "Before I forget...thank you for taking care of Mack."

"It wasn't a problem." He brushed her hair out of her face and her eyes fluttered open. "What's really going on, Charlie?"

"Someone wants us dead," she said, slurring her words.

"Us?"

"Mmm-hmm, someone's always trying to kill the McKays. They never have, though."

"That's good to know...Charlie?"

Her eyes flickered shut, and he checked the prescription on the nightstand next to her. She wouldn't remember he had even been here in the morning. "You'll probably be having some interesting dreams this evening, sweetheart..."

Craig found Casey and Alexandra sitting at the kitchen table. He almost groaned, they were drinking coffee—Alex's coffee.

"Is she asleep?" Alex asked, clearing a place for him to sit.

Craig took a seat and grinned. "Out like a light." Charlie had started talking nonsense—very sexy nonsense—and he'd had to leave while he'd still been able to.

"How much did you hear before you knocked?"

Casey asked. "Damn it, Alex, don't kick me under the table. You and I both knew he was standing there."

Alex closed her eyes. "A bit of tact, Casey, please."

She snorted. "*Me*? You're the one who kicked—"

Craig cleared his throat. "I heard enough to know Charlie is wasting her talent at the diner. She's a superb actress."

Casey pursed her lips. "You don't sound angry about it."

"Nah. I would have done it if she asked me outright." He shrugged. "I'll say this, though, if I wasn't so impressed...I'd be pissed." He sipped his coffee and ignored both sets of narrowed eyes. He was honest. About most things anyway.

"Great. So, has Noah found out anything yet?"

"Casey!"

"What now, Miss Priss?"

"It's fine," Craig said with a smirk. "And, no, he hasn't called me with anything. I don't know if I should say this, but I don't think he agreed to do this for honorable reasons."

"I counted on that being his biggest motivator," Alex said.

He blinked. "I'm sorry, what?"

Alexandra sighed. "For whatever reason, those two hate each other, and this will give Noah the power to hurt Fletcher."

"That's a shitty thing to do," Craig said. What kind of person would let someone take a potshot at their sister?

"Trust me. It's the best way. Fletcher's anger will be so focused on whatever Noah shoves down her throat, she won't feel the blow as bad."

"If there's anything there in the first place. You're forgetting we're going on Jasper's judgment here," Casey said.

"You, dear sister, are forgetting Jasper would die if anything bad happened to Fletcher again. The man's hair went completely white over the summer," Alex said. "Though, truth be told, I'm having certain inclinations where the good sheriff is concerned."

"Could you ladies fill me in here? I'll just ask around," he said when they didn't speak up.

"A while ago someone poisoned Fletcher—"

"I know that part." He grinned. "Small towns love fresh ears. I've heard that the sheriff is BFFs with his deputy."

"Yes, I suppose you could say they're best friends." Alex frowned. "He's her *only* friend outside the family."

"Fletcher doesn't trust people real easy," Casey explained. "And she makes most people uncomfortable with that hot temper of hers."

Alex nodded. "That's why she's such a good deputy, though. People are too wary of her to commit a crime."

"What about the two of you? What's your story?" Craig pointed to Casey.

"Why?"

"I can just—"

"Ask around? Fine. I'm Casey McK—Keller, damn it, and I'm twenty-seven. I left home for a while…but now I'm back. I'm married, own my own garage, and have a brother-in-law I can barely stand. How was that?"

"Great. Thanks." Craig chuckled, then motioned to

Alexandra. "You're next."

"This is ridiculous."

Casey smirked. "Problem, Alexandra?"

"If you insist. First off, a *lady* never discusses her age," she said looking pointedly at Casey, who shrugged. "I own my own business as well, obviously; I am a respected member of the community and have a seat on the town council."

"Boring," Casey said, then motioned to Craig. "Your turn, Mr. Nosey."

"Okay. Craig Sutton, early thirties, and single. I served on a SWAT team for a while, then went into the security business. I sold said business a few months ago and moved here where my old college roommate lives and a bar was up for sale," he said, then sipped his coffee. "So, what can you tell me about Charlie?"

Casey crossed her arms over her chest and leaned back in her chair. "Not a damn thing!"

Chapter Nine

Charlie fiddled with the centerpiece on Alex's kitchen table and again asked, "Is that all he said?" She was grouchy; she hadn't gotten much sleep with Alex waking her up every hour. But the dreams she'd had when she *had* been asleep were hot enough to have her checking the sheets for scorch marks. And they all revolved around the man in question.

Casey rolled her eyes. "Yes, you know everything Craig told us. He's either exceptionally honest or a high-caliber liar. I would have recorded the conversation if I'd known I was gonna be interrogated."

"I can't believe he knows I was playing up the situation. How can I look at him again without feeling guilty?"

"He *laughed* about it. He even said he was impressed. Don't worry."

"You're right." Charlie combed her fingers through her wet hair. Her head didn't hurt as bad as it had last night; she was pretty sure the hot shower had helped. She didn't have to worry about work because the diner was closed until the glass for the windows arrived. Speaking of which…"I can't believe Pops ordered bulletproof glass." Her father was an ex-FBI agent, and some habits died hard.

"It's typical. He gave the crew special instructions to fireproof the garage when we rebuilt it." Casey shook her head and smiled. "You've gotta love him."

"Amen!" They clinked mugs in agreement, then Charlie sighed. "I need to go get Mackenzie. I don't like her being away this much."

"I meant to ask you about that..." Color swept up Casey's neck to her cheeks.

Charlie blinked. "Okay?"

"Ryan and I are meeting Jake up in DC next week, and we thought we could take Mack. I know, I know, it's a big deal. We'd only be gone for four days, and there's tons of cool stuff in D.C. Remember when Pops took us? We had a blast."

"I don't know, Casey. I mean, I want to do that stuff with Mack." Charlie had a long list of the places she wanted to take her daughter; the point was, *she* wanted to take her.

"I get it, I do. But she's still young, so she won't remember any of it; you can take her again. This way, you'll have time to regroup, relax, and of course, and this is the biggy...I'll have an excuse not to be alone with Jake—there I've said it."

"That's what all this is about, isn't it? You don't want to hang out with your brother-in-law." Charlie laughed. Jacob Keller may be Ryan's twin, but that's where the similarities ended. "I happen to like Jake, and so does Fletcher."

"Yeah, well, you like everybody, and Fletcher kicked his ass."

"True as that may be...Casey?"

Casey's gaze was blank, no doubt lost in Keller land.

Charlie sighed. It was like trying to talk to a five-year-old. Heck, Mack was a better listener. She called her sister's name a couple more times, then waved a hand in front of her face.

"Sorry, my mind kept running after my mouth stopped. What'd you say?"

Charlie shook her head. "Okay, you can take Mackenzie with you, but only if you promise to be on your best behavior."

Casey threw her arms around her. "Thank you!"

She grinned, then shook her head when Casey ran out of the room to call Ryan.

Charlie would miss her baby something terrible, but this might be the best time for Mack to be away. And maybe Charlie could get a few things accomplished, like finding out who was behind breaking her windows and—who could possibly forget—putting Rick's remains on her doorstep.

****

Charlie pulled into her parents' driveway half an hour later. She smiled at the log cabin on steroids. She'd fallen in love with the wraparound porch the moment she'd seen it. She took her time going up the steps; if the wind was just right, she could imagine her sisters laughing.

The moment she walked into the kitchen she was embraced by both the heat of the oven and the tantalizing aroma of fresh baked bread. Her mouth watered; her mother's banana nut bread was to die for. It had won the blue ribbon at the county fair five years running. Charlie studied her mother before she announced herself. As beautiful as ever and still in love with Pops McKay.

When Savannah Walker had first come to Blue Creek, she'd been hired as principal of Blue Creek

Elementary and Middle School; Mildred was her secretary. Her first meeting with the "McKay heathens" hadn't been pleasant, but Charlie had liked her at first sight. She had kept that information to herself, of course; her sisters wouldn't have approved. They— Casey and Fletcher anyway—had labeled Savannah prissy-pants-principal, but she'd proved them wrong, then shocked everyone by becoming their mother.

"Charlie!" her mother said when she turned and found her there. They hugged for a minute, then sat down at the table.

"Where's Mack?"

"Your father took her to preschool this morning. We figured she'd have fun, and you needed the rest."

"Thank you." She stood.

"Charlie, honey, why don't you stay and keep me company for a little while?"

"I'm sorry, Mama. Of course I'll stay." She sat back down, a wave of guilt rushing to her head. She had been neglecting her parents.

"I feel like I haven't had a one-on-one with you in weeks."

"I know, I'm sorry."

"Oh, honey, don't be sorry. That's life. We all seem to be busy, and with everything that's going on with you, I figured you're pretty swamped." She got up and fixed a plate of banana nut bread and a glass of milk for the both of them.

"True," Charlie said once her mother took her seat. "This hasn't been a normal couple of weeks. It's still no excuse not to talk to you." She took a bite of the bread and moaned; it was the best.

"Don't worry about it. Really. Your father and I are

pretty busy ourselves. With Jebb in high school now, both his cell phone and the home phone are constantly ringing. I had your father have a talk with him about sex."

Charlie coughed.

Savannah smirked. "You should have seen it. Your father was too cute, fumbling over his words, making himself sick. Literally."

"He threw up?" It wasn't really a question. Her father tended to work himself up into such a state that he made himself sick. He'd been that way for years.

"Yep, both he and Jebb were terribly embarrassed by the entire thing. Served Emmit right, considering I had to tell you girls. Of course, I had the advantage of having been a teacher."

"How could I forget? Fletcher's eyes almost popped out of her head when you showed us pictures and explained about the intimate act of sex." None of the sisters had had the heart to tell their mother that they knew what sex was. Most teens did nowadays, but they had known because they'd wanted to know. Alex had heard their uncles talking about it and told her sisters. Charlie had gone to the library and Casey and Fletcher...well, they did what they did best in those days. Broke into the upper-grade classrooms and found all the information they could carry. "By the way, did Fletcher talk to you about Daemon?"

"We knew she was seeing him, if that's what you mean. Not that we liked the idea."

"Why? I thought Dad had done business with Daemon."

"He did, but business is business; his daughters are another matter entirely."

"What do you mean?"

Savannah fiddled with her napkin.

"Come on, Mama, talk to me."

"Fletcher isn't like you girls, honey."

"At the risk of sounding repetitive, what do you mean, exactly?"

"You, Casey, and Alexandra are strong, independent women…"

Charlie's mouth fell open.

Savannah smiled. "Yes, darling, you're strong, stronger than you give yourself credit for. I admire that about you."

"You do?"

"Of course! You made a life for yourself and your daughter despite so many people outside this family thinking you'd fail. You have your own home and family, and the diner is doing better than it ever has. And through it all you've been a good friend, daughter, mother, and sister. Plus, you did it all with a smile. Yes, honey, you're strong."

Tears glazed Charlie's eyes. "You don't know how much it means to me to hear you say those things." Charlie couldn't believe her mother thought that way. She said as much.

"Your father and I both do. Casey's the stubborn one, with a loyal streak a mile wide. When she loves, she does it completely. Alexandra is the savvy businesswoman with decent judgment and a good heart beneath the steel."

Charlie laughed. "Agreed."

"You're the strong one, not so much physically like Casey or Fletcher, nor shrewd like Alexandra, but emotionally. You're a rock and one of the kindest people I know. You have a wholesome beauty that even if overlooked cannot be denied. When you girls were teenagers, your father used to say that he wished his girls weren't so beautiful; then he wouldn't have to shine his shotgun."

"Pops wouldn't hurt a fly." But Charlie was touched. It was a wonderful to know her parents felt that way about her. Everyone needed to hear something good about themselves now and again. Which reminded her. "And Fletcher?"

"I didn't think you'd forget. Always the mother hen." Savannah sighed. "Fletcher's different."

Normally Charlie wouldn't pry, but she had a feeling her mother had more to say. "Come on, Mama, talk."

"Another of your little traits. Who can say no to Charlie? Oh, well. Fletcher really is beautiful if she would just let herself be. She's physically strong, which throws most people off because she so tiny, but she can protect herself that way. That's what she does; she'll go to any length to protect the people she loves—and, of course her heart."

"That's why she's so upset about Daemon's death? Because she'd let him in?"

"You know what I hate? People talking about you behind your back!" Fletcher said from the doorway.

Savannah stood. "Fletcher, honey…"

"Don't 'Fletcher, honey' me. I've been here for most of your little visit," she snapped, then went out the swinging door. The pounding of her boots against the stairs echoed in the kitchen.

Savannah sat back down and rubbed her temples. "Oh, Lord."

"It's my fault. I'm sorry, Mama." This is what she got for putting her nose where it didn't belong.

"It's not you, honey. You wanted my opinion."

Charlie shook her head. "But if I hadn't pried..." She looked up when Fletcher came through the kitchen carrying two duffel bags. This was not a good sign.

"I'm moving out" was all she said.

Charlie stared out the window as Fletcher threw her stuff in the back of her truck and sped off.

"She's going to her cabin; no need to worry." Savannah's eyes didn't leave the window.

"Of course you're worried."

"You're right, but *you* don't need to worry. I'll tell your father about this later." She bit her lip.

"What is it?"

"They aren't speaking right now. I think it has something to do with Daemon, but I'm not sure." Savannah half smiled. "Do you still want to know about Fletcher?"

****

Charlie pulled up to her house around dusk. It had been four days since she'd been in her mother's kitchen. The windows for the diner—bulletproof, no less—had arrived today. Charlie had cleaned up after her father and the workmen. Pops hadn't said much, and she didn't ask him what was wrong. He'd tell her if he wanted to. She'd always lent her father an ear if and when he needed.

Sighing, Charlie unbuckled Mack's safety seat. She was only half listening to Mackenzie, who had the tendency to be a chatterbox when she was tired.

"...I really, really like Pepper a lot," Mack said and took a deep breath.

"What, honey?" She opened the front door and typed in the code for the alarm.

"Mama, you don't have your listening cap on. I said, I really like Pepper a lot."

She snorted. "Yes, Craig is a very nice man." Charlie didn't know if she should let her daughter get attached to Craig Sutton. Heck, she shouldn't get attached to the man either. But it was difficult when everywhere she went…there he was. He turned up at the diner, at the hardware store, and every time she had gone over Alex's, he'd come in for something: a cup of coffee or a chat. It was hard to get someone out of your mind when they weren't long out of your sight.

"Could we have him over for supper again?" Mack asked when they entered the kitchen. "Pepper's fun! He likes playing Clue Jr. and reading books. Maybe he likes movies like us. Wouldn't that be great?"

"I don't know, honey. Craig's a busy man."

Mack climbed up on a barstool while Charlie started making dinner. "Why?"

"He's trying to open a business, sweetheart. It takes a lot of work to get things started."

"What kinda biz…bizn?"

"Business? Craig's opening a bar. Remember Shmittie?"

"That old man who you said wasn't Santa Claus?" Mack asked narrowing her eyes. "He looked like Santa—even his face was furry."

"Yes, that's him, but he's not Santa. He did own the bar, but he sold it to Craig."

"Why? It's because he had to go back to the North Pole, isn't it? I know you said he wasn't Santa, but I'm smart—everyone says so."

"Yes, you are smart, Mack, but you're wrong about Shmittie; he moved to Florida."

Mack gasped. "Where Cinderella lives!"

Charlie laughed. "Not quite."

"Hmmm, okay." Mack started fidgeting with the stack of mail on the counter. "Look, Mama, it's for me." She held up the pink card and pointed to the letters. "I can spell my name, and that says me."

Charlie smiled and took the envelope; Alexandra had probably sent it or their mother. Opening the flap, Charlie read the letter and trembled.

"What does it say? You know I can't read big words yet. Just small ones like cat or dog...or..." Mack clapped her hands. "Or the bestest word, pony!"

"I—it's a hello from Santa. He's saying he hoped you liked his presents this year." Charlie lied. They'd been talking about Shmittie and Santa, hadn't they?

"Oh, wow! Can I see it?" Mack made a grab for the letter, but Charlie snatched it away.

"Uh, no, honey, I want to clean it up a bit. You know what? I'll laminate it so you can put it in your treasure chest." She would make a brand-new card.

Mack stared at her for a moment, then shrugged. "Okay, Mama."

"Why don't you go and—" The doorbell rang, and Charlie jumped.

"I'll get it!"

"No! I'll get it. You go wash up for dinner." Charlie waited until her daughter had left, then went to the door. She looked through the peephole and sagged against the door.

"Thank goodness it's you," she said and dragged Craig inside.

Craig grinned. "Now, that's a greeting if I ever heard one."

"Good, great." Charlie shoved the card under his nose and shut the door. "Look what someone sent to Mackenzie."

Raising an eyebrow, Craig took the card and looked it over.

The outside showed a picture of Mackenzie with her eyes cut out, which was bad enough, but the inside was even worse. She didn't think she would ever get those words out of her head.

"Jesus," Craig said, and Charlie read the inside of the card again.

Little girls are a father's dream
And like his, her blood will stream!

It was signed "An avenging angel."

"Who the hell would send something like this, much less to a child?" Craig hissed.

"There wasn't a return address...I should call Jasper."

"That would be a good idea. Where's Mack?"

"She's washing up for dinner. I told her it was a card from Santa and that I'd clean it up and give it to her later." She was moving around the kitchen, but for the first time she could remember she didn't want to cook.

"Good thinking. She only touched the outside of the card, right? I'm thinking about fingerprints," he explained.

"Yes, just the sides." She got out a sandwich baggy and let Craig drop it inside. She'd give it to Jasper later. Right now, she had to figure out what to do about dinner and her daughter. Luckily, she'd agreed to let

Casey take Mackenzie to D.C. with them. What would she do after that? She flinched when Craig put his arms around her.

"Hey, we'll figure this out." He kissed the top of her head and let her go. "Okay?"

Charlie nodded.

Mack ran back into the room and came to a quick halt. "Pepper!" She jumped into his arms, and he gave her a big hug.

"Hello, sweets," Craig said, then put her down. "How are you doing today?"

"Santa sent me a card!"

Charlie could only stare. Her little girl took two of Craig's fingers in her hand, led him to the couch, then sat on his lap and told him all about her day. Now what was she going to do about that?

Chapter Ten

"Are you listening to me, girl?"

"Yes, Jasper," Charlie lied. She couldn't stop thinking about how Craig and her daughter had gotten along last night. She wasn't jealous of Craig for getting all of Mack's attention, and she wasn't jealous of Mack for getting all of Craig's attention. She wasn't. No, she was worried. The thought that a little dash of pepper was all they'd ever need played in her head like a relentless jingle, drowning out everything else.

Jasper huffed. "No, you ain't! This here is important."

"Yes, I am. Darn it, Jasper, I heard every word you said. Mackenzie is in danger. Someone is definitely targeting me, blah, blah, blah. Tell me something I don't know. Contrary to popular belief, I. Am. Not. Stupid."

"Now, now." Jasper sat up in his chair. "I know you're not. But hellfire and tarnation, this is serious."

They were in his office at the sheriff's station and the door was closed, but everyone would be trying to listen in on their conversation; this was a gossip goldmine.

She sighed. "I know, Jasper. Mack's going with Casey and Ryan to D.C. for a few days. They leave tomorrow morning."

"Going to see Ryan's brother, right?"

"Yes, and that will give us four days to try to sort this out." She didn't think they could find the person responsible, but she could hope.

"That ain't long enough. We still don't have a clue what the hell's going on. We're nowhere with the grave robbing, and we ain't figured out who smashed your windows. Even with the cameras your dad put in all those years ago, we can't make nothing out. And now this." Jasper shook his head. "Four days. Hell, it took the good Lord seven to create the world, and I certainly don't have his resources."

"I can't sit here and do nothing, and running isn't an option. First of all, it didn't work out well for me the last time. And secondly, whoever it is would probably wait until I came back." Charlie shoved both hands through her hair and squeezed her eyes shut for a moment. "I feel so helpless."

"We'll find whoever's doing this. People almost always slip up."

"Yeah, well, 'almost' isn't good enough." She got up to leave but stopped when Jasper called her name.

He fiddled with his badge and looked anywhere but in her eyes. "You, ah, haven't seen Fletcher in, oh, I don't know, the last week, have you?"

"Hasn't she come in to work?"

"She took her vacation time," he said, then mumbled, "Not like the girl's ever gone on vacation before."

"The last time I saw her, she told Mama she was moving out and left the house in a huff. She overheard us talking about her."

"Figured it was something like that. Oh, well, she'll turn up," Jasper said. They both knew he was lying.

****

By the time she went to pick up Mackenzie, Charlie was mentally exhausted. Twice while running her errands, she'd walked into a store and people stopped talking. She wasn't deaf or dumb; they'd been talking about her. She couldn't really blame them, could she? She was great gossip right now. What *did* surprise her was their topic of conversation; they weren't talking about her relationship with Rick Randle, the fight with Marylou, or even the fact that someone was sending her rotting corpses. No, all they seemed to care about was the nature of her relationship with Craig Sutton.

Charlie rolled her eyes as she buckled Mack into her car seat. This was why she didn't date. Fantasize? Sure, she did, but she didn't actually *date* anyone. Had guys asked her out in the past five years? Yes, they had. Had she accepted any of their offers? Nope. She'd spent enough time being the center of the town's attention, and she didn't want to do it again. Not to mention she didn't trust men or, more accurately, didn't trust her instincts when it applied to the opposite sex.

She could never forget what had happened with Rick nor how blind she had been where he was concerned. She had dated some guys before going out with Rick, but she never felt for them what she had for him. She had been so sure he was "the one." Charlie snickered now, thinking about the "*one* bad apple," and everyone knew what happened there.

"Do you gots a headache, Mama?" Mack asked.

"No, baby, I'm just thinking," she said and started the drive home.

"You knows, I been thinking too...I don't have a daddy, and I think we should ask Pepper if he wants to be my pops," Mack said with a happy clap and giggle.

Charlie swerved, then straightened, and pulled onto the side of the road. "Mackenzie Annie McKay—"

"Pepper's been at our house lots and lots, and we don't have men people over lots and lots. Men people don't come to our house, 'cepting for family, but Pepper does."

"That may be true, but Craig has only been helping us," Charlie began. She hated this conversation. Detested this topic. She always felt like a failure after the "daddy" debate. Not to mention it confirmed her worry over how Craig and Mack had gotten along last night. This was why she didn't have "men people" come to the house.

"Yeah, but Pepper gave you a hug—I saw it! And Steffi Young said her mama told her daddy that you and Pepper were probably tearing up sheets together, and Steffi said only mommies and daddies do that."

Charlie squeezed her eyes shut. People were talking about her sleeping with Craig, and they didn't care who overheard. "Baby, that's not true, about the sheets, I mean. And what have I told you about gossiping?"

"You said, 'It ain't nice, Mack,' " she grumbled. "But Steffi isn't a gossip, and Pepper *did* hug you."

"Yes, he did. He's a friend, honey." Yep, that's what she kept telling herself.

"Daddy Warbucks and Ms. Grace was friends too, but they got married and adopted Annie. And you said Uncle Ryan and Auntie Casey was just friends, buts they got married too."

"Sometimes that happens, yes, but that's not what's happening now." Charlie shook her head and climbed in the back seat with her daughter.

"Why not?" Mack asked. "Everyone says I'm a good girl, and they say I need a daddy."

"Remember how I told you finding a daddy is a hard job and it takes lots of time?" She waited for Mack's nod. "Well, we've haven't known Craig for long, and he and I aren't dating."

"But you never date like on the movies."

"I know, honey. I just haven't found—"

"Your prince? I knows, Mama, but those is pretend. You even said so."

"Yes, they are, but that's not what I meant. Finding a daddy is a big job. First, I have to like him and he has to like me. But more importantly you have to get along with him—"

"But *I* likes Pepper, and he likes me and you," Mack pointed out. "We all likes each other, so I don't see what's wrong."

"That may be true, Mackenzie, but Craig and I aren't going to get married." There, she said it. She was the bad guy.

"Why not?" Mack shouted. "I need a daddy. Everybody has a daddy but me."

"That's not true. I didn't have a father until I was eight, and I turned out okay."

"I gotta wait till then? That's a hundred million years away," Mack whined.

Charlie took a calming breath. Sometimes she didn't have the right words. Her temper was trying to flare up, but she didn't want to yell at Mackenzie for wanting a father. She herself had been desperate for a family.

"You're being shellfish. Like when I don't wanna share my doll babies; you don't wanna share me with nobody!" Mack's eyes filled with tears. "If Pepper was my daddy, I wouldn't want any Christmas presents at all."

"It's not that simple, Mack," Charlie said over the lump in her throat. Was she being selfish? Did she want to keep Mackenzie all to herself?

"Why?"

"It's just not." Charlie climbed back up front. Tamping down her frustration, she looked at her daughter in the rearview mirror. "Honey, there's a lot of grownup stuff going on right now. Things that are hard for me to explain."

"Like Pepper being my daddy?" Mack asked, then mumbled, "If Auntie Alex was my mama, she'd get me a daddy."

Charlie ignored that sting. "Look, it's best if you don't get attached to Craig."

"What's 'tached?"

"It means don't start pretending he's going to be your daddy. He's a friend. Kind of like an uncle."

"Like Jaspy?"

"Sort of, yes." Charlie nodded starting the vehicle again. "Like Jaspy. Now, let's talk about your trip."

Mack gave a dramatic sigh. "Ohskay."

****

Charlie slammed down the phone. "That's it!"

"No one's heard from the little witch, I take it," Alex said and finished braiding Mack's hair. "All done, sweetheart."

"Thanks," Mack said, patting her head. "Pepper

braided my hair too."

"Did he now?"

Charlie glared at Alex. Her sister's tone was saying "interesting," and that couldn't be good.

"Yep. He did real good too. I'll miss him when I'm gone."

"That's enough, Mackenzie," Charlie said. "Why don't you go make sure you have everything packed for your big trip." She went to the fridge. Bless Alexandra for bringing a bottle of wine. She poured herself a glass and refilled Alex's. She was surprised to see Mack still standing there.

"You're mad at me?" Mack asked in a small voice, making Charlie want to growl.

"No, I'm not mad at you, honey, but I've told you twice—"

"I know, I'm not supposed to get too 'tached to him."

"Exactly! Now go check your things." Charlie pointed toward the bedrooms and rolled her eyes when her daughter finally went.

"What was that all about?" Alex asked.

"I don't want her to get too close to Craig. That's all."

Alex took a seat at the kitchen table and smoothed her skirt. "Why not?"

"I have my reasons."

"Fine, don't tell me."

"Fine, don't tell me," Charlie mimicked. Why did she have to explain her reasons to anyone?

Alex's eyes darkened, and her ever-ready emotional wall went up.

Charlie sighed. "Look. Craig's a nice and

handsome guy, but there's something about him that bothers me." His interest in her sister was what bothered her. Big time.

"What? Craig's a nice man, and Mack adores him. Besides, you said he's a good kisser and you haven't exactly been with anyone."

"Yeah? Look where seeing someone got me."

"A child you love."

"Yes, I love Mackenzie. Honestly, I don't know who I'd be without her. But there was a price, and now somehow it feels like I'm paying for it again. 'The past has a way of being unearthed, no matter how deep you bury it.' " Charlie repeated the words left with Rick's body. Like she'd ever forget them.

Alex sipped her wine. "You can't let the past run your life."

"I feel like the past is kind of like a spiderweb."

"A spiderweb?"

"Un-huh, you know how when you see a spiderweb, you walk around it because you know that somewhere the nasty little spider is waiting? And this isn't *Charlotte's Web* we're talking about here."

Alexandra snickered. "So the past is more like the spider than the actual web."

"No! If you'd let me finish—"

"By all means…please continue."

"You know the spider is waiting. Sometimes they're poisonous—not to mention icky—and the past is like that sometimes too; it can bite you. Naturally, you'd avoid both. But"—Charlie held up a finger when Alex opened her mouth—"the web itself often goes unseen, and if you walk into one, it takes forever to get it off you. Or out of your mind, in cases like this."

"Sadly, I think I understood that."

"If Fletcher were here, she'd know exactly how to put it," Charlie said, then groaned.

"What now?"

"No one has seen or heard from Fletcher in days." Charlie had always hated hide and seek.

"Casey hasn't talked to her?"

She shook her head. "Mama said she'd gone by the cabin a few times, but Fletcher wasn't there."

Mack came into the room wearing her princess pajamas. "I saw Auntie Fletcher today."

"Where?" Charlie and Alex asked at once.

"It's okay, honey. You can tell Mama," Charlie reassured.

"She had lunch with me at school. Mrs. Williams didn't mind."

"Did she now?" Alex said, then under her breath, "Typical, just typical."

"What'd she say?" And why couldn't we have talked about this on the ride home instead of the "daddy" subject?

"I'm not 'sposed to say."

"Honey, it's important you tell us what she said."

Mack chewed her bottom lip, then nodded. "She told me I didn't have nothing to worry about 'cause she was workin' hard to fix everything. She gave me—hold on, I'll get it." Mack ran back to her room and came back with an envelope. She handed it to Charlie. "I'ma supposed to give it to Uncle Jake when I sees him."

Charlie had no qualms about reading the letter. What was Fletcher thinking using her daughter as a go between? She moved so that Alex could read along with her. She'd know her sister's chicken scratching anywhere.

Jake,

I have a huge favor to ask you. You. Owe. Me. Remember? But the favor—which you better do or there will be consequences—is keeping Mack out there with you for as long as possible. Things are going to hell in a handbasket out here, and Mack doesn't need to be in the thick of things. You'll think of something, I'm sure.

I don't know what Ryan's told you, but someone's coming after Charlie. I've done what I can to divert as much attention as possible, but it's not enough. I've been intercepting threats for a few weeks now, but I can't be everywhere and do my job too. I've taken my vacation days, and by the time you get this, I'll have gone to ground. You know what I mean. Remember our conversation at Casey's wedding? Exactly. Be on the lookout. I'm trusting you with my niece, so don't fuck this up.

Sincerely,

Fletcher J. McKay

"I'm gonna kill her!" Charlie growled, then winced when Mack started crying. "Oh, honey, I didn't mean it. Really, I'm not going to hurt Fletcher." Much.

"I shouldn't have told you. It was a secret." Mack sobbed. "Auntie Fletcher will be so upsets."

"Baby, it wasn't right of Fletcher to ask you to keep a secret like this."

"She ain't bad," Mack hissed. "She ain't—I know it!"

"No, honey, she just..." Charlie didn't know what to say. She closed her eyes tight for a moment, then put the letter in the envelope and picked up her daughter. Setting Mack on the counter, Charlie cleaned off her face and kissed her heated cheeks. "Now, do you think you can do something for your mama?"

"Whats?"

"You're going to give this to Uncle Jake, like Auntie Fletcher told you, and pretend we didn't ever see it."

"Like it never happened?" Mack asked, blowing her nose into the tissue Charlie held to her.

"Exactly!" Charlie kissed her daughter again and set her down. "How about you go brush your teeth, and I'll be there to tuck you in, in just a minute."

"Deal!" Mack gave her a high five and skipped out of the room.

"What are you thinking?"

"Fletcher knows more about what's going on than we do—which is *so* typical of her. But if she's this worried about Mackenzie's safety, then there must be a reason." And it scared Charlie spitless. "I have to agree with her about Mack staying away longer. I don't like it, but it's probably the safest thing to do right now."

"What happened to the 'I'm gonna kill her' part?"

"I'm mad she was going behind my back, but her heart's in the right place." And if Charlie were being honest about it, Fletcher's heart was almost always in the right place.

Alex shook her head and grabbed her purse. "I'm going home and going to bed before I say something I might regret."

She sighed. "Oh, Alex."

"I'll talk to you tomorrow, and don't forget to set the alarm behind me," she said before she shut the door.

After Charlie set the alarm, tucked Mack in bed, and read her a story, she made a phone call.

"Hi, Mildred. It's Charlie. I'm sorry it's so late. Yes, I'm fine. I was wondering if I could ask you a small favor..."

Chapter Eleven

Ryan closed the hatch of his luxury SUV. "We'll call when we get to the hotel."

"Thanks, Ryan." Charlie smiled. She loved her brother-in-law to pieces. He was the best thing that had ever happened to her sister, after being adopted by Pops, that is. Ryan got in the passenger seat, and Charlie turned to Casey. "You're driving?"

Casey smirked. "Of course."

"How'd you do that?" She looked between the couple.

"That's privileged information." Casey winked. "I'll take care of Mack."

Charlie nodded. "I know you will."

"You take care of things here," Casey said, then hugged Charlie and hopped in the driver's seat.

Charlie crouched in the backseat to speak to Mackenzie. "You be on your best behavior, sweetie. Listen to what the grownups say, and make sure you do what you're told. Okay?"

"I got it, Mama. I'll get four stars for sure." Then Mack leaned in and whispered, "My tummy feels funny, not like a tummy ache—"

"Like there are butterflies in there?" The same thing was happening to Charlie.

Mack's gaze went wide. "How did butterflies get in my tummy?"

"No, it's a way to describe how you're feeling. Now, are you all set?"

"You bet…I love you, Mama."

"Oh, baby, I love you too," Charlie cooed and kissed her daughter on both cheeks. "We'll have a party when you come back. How does that sound?"

"With cake and ice cream and everything?"

"The works!" She kissed Mack's forehead, then shut the door, and waved until they were out of sight. She wiped her tears away on her sleeve. She missed her baby already. "Okay, Charlie girl, suck it up! We have a little sister to find."

She was almost at the side door of the B and B when Craig called her name. She closed her eyes and turned around. She met him halfway, straightening her wool cap and jacket as she went.

"Hey, Charlie," Craig said again.

"Hi." She hoped her smile didn't look as fake as it felt. She had a lot of things to do, none of which included him.

He rocked back on his heels. "How is everything? Mack?"

"Everything's fine, and Mackenzie just left on a trip with Casey and Ryan," she said relaxing a bit; she was a sucker for people who liked her little girl.

"I see."

"If you'll excuse me, I need to go talk to my sister." She would have turned if he hadn't taken hold of her arm.

"Charlie, what's wrong?" His question was so sincere, she was glad she was wearing sunglasses; they gave her the edge she needed to say what she had to say.

"Nothing...Look, Craig, I don't think it's a good idea for this"—she motioned between them with her free arm—"thing to continue." There, she'd said it. She had to squash this issue. For Mack and for her own sanity.

"This thing between us?"

"Yes, a fling, an affair, whatever you want to call it."

He let go of her arm and took a step back. "Oh, I thought we were becoming friends."

He turned to walk away, and Charlie said, "Do I look stupid?" She wasn't as naïve as she'd once been; her rose-colored glasses had been destroyed years ago.

"I'm sorry?"

"You heard me. Do you think I don't get it? I've seen *Jerry McGuire* too, you know. You like my kid, and I'm the side dish. Which, hey, I don't blame you. I have a great kid, but no one—*no one*—plays Charlie McKay. Especially, someone who has the hots for my sister!" Charlie pointed to the house where Alexandra was no doubt staring out the window.

Craig crossed his arms over his chest. "Let's get a few things straight, sweetheart. Yeah, I like your kid. What's not to like? And I like Alexandra...as a person. You're the one I'm attracted to. But you know what, *Ms. McKay*? I don't need your shit." With that, he stomped away.

Charlie slammed into her sister's kitchen and yanked off her jacket, hat, and sunglasses. Alexandra was getting ready to host a luncheon for the lady's league, but Charlie didn't care. The nerve of the man!

Alex came rushing into the kitchen. "What's wrong now?"

"Nothing."

"Okay, then why're you crying?"

"I'm not." Charlie swiped the tears from her cheeks. "I guess I am. Stupid, stupid, stupid." Maybe she was a fool.

"What happened?"

"I told Craig I don't want him, and he told me he didn't need my shit." Why wasn't she relieved? Because she was a liar, liar pants on fire—she did want Craig, but...

Alex raised a brow. "That was short-lived."

"Shut up, Alexandra. If anyone doesn't need crap, it's me not needing yours."

"Why are you biting my head off? I was in here minding my own business. I didn't do a thing," Alex said with a touch of ice.

Charlie ignored it. "You didn't have to. God, don't you get it? I do not compete with my sister."

"All right, Fletcher. I get that."

Her sister's superior tone got her back up. "I'm not Fletcher!"

"Really? You sound like her, making asinine accusations. Yes, Fletcher J. McKay."

"Oh, be quiet...and it's not an asinine accusation. Craig always asks about you. And you act like you don't even notice him. Which, being that *I know you,* is a sign you're interested. So there."

"I'm not attracted to him, Charlie. I swear." Alexandra's voiced hitched, something it rarely did, and it stunned them both.

"That's what Craig said."

Alex smoothed a hand down her skirt. "He said I wasn't attracted to him?"

"No, he said he likes you as a person, but that's it." Could she believe that? Charlie didn't think so. If a guy had a pulse, he was attracted to Alex.

"What are you so upset about?"

"Let's drop it, okay? We need to figure out where to find Fletcher."

"Fine with me. But I have to stay here, and what about the diner?"

"I've got that covered."

"Oh?"

"I called Mildred last night and asked her how she felt about running the diner for a week or so. She loved the idea." Which hadn't surprised Charlie. When Ida Mae had run the diner years ago, it had been a hotbed of gossip. Mildred would be right at home.

"That's good for you, but I can't let anyone run this place."

"No, you could never give up control."

"What's that supposed to mean?"

"Nothing, sorry." She shrugged. "I'll enlist Jasper's help."

"He's the sheriff, Charlie. He can't drop an investigation to hunt Fletcher down. I say we let Fletcher do whatever she's planning to do and play catch-up later."

"Maybe you're right. I need to look into a few things anyway." Charlie put on her jacket and cap.

"Of course I'm right. I'll come over later though, okay?"

"Sounds good." Charlie slipped on her sunglasses. "Six-ish?"

Alex nodded. "I'll bring the merlot."

Once she was in her vehicle, Charlie let loose a

growl. She had no intention of sitting around and waiting for things to surface. What was up with Alex anyway? She started the ignition and pulled out of the drive. How could she find Fletcher? She shook her head; she didn't think like Fletch—didn't know how—but she knew someone who did.

****

Jebb buckled his seatbelt. "As much as I appreciate you getting me outta school early, Charlie, I don't think the folks are gonna be happy."

"Don't worry. I'll talk to them. Besides, you're only missing two classes." She'd never intentionally missed a class in her life, but that was because she hated makeup work.

"What's up, anyway?"

"I need to find Fletcher."

"Oh, is that all?" Jebb rolled his eyes. "Are you nuts? She doesn't wanna be found, and if she doesn't wanna be found—"

"You're the second person to ask if I'm nuts in a matter of hours, and the answer is no; I'm freaked out, Jebb. I know you know what's going on; that's why I picked you."

He sat back in his seat and stared for a moment. "Picked me for what?"

"You think like Fletcher, and that's what I need."

"I…ah…you can't tell Ma or Pops…"

"Promise."

Jebb puffed out his chest. "I put a tracking device in her tablet case."

"Tablet case? Why there?"

"Fletch can't live without her show. She streams it."

"You're a genius." Fletcher loved *Murder She Wrote*; she owned every episode ever made in every medium available.

"I know." Jebb grinned. "The app on my phone tracks it, but…" He put his arms behind his head and looked at Charlie. "I checked this morning, and she was in her cabin."

"Mama's been there several times already." Her brother, she was now realizing, was one cocky kid. There was no denying he was part of their family.

"I betcha she didn't check the bunker. No one knows about that."

Bunker? What in the world? "But you do?" Charlie turned onto the dirt road that wound deep into the woods to Fletcher's cabin.

"Yeah. She told me if there was any big trouble, I was supposed to go hide there," he said, then hit his head on the roof of the SUV when he sat up straight. "I can't go with you. She'll know I told you, and she'll be pissed. She might smack me or something."

She pulled in next to the cabin. "Have you ever seen me pissed off?"

"Can't say as I have, Charlie. You and Ma are the sweetest ladies in town."

"Well, me pissed off beats Fletcher's pissed off any day. Got it?"

He smirked. "Sure, if you say so."

Charlie followed Jebb through the cabin. It was a decent size. A bedroom, a bathroom, a small den, and a kitchenette. Fletcher had built it from the ground up. It had taken her a couple years, but she'd done it with no one the wiser. Jebb stopped in front of the fireplace and pushed in the third brick from the left. How dramatic.

Her eyes widened. The wall of the fireplace slid apart and a set of steps appeared. She followed her brother down a small flight of stairs, jumping when the wall closed behind her. The steps led to a small tunnel.

"We're only about seven feet underground." Jebb took Charlie's hand and led her about six feet, then stopped at a door, and pressed in a code. "It's the day Ma and Pops were married," he explained, and the door slid open.

There Fletcher sat with her back to them. A wave of warmth hit Charlie in the face the moment she stepped inside the room. Her sister was in a tank top and pajama pants. Her hair was in its twin braids.

"You are a bullfrog, bullfrog," Fletcher told Jebb. She and Casey had given him the nickname the day he was born. Jebbediah sounded so much like Jeremiah that they couldn't resist; Charlie had always thought it was kind of cute, but right now she was not thinking happy thoughts.

Jebb flung himself on the extra cot. "Saw us coming, huh?"

Charlie stepped up close to her sister. "Fletcher Jamie McKay, I'm so mad at you. Do you know what you've put me through? First of all, you hurt Mama's feelings, and that is unacceptable; then you go in your going-to-ground mode and don't tell anyone where the hell you are. Jasper's hair's already white. Do you want the man to have a heart attack? You're being astronomically selfish and I've had enough!"

"Charlie, I—"

"*No! I. Am. Not. Done!*" Charlie released her pent-up frustration. "How dare you play on other people's concern for you! I don't know what really went on between you and Daemon, though I have a feeling you left a whole heck of a lot out. But more than that, I think you've been omitting things left and right, and I'm sick of it. Do you understand me?" Charlie took hold of the arms of Fletcher's chair boxing her in.

"Going behind my back is a crappy thing to do, but did that faze you? No! You're Fletcher-flipping-McKay." Charlie lowered her voice and ignored the tears filling Fletcher's eyes. "And if you ever, *ever*, use my daughter as a go between or tell her to keep things from me again, I will not be held responsible for my actions. Do I make myself clear?"

Fletcher bobbed her head.

"I...ah...think I'll wait upstairs," Jebb murmured. When no one complained, he couldn't get out fast enough.

"Who pissed you off? Besides me, I mean?" Fletcher asked with a sniff. "And why isn't Alex with you?"

"What do you mean, 'Why isn't Alex with me'?"

"She obviously told you what was—ah, how'd ya get here?"

"I took Jebb out of school and forced him to talk. His mindset's the closest to yours, so I figured I'd use that to my advantage. And what do you mean 'Alex obviously told me'? You better answer me, Fletcher, or I swear to God I'll shave your head in your sleep." Charlie thought it was a silly thing to threaten until all the color drained from her sister's face.

Fletcher cleared her throat. "We had a plan. She'd tell you what was going on as soon as we knew everything was in place. Then you guys would come here, and we'd work shit out."

"She knew about the letter?" Charlie sat down hard. Alex, her best friend on the planet and sister, had lied to her. "She was right there when Mack handed it over. She was as pissed as I was. She—"

"Give her some credit. You know how sly Alexandra is. She didn't think right then was a good time to tell you; so she didn't tell you. I'm sure she had her reasons." Fletcher sat down next to Charlie and gave her a half hug.

"After giving me the runaround for the last couple days, they'd better be the best reasons ever. And why the heck are you here? Mama's worried sick. And what's going on with you and Pops?"

"Ma will be fine; she knows I'm working. Jasper and I had a disagreement, and I ain't talking to him. As for Pops"—she shifted on the mattress—"we ain't seeing eye to eye 'sall."

"And Daemon Randle?" Charlie pushed.

Fletcher got up to pace. "I can't talk about that right now."

"All right. Were you really intimate with him?"

Fletcher nodded.

Charlie pulled her down on the cot and hugged her. Her poor sister. "I'm sorry, honey." And she was. She wouldn't say anything about Jasper's accusations or what her mother had told her. Not yet anyway. She would have to tell Noah to back off for now; she didn't want to cause Fletcher more pain.

"I'm sorry too, for a lot of things. If you read the letter I sent Jake, you know I intercepted some stuff," she said, her cheeks flushing. She retrieved a bag marked "copies" from the desk, then pulled out a stack of papers and handed them to Charlie. "I wanted to spare you these."

Charlie read through the letters, and her stomach turned.

"They all say pretty much the same thing. 'Should have killed you when we had the chance,' 'This isn't over,' and my personal favorite, 'Crimes of passion are punishable by death.' Yep, we've got us a real fucking poet."

Fletcher's attempt at humor did not ease Charlie's worries. She rubbed the chill from her arms. "When did you get these? Where did you get these?"

Fletcher sighed. "They started showing up at Mack's school at the beginning of the term. Hence, Mrs. Williams's sudden case of the flu. They were all addressed to Mack."

"Oh, God." Charlie choked back tears. They'd sent the letters to her little girl! The bastards. Poor Mrs. Williams. "Why didn't you tell me? Why didn't Jasper tell me?"

"We didn't want to worry you. I know it's a shitty excuse, but we wanted to put it off as long as possible. One of the letters had a partial print, but it didn't pan out."

"Why?"

"It was Rick's print."

Charlie's brows bunched. "Rick's? But how?"

"He was missing a finger."

"What? They took it off his body?" Oh, how revolting. But, honestly, what did she expect? Someone dug the man up and dismembered him. A finger would hardly give such a person pause.

"The body hadn't been exhumed at the time. Rick's finger was cut off when he was murdered. It wasn't a well-known fact. The police figured whoever robbed and killed Rick cut the finger off to get that big-ass gaudy ring he always wore and then decided to keep a trophy. What can I say? People are screwed in the head. Considering how hard it is to get a print off a decomposing finger, the sick son of a bitch had to have kept it in a freezer—probably right next to the fish sticks. Fucking nasty."

Charlie shook off the image. She wouldn't let herself feel sorry for Rick. "How did you know about the finger in the first place?"

"I read the police report. Remember when I first started losing my mind? It was right after I'd requested Rick's case file."

When someone had started drugging her. Fletcher didn't need to say it, but Charlie couldn't forget. The scars marring Fletcher's flesh were a testament to how good a job the psycho had done.

"I forgot about you looking into his case." She had let herself forget. "Fletcher...are you saying Rick's murder had nothing to do with a robbery?"

Fletcher shrugged. "That's what my gut's saying."

"What about..." Charlie waved her hand in the air. She couldn't absorb what she was hearing. It was too crazy.

"The handwriting on the letters sent to Mack's school matches the handwriting on the letters I received last year."

"And we have no idea whether they were written by a man or a woman?"

"Noah's handwriting expert concluded there were two different contributors, but Pops had Jasper send the letters to an old friend at the FBI and his results were different."

"But how can that be?" Charlie rubbed her head. This was getting worse and worse.

"Whoever is doing this is a world class forger—go fucking figure, huh?"

"What does that mean, exactly?"

"There are two different writing styles, okay? One is feminine and one male—"

Charlie rolled her eyes. "I know that."

Fletcher sighed. "I know you know that. What I'm trying to say is that there aren't two different people. One person is writing both."

"So is it a man whose been writing them or a woman?"

"That's what they can't figure out."

A giggle escaped Charlie's lips. "Which witch is which?"

"Uh, have you cracked?"

Charlie took a deep breath. "Not yet. So, what's the plan?"

"We don't have one at this point. It's all kind of wait and see."

"Fletcher! What aren't you telling me?"

"We've been trying to trace them—"

"How could you trace them if you don't know who they are?"

"They, ah, kinda bugged your house."

Charlie paled. "Someone has been listening to me and Mack? Spying on us? And you didn't feel the need to tell me?" Charlie screeched. "How long ago, Fletcher? How long have they been listening?"

She winced. "I figured it out the last time I was there."

"I understand you weren't in your best form that night, Fletch." Charlie started softly because she remembered what a wreck her sister had been. "But why not tell me the next day?"

"That's one of the reasons I'm not speaking to Jasper." Fletcher huffed. "He said it was best if you didn't know, and I told him he could take his badge and shove it up his ass."

Charlie shook her head. "It amazes me that he doesn't fire you." That man wasn't even getting a birthday card from her. "Can you get the bugs out or whatever?"

"Not without whoever put them there knowing."

Chapter Twelve

Someone had bugged her house. Charlie still couldn't believe it. Jasper hadn't wanted her to know. "Jerk," she mumbled. She had dropped Jebb off at home and was now headed for the B and B; Alexandra had a lot of explaining to do.

She sighed, remembering how much she had longed for a family. She had wanted so badly to take care of someone—like her favorite redheaded orphan had taken care of Molly in the movie. Charlie had tried forming similar relationships at the different orphanages and foster homes she'd been placed in, but those places weren't permanent and her heart broke each time she had to say good-bye. Eventually, she had given up and instead set her hopes on being adopted by a family who needed her.

"Be careful what you wish for," she whispered, then snorted. Who was she trying to fool? She wasn't sorry...could never be sorry. She had read the first letter from Pops and had known in her gut that this family needed her; it had only taken seconds after meeting them to know she was right. Becoming a McKay had made her part of something special.

She could understand Mackenzie's desire for a father. Charlie too had cried herself to sleep many a night hoping for a family, but once Pops adopted her, she hadn't thought much about having a mother. More because, at that time, she'd still seen Anita as having been her maternal figure, and Pops had done a fine job playing both parental roles. It wasn't until Savannah came into their lives that Charlie realized what they had all been missing.

Maybe that was why she hadn't actively looked for a father for Mack. Perhaps she wanted to prove that she, like Pops, could do both, be both. But, then again, she might be trying to spare Mack the pain if things didn't work out. It was horrible to have your heart's desire within reach, and then have it taken away.

She shook the thoughts out of her head. What she needed to do now was find her anger again. Yep, she was mad at Alexandra and she needed to be fired up for that, not throw a pity party for herself. She turned the station to one of Fletcher's favorites and let the music get her back in the right frame of mind.

She pulled into the B and B's parking lot, shivering when she got out. The weatherman said it was going to snow tonight. She wished Mack were here. They loved making snow angels and having snowball fights. Then they would go inside, snuggle in front of the fire with cocoa, and watch a movie.

"Alexandra?" Charlie called when she entered the B and B. Dusk was settling in, so she hit the light switch.

"She isn't here."

"Darn it, Craig, I can see that," Charlie said after her heart removed itself from her throat.

"Sorry."

"That's fine." She rubbed her forehead. "I wanted to yell at her, is all."

He got up from his seat at the table. "Seems to be

going around."

"What do you mean by that?" What she really wanted to know was what her body meant by getting hot and bothered. Though, she couldn't blame her hormones. The lamplight highlighted the red in his brown hair and made his blue eyes seem black. He was sexy as sin, but that was beside the point.

Craig stepped closer. "I meant first me this morning, now Alexandra. Seems it's going around."

"You forgot Fletcher—I yelled at her too." Yes, and she'd done a darn good job of it. *Stay mad, Charlie girl.*

"Definitely going around," he murmured, trapping Charlie against the wall. She squirmed a bit, but he didn't budge.

"What do you think you're doing?" Charlie had a good idea, but...but...Oh, wow, was this happening?

He slid his hands up her arms and around her back. "Showing you something."

A little breathless, she asked, "What?"

"That no matter what you think I feel for anyone else, I promise it's your thighs I want to slide between."

Her face flamed. "You can't say things like that."

"Can't I? It turned you on, didn't it? Admit it, sweetheart. I've figured you out." His erection pressed against her stomach, but she wouldn't let herself react. Then he leaned down and gently bit her bottom lip.

She whimpered. "You need your head examined," she said. Then he sucked on her lip again. Oh, God, was she that obvious?

"It's you I want to examine." He caressed her breasts through her sweater and gave them a gentle squeeze. "Every inch."

Oh, screw it! Charlie yanked his head down so she could attack his mouth. She loved sex. Missed sex. God, she wanted this—wanted him—so, so much.

Craig maneuvered her hands from his ears to around his neck and lifted her up. She kicked off her shoes and wrapped her legs around his waist.

Charlie pulled her mouth from his. "Now, Craig!"

He set her down on the kitchen table and tore her sweater over her head. Cold air sent goose bumps across her naked flesh, and Craig swore when he realized she wasn't wearing a bra. He kissed his way from her clavicle to her breast, then latched onto her nipple.

Charlie held onto his upper arms, her fingers digging into his sweatshirt, and threw back her head. She whimpered when he switched breasts. He was rough and untamed, and she couldn't get enough. Pushing him back, she helped relieve him of his shirt. She used her nails on his bare chest, then leaned in and bit at his pecs. She loved his chest.

He pulled down the zipper of her jeans and growled, "I want inside."

Charlie lifted her hips, and he pulled off both pants and panties in one motion.

"You're beautiful."

"Thank you," she said, blushing. "Now...can we get back to where we were?" She could have this, she deserved this, and she wouldn't let herself think about consequences.

"Shit, yeah." Craig took a condom from his back pocket.

"Always prepared, are we?"

He grinned, popped the buttons of his jeans, and

shoved them to his knees. He pulled her legs to the edge of the table, then sheathed himself.

Charlie swallowed. He was big. Not lengthwise, though that wasn't anything to laugh at, but in girth he was…well? This might hurt.

"I'll fit," he assured her, spreading her thighs wider and standing between them. "Do you want me to go slow?"

"No," she mumbled, sucking in a breath when he fixed his forearms under her shoulders and thrust inside her. Hard.

Craig's mouth caught her guttural moan; one thrust and she crested. Her feet were hot and her fingers damp, but Craig was still kissing her and holding himself absolutely still. His tongue was sweet and tasted of coffee. She bit his bottom lip, dug her heels into his firm butt, and said, "MOVE!" Orgasm number two, here she came.

He did as she asked, and Charlie gasped. Holy moly, he was getting bigger inside her—stretching her. The delicious pressure began to build again, and she licked her lips. She wanted harder, faster, more, so she pressed her mouth to his ear and whispered her desires.

Craig squeezed his eyes shut for a second, looked into Charlie's dilated pupils, and let himself go a tad crazy with lust. Her words fueled him as he took hold of her hair, arched her neck, and sucked at the pulse throbbing there. He tongued his way back to her mouth where he sank in, then started thrusting his hips in a primal rhythm.

He dug his toes into the cold floor for purchase while he hammered into her. On the last thrust, he held himself still, sweat sliding down his back, then swiveled his hips, groaning when Charlie convulsed around him. His own growl echoed in the kitchen as he too climaxed.

Craig lifted her in his arms and sat down on the nearest chair with her in his lap, without breaking contact. She wrapped one arm around his shoulder and the other under his arm, resting her head above his pounding heart. He looked down and snorted.

"What?"

"You have a tattoo." Who would have thought? Little Ms. Charlie had a tattoo.

"I couldn't let Fletcher go alone the first time, now could I?"

"I guess not. But why did you get a…what the hell is it?" Craig angled his head to try and figure it out. Her sigh caressed his neck. His stomach flipped. Oh, shit.

"You'll laugh." Charlie pouted.

Craig cleared his throat. "No, I won't."

"It's half of a heart-shaped locket."

His lips twitched. "More of your favorite movie?"

"No."

"Oh, like the one you wear then?" He fiddled with the necklace she wore around her creamy throat. He kissed her collarbone and waited for an answer.

"Mama gave us all jewelry the first Christmas we were together. And I got a locket like Annie had."

"So that's what your tattoo is of?" he asked, planting soft kisses on her brow. She was soft and sweet in his arms; he could hold her like this forever.

Charlie shook her head. "It's only half a locket. Alexandra was supposed to get the other half, but she chickened out. Oh, no!" Charlie dislodged herself from Craig. "I was supposed to meet Alex at *my* house."

"What time?"

"Fifteen minutes ago...She's gonna throw a fit."

Craig stood, disposed of the condom, and pulled his jeans up while Charlie dressed.

She was slipping on her shoe when she stopped and looked up at him. "I just had sex on my sister's kitchen table."

He kissed her slack lips before he shoved his head in his sweatshirt. "Crazy feeling, isn't it?"

Snowflakes smacked him in the face as soon as he stepped outside. He followed Charlie to her vehicle, then she stopped, spun around, grabbed him by the shirt, and kissed him. She giggled when she let him go and said, "I just had sex."

He grinned with an aw-shucks shrug and opened the passenger side door. "I'm coming with you."

She paused a moment. "Okay, if you want to."

They rode in silence for a couple of minutes before Craig noticed smoke billowing in the air. "Where the hell is that coming from?"

"OhmyGod! It's coming from my house," she shouted, and the vintage SUV roared with the power of her foot against the accelerator.

****

Craig dragged her toward the house, and her father ran toward them. Fire trucks rounded the corner, their sirens piercing the ominous silence. Charlie sucked in air when Alexandra ran to meet them. Charlie grabbed her damp, smoky sister and hugged her as hard as she could.

"Fletcher," Alex said coughing.

Charlie's brows pinched. "What about her?"

Alexandra coughed again and pointed at the

flames.

Her breath caught. "OhmyGod." Charlie turned to Craig, who nodded and headed for the burning house. Had those been tears in his eyes?

"Charlie? Alexandra? Are you all right?" Pops voice was thick. He grabbed them both and held on tight. Then their mother's arms joined in.

"Dad, Fletcher is still in there," Alex said.

Charlie used all her weight to keep her father still. "Craig's gone in after her, and the firemen are here too."

A few minutes later, Craig came back carrying Fletcher's limp body. This wasn't happening, not again. Then she heard it—the most beautiful thing in the world.

"If you"—cough—"don't put me the fuck down"—cough—"I's gonna shoot you."

"Whatever you say, little beast." Craig laughed and dropped Fletcher into Pops' arms.

The McKays enjoyed another group hug while the firemen doused the flames. Charlie turned when Craig cursed. Her mouth dropped when he took hold of Alexandra's shoulders, rubbing his hands up and down her arms and asking if she was all right. Charlie's eyes met Alex's, then she growled low in her throat and shoved Craig away from her sister.

"Shit, Charlie," he said, regaining his footing.

"Please tell me I didn't just have sex with someone infatuated with my sister!" She was not this gullible—she had promised herself she would never be that stupid again.

Pops stepped forward. "What in the hell is going on here?"

"Emmit," Savannah began, "mind your business."

"Oh, Charlie, what have you done?" Alex said.

Charlie glared at her sister then turned to Craig. "Tell me you're not obsessed with Alexandra. Tell me you're not fixated on my sister." The look in his eyes spoke volumes. She wanted to cry and throw up at the same time.

"I'm sorry, Charlie, but I can't tell you what you want to hear. I am fixated on her," he began, then grabbed Charlie when she would have run.

"How could you?" Charlie whispered. She wanted to get away from him, from Alex, and from the pain coursing through her chest—her life going up in flames around her.

"She's the reason I came here, the reason I moved my life here!" He took a deep breath, then said, "Alexandra's my sister."

Chapter Thirteen

"*What?*" all of the McKays asked at once. Except Alexandra, who sat down on the cold ground.

Craig pressed a kiss to Charlie's temple, then sat next to Alex. He brushed her loose hair out of her face. "I've been looking for you since the day they took you away." The truth was out. His sister. His.

"I...I don't know what to say," Alex whispered.

"You have proof of this, don't you, son?" Emmit asked.

"He's got proof," a voice bellowed.

Craig smiled.

"Who the hell invited you?" Fletcher hissed.

Noah glared at the youngest McKay.

Emmit pointed to him. "You know this for a fact, Noah?"

He nodded. "If Craig says she's his sister, then she is. He's been searching for her forever; he wouldn't make a mistake. Hell, I knew you were up to something; I should have put two and two together."

Craig grinned at Alex and cocked his head toward the other man. "Noah's our cousin, by the way, on Mother's side."

Noah inclined his head. "Would've been nice if you'd told me all this in the first place, Craig, but what else should I expect from you?"

"Great! Now we're one big happy fucking family,"

Fletcher said, then stomped away.

"Go see the paramedics first," Savannah called out after Fletcher, then turned to Alex. "You need to let them have a look at you too, honey." She helped Alex up, then dragged her husband with them, calling over her shoulder, "You can talk tomorrow."

Craig went over to Charlie and tried to embrace her, but she pushed him away.

Charlie's gaze was fixed on her house. "The home I made for my daughter is gone—destroyed. Ashes in the wind," she murmured, using her sleeve to blot the tears. "Someone out there almost killed my sisters, in my own house. The last thing I need in my life is a man using me to accomplish his goals; I've had enough deceit to last three lifetimes, and I don't plan on adding to it."

"I didn't set out to deceive you—"

Charlie snorted.

"I'm here to stay, Charlie. Alexandra's my sister, and I'm not losing her again," Craig said. He was angry at himself, at the destruction of the fire, and at Charlie. Didn't what they'd shared not an hour ago mean anything? He asked her that very question.

"It was only sex, right? Good sex, but that's all. You're Alexandra's brother, and that's fine. But you used me and lied to me. And worst of all, you wheedled your way into my daughter's heart...into her life for your own benefit."

"Now, wait just a damn—"

Charlie raised her hand. "Stay in Blue Creek or leave. I'll take Rhett Butler's stance on the matter."

He could only stare as she walked away from him.

"Need a ride, old friend?"

He forced a smile. "Noah, what I need is a miracle." He'd gotten his sister, but what had he lost?

****

Craig kept his attention on Alexandra, ignoring Fletcher's leer. They were in his apartment, sitting around the kitchen table drinking the coffee his sister had brought over in a thermos. She told him she had to bring Fletcher because Charlie refused to come, not that he could or would blame her.

"We're here. Get to talking," Fletcher instructed. "You have physical evidence to prove you two are related?"

"I have the DNA test right here," Craig said and handed the paper over to Alex.

Fletcher leaned in to get a look at the document. "It says ninety-nine point nine percent positive."

Alex rose a brow. "How'd you get my DNA?"

"You gave blood several months ago; I paid off one of the lab techs."

"You do know that's illegal, right?" Fletcher asked, but they both knew he was aware of the law, having been a SWAT officer.

"When has something like that ever stopped you, Fletcher McKay?" Alex rolled her eyes.

Fletcher smirked. "Just making an observation."

"I'm sure Craig appreciates it. Can you tell me what happened? How did I end up in an orphanage?"

Craig sighed. "Do you remember anything about our mother?"

"No, most of my early memories are of Casey and Fletcher."

"I figured as much," he said, then stared at her a moment before shaking his head. "You don't know how long I've been waiting to do this—talk to you like this. I'm sorry I didn't come clean sooner, but I wanted to get the bar up and running, have a foundation to work with, and get to know you in the process." It was the truth. After what Charlie had said last night, he figured the least he could do was be honest.

"I would have done the same," Alex said.

"You come by it naturally. Mother was a suspicious person by nature. I have…ah…pictures of her—of us—if you'd like to see them." Craig grabbed the photo album after she nodded.

He pointed to the first photo of a willowy woman with long dark red hair and a beautiful smile. "This was our mother. The first time I saw you I was stunned by the resemblance. You have her eyes," he said, turning the page to a portrait.

"He's right, Alexandra. You look exactly like her. It's creepy."

"Fletcher—"

"This is you the day you were born," Craig said before they could start bickering, not that he didn't get a kick out of that. "It was just me and her then; she and Dad had been divorced almost a year before that." Craig had been so happy that day. He was officially a big brother.

"Did you meet the man who she was with?"

"The sperm donor," Fletcher mumbled.

"Yes, I remember him, and I can honestly say I was glad when she kicked him to the curb." Craig put her hand in his. "I know all about him, Alexandra, so you don't have to say a word."

She looked at their joined hands. "I wasn't going to."

He gave her hand a squeeze, then let it go.

"How'd your ma die?" Fletcher asked.

"She had a bad heart, and it gave out on her."

Alex sat straighter in her chair. "Couldn't the doctors have done something for her? Surgery?"

Craig shook his head. "Mother didn't like doctors or hospitals."

"What was her name?" Alex asked.

"Rebecca, Rebecca Alexius Reed. She didn't take Dad's name when they married. She said she wouldn't submit to the roles society forced on women." Craig laughed. His mother had been her own woman.

"She was a hippy?"

Fletcher snickered.

"In her way," Craig said, glancing between the sisters. "Lucky for us she didn't name us Moon Cloud or something. She called you Firefly though, because of your hair."

"My given name was Alexandra though, wasn't it? No one ever told—"

"You weren't born in a hospital. Mother had a midwife come to the house. My dad made her go to a hospital when I was born, but she wanted a home birth with you. I have your birth certificate."

Both Alex and Fletcher sat up straighter.

"You do?" Alex asked.

"Yeah, I always thought they made a copy of the original," he said and went to grab a folder from his desk.

"You okay?" Fletcher whispered to Alex.

"A little overwhelmed, but fine for the most part."

He gave it another moment, so they wouldn't know he had been eavesdropping, then came back with a slip of paper. "Here."

Alex took the certificate, then said, "In this state your original birth certificate is sealed after adoption, but when I petitioned the court to unseal it, they were unable to locate it. Error of the clerk, they said. Or some such nonsense."

"Then, if you don't mind me asking, how did you find out about—"

"My birth father?" she asked without looking up.

He sat back in his chair. "Yeah."

"We have our ways," Fletcher said.

Alex nodded, then glanced at her sister. "For a while, I thought Miss Tina may have had something to do with—"

Fletcher snorted. "Yeah, right! This is a *legal* document; that woman didn't have the connections."

"True."

"Who's Miss Tina?" Craig asked.

"The lady who ran the home we were in."

"An unstable lady—"

"Did she hurt you?" he demanded.

"No, she didn't bother with us," Alex said, and a look passed between the sisters.

Fletcher poured herself another cup of coffee. "What happened after your mother died?"

"Dad took full custody of me, but he wouldn't take a child that wasn't his. It was a point of contention in our entire relationship. Mother only had one brother, and Uncle John was in the FBI. He was gone on assignment a lot, and our aunt was troubled, so she couldn't take you. Social Services took you away, and that was the last time I saw you."

"I'm sorry if this sounds hateful, but I'm glad I

ended up where I did. I had a happy childhood, and my life is how I want it."

"Aside from people occasionally trying to kill us, our lives are pretty perfect," Fletcher said.

Alex smirked.

Craig nodded. "I understand. I'm not expecting you to claim our mother or even myself, for that matter, but I'm here nonetheless. I've waited twenty-some years to be sitting here with you. I never forgot you or gave up hope; you'll always be my baby sister."

"Thank you, I—"

Fletcher's cell phone rang. "McKay. Yeah, Jake, it's me. Good. Good. No, that's excellent. Things have gone to hell in a handbasket here. Someone burned Charlie's house to the ground—arson. Oh, that's just great. Yep, this sicko means business. Don't you yell at me, Jake Keller, or I'll kick your ass. Fuck you too. Bye." Fletcher set down her phone and grinned.

Craig didn't know how to respond, so he followed Alexandra's lead. "Jacob got your note, I take it."

Fletcher nodded. "He's gonna keep Mack for at least two weeks."

"That's good then. What about Casey and Ryan?"

"Seems Charlie was busy on the phone last night. She's brought Casey up to speed. Course, big sis is on her way home as we speak, left at the ass crack of dawn this morning." Fletcher grinned.

"Oh, wonderful."

"What's 'wonderful'?" Craig asked. What the hell was going on?

Alex explained. "Casey's talked to Charlie, so she knows Fletcher and I went behind their backs to get Jacob to keep Mack with him. She's going to be livid.

Casey can be extremely annoying when she's on one of her rampages."

"Why'd you go behind Charlie's back?"

Fletcher narrowed her eyes. "Why did you?"

"I didn't."

His sister glared at him.

"Not intentionally."

Fletcher snorted. "You do know the road to hell was paved with good intentions, right?"

"Don't mind Fletcher; she's always defensive." Alex glanced at her watch.

"I'm not always on the defense!"

"Yes, you are. Look, I'd like to talk more about all of this, but I have an appointment, then I need to go check on Charlie."

"I understand." He paused. "How is she doing?" He needed to know. He hadn't got but an hour's sleep; he would have expected today's meeting with Alexandra to have kept him awake, but it had been thoughts of Charlie and her lovemaking that had plagued his mind.

"She's fine, considering…Are you coming, Fletcher?"

Fletcher grabbed the thermos before Alex could, put her feet up on the table, and grinned.

"Suit yourself."

Craig walked Alex to the door. "Do you mind if I hug you?"

"No, that's fine," she said and he wrapped his arms around her, holding her tight. Alex pulled back first with a strange look in her eye. "You used to brush my hair…I remember, and Rebecca called you 'her little man.' Am I right?"

"Yeah" was all Craig could get out around the lump in his throat.

"We'll talk more later," Alex said and closed the door on her goodbye.

Craig went back into the kitchen and sat down with a thump. He glanced up at Fletcher's questioning gaze. Alex had remembered him. It was a small memory, but a memory nonetheless.

He rubbed his stubbled jaw while Fletcher sipped from her mug. "Well?"

"You fucked up…big time."

"What are you talking about?"

"I'm talking about Charlie. You fucked things up. Big."

"I know." He rubbed his hands over his face, then narrowed his eyes. "Wait, why do you care? You told me you'd shoot me if I went near her."

Fletcher's smile was wicked. "I can't shoot you now that I know you're Alex's brother. She'd be really pissed; and she can be *such* a bitch when she's mad at a body."

"I guess I should be relieved."

She nodded gravely.

He smiled.

"Now, about Charlie…"

"What is or isn't going on between me and Charlie is none of your concern."

She burst out laughing. "Anything involving my sister is my business. Look, I wouldn't even be saying anything except someone's after her. I'd play up to your male ego and say she needs a big strong man to protect her, but I'm pretty sure my tongue would drop right out of my mouth, so I'll go with the truth. You were once a member of a SWAT team and a security expert, which makes you more than qualified to help. Jasper and I are doing the best we can trying to figure this whole thing out, but we can't do it alone. At least, not in a couple weeks."

"What am I supposed to do? Charlie isn't even speaking to me."

"I don't give a fuck what you do. Just get to doing it. I don't know…" She waved a hand in the air. "Win her over. Woo her."

"Listen, Charlie isn't going to be won over anytime soon. And besides, I have a bar to open." He'd finished most of the remodeling last week, but he still had to fix the lighting. Then hire employees.

"No, you listen, *little man*. Whoever's after Charlie would be more than happy to go through Mack to get her. Or any of Charlie's sisters. Do you really think last night was an accident? Do I need to remind you where Alexandra fits in Charlie's life?"

"What are you saying?" She'd had him at Mack. If anything happened to that child…he didn't know what he'd do. And God, Alexandra? He'd just found her.

"I'm saying, you do whatever it takes to get back in Charlie's good graces." She crossed her small arms over her chest. "Am I wrong thinking you care about her?"

"No, damn it, you're not wrong." He did care. Maybe too much, considering the woman wasn't speaking to him. "I'll try. That's as good as I can do."

"That ain't good enough. McKays are stronger than that."

"I'm not a McKay," he said annoyed.

"Of course not, but Alexandra *is*, and if you want

to get to know her, then you need to know us." Fletcher refilled her mug again. "Let me tell you a story. Once upon a time, there were three little orphans…"

Chapter Fourteen

Charlie was combing her hair when Alexandra came into her room. She was at her parents' house and had just gotten out of the shower. It had been a long day but a productive one. Everything that could have been salvaged from the rubble of her once-beautiful house had been. It wasn't much, but it was more than she'd expected. Her fireproof safe had held true, and her important papers had been spared—thank the Lord—but Mackenzie's treasure chest was gone. And that rankled.

Alex took a seat on the bed; she had always made herself right at home in Charlie's room. Heck, she had made herself at home in Charlie's heart years ago. With a sigh, Charlie pulled on a pair of sweat pants and T-shirt. She was lucky she always kept extra clothes here.

"How did it go this morning?" she asked, taking a seat next to her sister.

"I was going to ask you the same question."

"You wouldn't believe how many people showed up to help. Even Dana Randle came by."

Alex's brows rose. "And how did *that* go?"

"Better than expected," she mumbled, then sat up straighter. "That poor woman, Alex. She just buried Daemon, and there she was offering a helping hand. She told me she didn't think it would be a good idea if she was a part of Mackenzie's life. She said if it didn't bother me, she would rather Mack not know about her—it's too much."

"That's good though, right?"

"For me, yes, but the poor woman doesn't have anyone. You remember, her parents moved away after Rick made a mockery of the Thomas family."

Alex nodded. "The whole thing was quite scandalous. I wonder if she'll go live with them?"

"I think so; she mentioned she was considering a move." Charlie placed her hands behind her head and sank onto her old pillows. "It probably took all her courage to speak to me."

"I'm sure it did, poor thing; she's always been soft." Alex slipped off her boots and rubbed her feet. "Did you talk to the insurance agent?"

"Yes, he said he talked to the fire chief, and everything was in order. I called Casey and filled her in on what was going on. I told Mackenzie too; she was crying something awful, but then Jake said he'd take her on a special trip to Disney World, and she was all better." Charlie wished she had that capability.

"Oh, is that how he did it?"

Charlie eyed her sister. "What do you mean?"

"Jacob called Fletcher earlier, but either she or he failed to give details. Casey's on her way home. I assume Ryan's coming with her."

"Of course. Ryan was just as upset as Casey was." Charlie giggled. "Well, maybe not as pissed as Casey was." Their brother-in-law was the sweetest man they knew. It still drove Casey crazy that her husband was the more rational of the two of them.

"I'm sure we'll hear all about it." Alex fiddled with her charm bracelet. "I *am* sorry I lied to you about

Fletcher's letter to Jacob, even though technically I only withheld information."

"I was upset when I found out, I'll admit, but after everything that's happened, it's the least of my worries." Charlie kissed Alex's cheek and jumped off the bed, happy when her sister followed her downstairs.

"Where is everyone?" Alex asked when they entered the kitchen.

Charlie started getting out the makings of dinner while Alex went to the coffee pot. She hid her smile. Alexandra didn't cook, never did—couldn't, if they were being honest—but she made the best coffee. Charlie still didn't know her sister's secret to that.

"Jasper invited the parents and Jebb to dinner, so it's only going to be us."

Alex leaned against the counter while the coffee brewed. "Fletcher didn't say anything."

Charlie smirked. "That's because Fletcher wasn't invited."

"Interesting."

"I think he did it on the spur of the moment to get them out of my hair for a while. Where is Fletcher anyway?"

"The last time I saw her was at Craig's."

"You left her there alone?"

"Yes."

"Was that wise?" Charlie wanted to hear what happened this morning, but she didn't want to talk about Craig. She was having a hard time not thinking about him as it was. Last night, he had taken her places she had never experienced. She didn't regret it—how could she when it had been so right?

"She won't shoot him, if that's what you're

worried about." She poured a cup of coffee, then took a seat at the table. "But she is up to something, and I for one would be interested in knowing what."

"Good luck with that! So...how *did* it go this morning?" Charlie had to ask. It was important to Alexandra and therefore important to her.

"He *is* my brother."

It was said in such a low tone, Charlie stopped what she was doing and sat, taking Alex's hands in hers. "Oh, honey."

"He had pictures of us...and my mother. Her name was Rebecca Alexius Reed and...and she was a hippy. A *hippy*, if you can believe it."

"That's not so bad." Charlie held back a smile. Alexandra had always prided herself on being a lady.

"No, it's not. Not really. Craig said she called me Firefly, and goodness, I look like her clone. It was eerie seeing myself as the mirror image of a dead woman."

"She must have been quite lovely then." Charlie smiled and got back to her feet once Alex had composed herself. Tacos sounded good for dinner.

"Yes, she was," Alex said.

"You know, with all the bad stuff that's been happening, it's nice to hear some good news for a change." And wasn't that the truth.

"I suppose it is."

Charlie pulled out a frying pan, then glanced over at Alex. "Was there something else?"

"Yes, but I'm not quite sure how to put it."

Charlie snorted. "When has that ever stopped you? Just say whatever it is that's on your mind."

"All right...Do you think Jasper could have something to do with all of this? Covering for someone, maybe?"

Charlie dropped her spoon. "What? Where the heck did that come from?" No way.

"Think about it, Charlie…just for a second. Why would Jasper make Fletcher leave the bugs in your house? Why did he tell Fletcher to keep the notes sent to Mackenzie's school a secret? Why wouldn't he tell the Thomases about your relationship with Rick Randle? And why the hell would he go out of his way to have Rick sign those papers for you? Did you notice the date on those forms?"

"I—"

"They're dated the day of Rick's death. How's that for coincidence? And if he was spying on Rick for the Thomases, what else was he doing for them? To what extent did the favor he owed them go?"

Charlie sat down hard. Everything Alex was saying made sense. But what could Jasper's reasoning be? Charlie stared at Alex; her sister was having a hard time voicing this. "What else?"

"Why did he go into such a song and dance to us about Daemon Randle? The man doesn't talk about things like that. Also, he knows way too much about the goings on in this town, and he holds a lot of leverage, being the sheriff. Plus, he knows where the cameras are at the diner."

Charlie dragged her hands through her hair. "If what we're thinking is right…"

"The question is, if he *is* involved, why?"

"I don't know." Charlie took a calming breath. "Fletcher would know. She'd know if Jasper was mixed up in this."

"Fletcher would never believe it. That's why we

can't tell her."

A ball of nausea rolled in her stomach. "I hate to say it, but you're right. She can't know what we suspect."

"When Ryan and Casey get here, we'll see what they think."

"We are here," Casey said from the doorway, making them jump. She looked at her husband. "Ryan, didn't you say Jasper has a file on everyone in Blue Creek?"

"Yes, he does, but there's no way he's involved," Ryan said as they both sat at the table.

"I don't know what to think," Charlie said. She decided cooking would help her deal with this, so she got up and set about making tacos.

"I'm not saying Jasper's guilty of anything…not exactly," Alex clarified. "But I truly believe he *is* keeping something from us."

"You think he knows more than he's sharing?" Casey asked.

Alex nodded. "At the very least."

"If he's keeping secrets, I'm sure he has a good reason."

Alex cocked her head to the side and looked at Ryan. "What reason could he possibly have?"

He opened his mouth, then shut it again.

Casey sat up straighter in her chair. "I think it's worth looking into."

"We can't say anything to Mama and Pops, either," Charlie said. "As much as I don't want to lie to them, they wouldn't believe us. They trust Jasper implicitly. We have to find proof before we tell them."

"Doesn't that very fact put an end to this

nonsense?" Ryan said. "Your parents trust him; I trust him too."

"You've never been deceived by someone you 'trust implicitly,' but we have," Alex said.

Charlie gripped the spatula tighter. "She's right, Ryan."

Casey took her husband's hand. "I don't think it would hurt to look into it."

He sighed. "Let me say for the record, I don't like this, but I won't stand in your way."

"Or tell Fletch," Casey added.

Charlie looked back and forth between the couple until Ryan nodded. She wasn't sure whether or not she was relieved. "That's that then. But how do we go about this?"

"What about Craig Sutton? I'm sure he has connections. What?" Casey asked when Charlie stiffened, and Alex bit her lip.

"You didn't tell her?" Alex asked Charlie.

"No, I thought you should."

"Okay, Charlie slept with Craig."

"Alexandra McKay, that's none of their business!" Charlie turned beet red. "What I wanted Alex to tell you was that we found out who Craig really is—"

"Besides the man you had sex with?"

"Casey," Ryan pleaded, but he couldn't hide his partial grin.

Well, poop! "He's Alexandra's half-brother," Charlie blurted out, then stuck her tongue out at Alex.

"*What!*" Casey and Ryan said simultaneously.

"It's true. He told us last night, and he showed me the DNA results and baby pictures this morning. I look exactly like my birth mother."

Alex jerked a bit when Casey and Ryan got up to hug her. Charlie smiled. Big sister wasn't as hard as she wanted people to think.

"So asking Craig is out," Casey said once they all took their seats again. "I'm loath to suggest it...but what about Noah? That Oakland Raiders wannabe might be our only ally in this."

"Apparently, he's my cousin."

"Shit, Alex," Casey began, "I go away for a day— one freaking day—and you turn up with a brother and cousin. Charlie finally gets some action, and someone goes all scorched earth on her house."

Ryan smiled. "Don't be crass, sweetheart."

"I don't have a problem asking Craig to help us," Alex said. "I have a feeling he will."

Casey looked at Charlie. "What about you? Are you all right with that?"

"As long as I don't have to see him. I don't like being used."

"He didn't do it intentionally, honey," Alex told her.

"All right, we need all the help we can get." Charlie narrowed her eyes at Casey. "You know, you accepted Jasper being the bad guy easily. I'd like to know why?"

Casey shifted in her chair. "What are you trying to say?"

"I think you're agreeing with all this because deep down you're jealous of Jasper's friendship with Fletcher; he's her best friend and you aren't anymore."

"Who the fuck do you think you are making that kind of accusation?"

"It makes sense," Ryan said, holding up his hands

in mock surrender when Casey glared at him. "You know how protective you are of your relationship with Fletcher."

"Oh, this is just great! My sister and my own fucking husband think I have ulterior motives. This is bullshit. Screw you! And you're not sleeping with me tonight, Keller; I'm leaving your ass here." Casey pushed out of her chair and slammed the door shut behind her.

"I'll talk to you ladies later," Ryan said and followed his wife outside.

Alex turned to Charlie. "I can't believe you said that."

"You were thinking it, Alexandra. Don't act like you weren't." Charlie shook her head and got up to start browning the ground beef.

"Of course *I* was, but I didn't think *you* were."

****

Craig sipped his beer and admired the new lighting from where he sat at the bar; he'd made a damn fine choice. He had spent the past twenty-four hours working to get things in order at his new place of business. He'd talked to the former employees and had hired all of them. They knew the people in this town and knew them well. That was a key factor in running a bar. His father always told him that if you didn't have good people working the crowd, there wouldn't be a crowd to work.

Pleased with himself, Craig grinned. The door opened, and he slipped his sweatshirt back on. He narrowed his eyes at the stranger. The man was pretty tall and, well…just pretty, for a man. Was that Armani?

"You must be Craig Sutton?" The man held out his

hand and grinned when Craig put a beer in it. "Ryan Keller."

"Ah, the dark-haired dame's husband."

"That's the one," Ryan said, taking a seat on one of the barstools. "The place looks good."

"Thanks. I should be ready for a soft opening by the weekend."

"This weekend?"

"Yep. Why?" Craig asked when the other man appeared put out. *Why do you care, Sutton?* Because this was Alexandra's brother-in-law and Charlie's— *don't think of her right now.* He'd tried calling Charlie about a hundred times, and he'd left as many messages. She hadn't called him back. He knew a lot more about the McKays after Fletcher told him the family saga. Shit, what a story.

"The thing is, we need your help." Ryan filled Craig in on the sisters' suspicions.

"You don't agree?"

Ryan shrugged. "Don't get me wrong. It wouldn't surprise me to find the canny old goat is keeping things to himself, but I don't believe the deception runs as deep as the ladies do."

"I see," Craig said and shook his head. "It's going to kill Fletcher if she finds out about this."

Ryan's smile was a bit sad, a bit guilty. "She got to you too, huh?"

"I don't know what it is, but she sends out that lost puppy signal underneath the badass attitude. But that's not the reason I'll help you."

"Are you in love with Charlie?"

Craig choked on his beer, and Ryan handed him a napkin. "Thanks."

"So?"

"No," Craig said. "But I care about her. And her kid." Love? Craig only loved two people, his sister and his cousin. Okay, he loved Mackenzie too, but that was different. Who couldn't fall in love with Mack? She was perfect.

"I understand."

"From the stories I've heard, I think you do," Craig said and saluted Ryan with his bottle. "Look, I don't know many people in town—"

"If you've aligned yourself with the McKays, you've taken a step in the right direction. But considering you're Alexandra's brother, my friendship comes with the package."

"Thanks," he said, uncomfortable with all the feelings. "What we should do is find out more about Jasper Hart. Where does he live?"

"Are you planning to break into the sheriff's home?"

Craig eyed him over the rim of his beer. "I am."

****

Craig waited an hour before going inside. The sheriff's security system was no joke, but Craig was grinning when five minutes later he was in the man's home. It wasn't a secret that Jasper Hart was a widower; his wife had died few years ago of cancer. Guilt crept up, but Craig squashed it. He'd met the man a couple of times in passing. It was hard to believe the wiry guy was a murdering bastard, but stranger things had happened.

The house was small and messier than he would have expected. He went through the sheriff's closet and drawers, then the bathroom and fridge. Checked the icebox twice. You never knew where people kept things. The least likely places were often the right ones.

Going to Jasper's home office, Craig put his baseball cap on backwards and, using his penlight, started going through the man's files. He used his lock kit to open the drawer. He'd just pulled out a small safe when the cold steel of a blade caressed his carotid.

People didn't usually sneak up on him; he'd been on the SWAT team, for fuck's sake. He hadn't realized how out of practice he'd become. He didn't move a muscle and most certainly didn't swallow.

Chapter Fifteen

"You've got one minute to tell me what the fuck you're doing in Jasper's office. And I warn you, if I think you're lying, I'll either arrest you or kill you. Either works for me."

"Fletcher?"

Fletcher twisted the knife. "Just call me judge, jury, and executioner."

Craig grabbed her arm and wrestled her to the ground. He breathed easily as he took the kitchen knife out of her gloved hand. Shit. What should he do? He wouldn't hurt her, but she'd kill him if he didn't think fast. He shifted position so that he sat at her side holding her arms with one hand. And there was his mistake.

Fletcher contorted, dislodged his hand, and flipped over. She brought her right foot up and kicked him in the chin, knocking Craig off balance. She reached inside her boot and pulled out the deadliest knife Craig had ever seen—and he'd seen a lot. She used his distraction to her advantage and knocked him down with her elbow. If the pain wasn't enough, then the crunch of bone was the telltale sign she'd broken his nose.

"Damn it," he hissed, blood trickling down into his mouth.

She took a handkerchief from her pocket and

pushed it on his face. "No sense in getting blood on Jasper's new carpets." She straddled his chest and put her blade against his pulse. "Let's say you and I play a little game." She pulled out a pair of cuffs.

"You broke my fucking nose." He didn't scream when she tweaked it, but he did see stars. Jesus.

"You're lucky I didn't break your fucking neck!" She helped him to his feet and put Jasper's desk back in order. "He'll never know you were in here."

"Noah was right about you." He was ready for the punch to the gut. He'd thought they were friends. Hell, he'd wanted to protect the kid. Lost puppy, his ass.

"Yeah, well, so what?"

"This is police brutality."

"I'm on vacation! And to think I…oh, never mind."

"You cuffed me," he pointed out as she escorted him to the garage.

"For your own safety." She shoved him in the back of her truck.

He waited until the garage door closed and she had put the truck in reverse to ask where they were going.

"To Alexandra's." She rummaged around the passenger seat, then threw him a towel. "I don't want you getting blood in my truck either."

He put the towel to his nose and grunted. "Why Alexandra's?"

" 'Cause I'm damn sure she put you up to this." And that was the last thing she said until they got to the B and B.

She pushed Craig down into one of the chairs once they were in Alexandra's kitchen. The last time he'd been in here he and Charlie had made love. He winced when Fletcher screamed for Alex to get her ass downstairs. He was surprised when she came into the room with her hair down; she looked even more like their mother with her hair loose. And he was even more shocked to see Charlie running in with her. They came to a halt. Yep, he had a broken bloody nose, and Fletcher had put that wicked blade against his throat again.

"Fletcher, honey, what do you think you're doing?" Charlie asked calmly. She glanced at Craig. Fletcher had beaten the crap out of him. Her little sister had lost her mind. Again.

"I've put up with a lot of your antics, but this is insane!"

"You haven't even begun to see *insane*, Alexandra." Fletcher sneered, then pointed to them. "Now you two are gonna tell me what the fuck you're doing having Craig break into Jasper's house."

"I—"

She looked down at Craig. "I didn't ask you, so shut up."

Alex took a seat across from Craig and pulled Charlie down next to her. "What are you talking about?"

"Don't play innocent with me!" She turned to Charlie. "Why?"

Charlie carefully explained Alexandra's suspicions and how they had agreed to look into Jasper. "I'm sorry, but think about it, honey. I know you trust Jasper—"

"You don't know a fucking thing!" Fletcher swatted tears away from her cheeks. "It ain't possible! Jasper isn't involved with this."

Alex crossed her arms over her chest. "For goodness' sake, let Craig go. This is ridiculous."

Fletcher looked around the place. "Granny Vaughn must be rolling over in her grave right about now. She'd be ashamed of you—both of you," she whispered. She flung the keys to her handcuffs on the table, then sheathed her knife. "You can have your brother and your twisted truths."

Charlie swallowed when Fletcher's tear-filled eyes landed on her.

"Alexandra excels at getting people to see things *her* way, but you forget how bad the repercussions are when her ideas backfire. If she hadn't fucked with your head, I know you wouldn't have believed any of this, Charlie. Or you either, Craig," she said and shrugged. "Sorry about the nose."

"Fletcher, sweetie, don't do anything—"

"What, Charlie? Crazy? Don't do anything crazy?" She shook her head. "All the information I've gathered is in the bunker. If you don't remember how to get in, ask Jebb."

"What are you going to do?" Charlie asked, though she was afraid of the answer.

"I'm not going to *do* anything the way you're thinking, but I *am* gonna call Jasper and tell him what happened." She looked at Alex. "Jasper was at the hospital the night Rick was dug up, just so you know, Miss Priss. He had that heart attack you're always saying I'm gonna give him, Charlie. I was with him when it happened, so I'm the only one who knows. He was planning on announcing his retirement after we caught the son of a bitch who's after you and Mack. Truth be told, he should be resting and recuperating.

That's the real reason he and I had a disagreement."

"Why didn't you tell us?" Charlie asked, horrified. She'd believed Jasper played some part in this, and here he was risking his health to help her. She *was* ashamed. What had they done?

"You should trust me," Fletcher said, pointing to herself. "A fucking recurring problem in this family."

"Oh, for the love of—"

Fletcher swiveled toward Alex, quick as a snake. "Fuck you, Alex! You really think the world revolves around you, don't you?" There was no humor in Fletcher's laugh. "Jasper's been covering for your ass since we were kids."

"I—"

"What, *Alexandra*? Cat got your tongue? Well, stick this in your craw...Jasper cashed in just about every favor he was owed to make sure you could open Granny Vaughn's, despite the fact it was tied up in Granny's estate until one of us got married."

Charlie shot a quick glance at Alex, whose face lost all color. She had wondered how Alex got around the will, but she'd never asked. "Fletcher—"

"No, Charlie, she needs to hear this. All this because you got it in your thick skull that Jasper was keeping secrets." Fletcher shook her head. "He damn well *is* keeping secrets—yours, mine, and Charlie's— but he does it to protect us. So you can have your brother, this town, and whatever else your cold heart desires; just make sure you take it back to hell with you when you go." The door slammed so hard behind her it shook the pictures on the wall.

"Fletcher!" Charlie moved to go after her, but Alex grabbed her hand.

"Don't," Alex whispered. "She won't listen." She let go of Charlie's hand and uncuffed Craig. She cleaned up his face, then walked away.

Craig rubbed his wrists and looked at Charlie. Tears were rolling down her pretty face. He pulled her into his lap. They sat there for some time.

"I'm sorry, honey," he whispered. If he'd been more careful, this could have been avoided. He said as much.

"No, she would have found out one way or another." Charlie gave him a small smile, then winced. Touching his swollen nose lightly, she said, "Got you pretty good, did she?"

"Yeah, who knew? I mean, sure, she talks about kicking grown men's asses all the time, but she's not even half my size." He shook his head. "Who the hell taught her how to fight?"

"Pops and Tiny. They taught all of us." Charlie ducked her head. "This is going to kill my parents."

"And Alexandra?"

"I know she's hurt—very much so—but she won't admit it. She doesn't show emotional weakness. And that's how she sees it, as a weakness. She'll talk about it when she's ready. Which will probably be never. Fletcher won't care, though. She meant what she said. She almost always does."

"What do you think she's going to do?"

"With Fletcher, one can never be sure."

"Charlie? I know this isn't the right time, but lately timing hasn't been my strong suit." He waited until her tear-filled eyes met his. His heart clenched. "Do you think you could give us a real chance? I mean, I know—" He didn't get the rest out because Charlie

166

latched her mouth onto his. Craig didn't care that his nose was broken or that kissing hurt like hell. Nope, he sucked her tongue into his mouth and relished the taste of her. He ran his hands over her back, then the porch door opened and someone cleared his throat.

Sheriff Jasper Hart stood there looking at them. Charlie got off Craig's lap and stood to face a man they had wronged. Tears were in his old eyes.

"Jasper," Charlie whispered, but the sheriff's eyes never left Craig's.

"I won't be pressing charges against you, boy. Fletcher asked me not to," he said and looked to Charlie. "You best put on a pot of coffee, girl, 'cause this house is about to be packed. Someone might want to go get Alexandra too." Jasper put his hat on the kitchen counter.

Charlie was quick to nod. "I'll make the coffee. Craig, why don't you go get Alex, then maybe clean yourself up a bit."

Craig decided to clean himself up first. He ran to his apartment, changed clothes, and washed his face. It only took six minutes for him to be knocking on Alexandra's bedroom door. Midknock, he realized Charlie hadn't exactly answered him, but there was no time to dwell on that.

"Yes?"

"Alexandra?" he began and entered the room. "Jasper's here, and your family are on their way." He closed the door behind him and turned on the light.

She sat in a chair staring out the window, tears running down her cheeks. He went to over to her and hugged her, surprised when she held him tightly. Charlie said Alexandra didn't like showing weakness.

So Craig figured she must be heartbroken. He rubbed her back and stroked her long hair.

"I used to do this when you cried. It always calmed you down," he whispered, then he stood her up and guided her into the bathroom. He used a washcloth to wipe the tears from her face.

"Did you do this too?" she asked, her voice raw.

"Yeah." He kissed her forehead, relieved when she gave him a weak smile. "Want me to wait here till you're ready to go downstairs?"

"Please."

He nodded and closed the bathroom door. When she came out, she looked like nothing had happened. Craig could almost believe he'd imagined her crying if his shirt wasn't still wet.

"Makeup," she said and led the way downstairs.

The voices of the McKay family vibrated the walls as they headed to the kitchen. When Alex walked in, everyone got quiet, but the displeasure in Emmit McKay's eyes was clear. Craig held his tongue and followed his sister to the coffee pot.

"All right, we're all here, except Fletcher. And where is she, I'd like to know?"

"Emmit, please calm down."

"I will, Savannah, right after someone tells me what the hell is going on!"

"Dad, take it easy," Casey said.

Jasper cleared his throat. "I reckon I'll go first...Got an interesting call from Fletcher about half an hour ago. Seems someone broke into my home."

"Oh, how awful."

"Yeah, Savannah, it is. Apparently, your daughters—with the exception of Fletcher—thought I might have something to do with all the bad things that have been happening to Charlie lately." He let that sink in for a minute. " 'Course, they're all dead wrong. But if you need proof, the night Rick Randle was dug up, I had a mild heart attack and was at the hospital with Fletcher. And no one knew that the only thing keeping this badge on me was my desire to help find whoever wants to hurt Charlie."

Emmit was on his feet. "Whose idea was all this? And who the hell broke into Jasper's house? You, Sutton? It was you, damn it."

"It was only because I asked him to," Ryan admitted getting a heated look from his father-in-law and a sigh out of Jasper.

"Ryan didn't believe any of it, Jasper, just so you know," Casey clarified.

"I'm the one who thought you knew more than you were telling us," Alex said, smoothing her skirt down. "If you look at the facts, it is rather suspicious, Jasper. And I'm sorry for doubting you."

"But after hearing her concerns, we all thought we should look into it. So we're all to blame here," Charlie said.

"Alexandra McKay, I can't believe this," Savannah said. "Jasper's our friend. No, damn it, he's our family. I'm ashamed of all of you for even thinking this."

They all turned when the screen door opened and Noah came in, crowding the room. "Sorry to interrupt."

"Who the hell invited you?" Casey wanted to know.

"Fletcher did," Noah said.

Craig caught a look that passed between Noah and the sheriff. Jasper held up five fingers, and Noah nodded. *Now, what was that about?*

"Fletcher hates your guts."

"Yes, Mrs. Keller, I'm well aware of that, but she called in a favor."

Casey snorted. "Yeah, right."

"It's true," Noah said.

"What favor?" Craig asked.

"Didn't see you there, cousin. Fletcher do that to your face?"

"Yep." Craig smirked when Noah laughed.

"I still don't know why the hell she called you. And where is she anyway?" Casey prodded. "I haven't talked to her since we've been back."

"She called Noah 'cause he's my replacement. As of twenty minutes ago, I'm no longer sheriff of Blue Creek."

Emmit shot to his feet again. "You can't be serious!"

"May as well take your seat, McKay, there's no going back now. Noah will be sworn in as interim sheriff tomorrow morning to make it official," Jasper said and motioned to Noah. "Go on, boy. Tell 'em the rest of it."

Charlie didn't let him answer. "Noah, what favor did Fletcher ask you for?" she asked, then jumped when Craig took her hand under the table. She squeezed his in return.

"That I would watch over her family or she would find a way to hurt me," Noah said, helping himself to a cup of coffee.

Savannah stood up. "And why, exactly, would you need to take care of us?"

"Jasper," Noah began, "are you sure you want me

to…Okay, Fletcher's gone."

"Gone where?" Emmit asked, standing and putting his arm around his wife's shoulders.

"She's gone, as in left town—probably for good."

"No," Savannah whispered and looked at Jasper.

"I'm sorry, Savannah. She wouldn't even tell me where she was going. You couldn't have stopped her," Jasper said and then had to excuse himself. Noah was right behind him.

"I'll go check on Mama," Charlie said after Savannah had left the room.

"No, you're going to sit right here at this damn table with your sisters and tell me everything! And I mean everything." Emmit slammed his fists on the table.

"Basically," Alex began, "you know—"

"Don't you take that tone with me, Alexandra McKay. 'Basically' is for the damn dogs. I want the truth."

"Emmit, there isn't more to any of this," Ryan said. He tried to put his arm around Casey, but she shrugged it off. Then she got up so fast, the chair fell.

"Casey, calm down," Charlie said.

Pops sighed. "Don't go getting worked up, Case."

"Fuck that, Pops. I only went along with this because I was jealous. Okay? You were right, Charlie. I was jealous that Jasper is Fletcher's best friend and not me. God, we suck!" she said, then let Ryan hold her.

Charlie eyed her family and rubbed her arms. She had played a part in all of this, going behind Fletcher's back, hurting not only her sister, but Jasper as well. What was she going to tell Mack? *Sorry, honey, Auntie Fletcher ran away because your mama's a fool.* Yeah, that sounded good. She glanced at Alex. If her sister was crushed, which Charlie suspected, you would never know from looking at her. Not a hair out of place, not an emotion betrayed.

"Maybe we should talk about what's happening to Charlie."

Casey turned in Ryan's arms to sneer at Alex. "Oh, you'd like that, wouldn't you?"

"Fletcher is throwing a fit as per usual, but someone is out there threatening Charlie and Mack's lives, and I think *that's* what we should be discussing. Because it seems like you've all forgotten," Alex accused.

"Alex!" Charlie hissed, her cheeks flushing.

Pops turned to Charlie. "Do you feel that way?"

"No, I—"

Alex rolled her eyes. "Of course not!"

"Someone is after you and Mack. That's worth discussing," Pops said.

Charlie glared at Alex. "I don't want to talk about it."

"We probably should go over everything that's happened," Casey said rubbing her temples.

"It's about time," Alex mumbled.

"Charlie?"

"What do you want me to say, Dad?" she said, standing up. "Do you think I've forgotten that some crazy person burnt down my home, vandalized my business, sent threatening letters to my child, gift wrapped Rick's rotting corpse and put it on my porch— my God blessed porch! Do you really think that's not going through my mind constantly? Do you think I don't have nightmares about it? That I'm not absolutely terrified? Well, I am; I'm scared spitless, okay? So sue me if I would rather focus my energy on something and someone I may actually be able to help!"

Charlie took a few deep breaths, ignoring their stares and said, "I'm going to talk to Mama." Craig gave her another squeeze, but no one else said a word as she walked out.

Charlie took her time walking to where her mother sat on the steps of Craig's apartment. She needed to calm down; she hadn't meant to go off on her family. She sighed when she took a seat next to Savannah. It was freezing outside, but neither of them mentioned it.

"It all started right here," her mother began, taking Charlie's hand. "I moved into this nice widow's apartment and took the job as principal. I remember the first day I met all of you."

"I fell a little in love with you that day," Charlie admitted.

Savannah smiled. "I remember so much of that time, but I don't remember not loving you all. Your father, Jebb, Mack, and you girls mean the world to me. I explained Fletcher to you as best I could, so I don't understand how this happened."

"I didn't even think about it, Mama. To be perfectly honest, I was too relieved that we might put an end to all this craziness." To the nightmares.

"Okay…I can understand that," she said. "I know you may think Fletcher is cruel to do this, and I'll admit I'm angry at her for leaving without a word, but it's her way. It's not that she doesn't feel—"

"It's that she feels too much, and it scares her. I don't know what I'll say to Mackenzie."

"Just tell her the truth, honey. I always do."

Charlie stared at her shoes. "Good point."

Savannah moved a hair behind Charlie's ear. "How are you doing? Really?"

She shrugged. "As good as can be expected. I feel awful about all of this. And I'm sure Pops will tell you about my little blow-up in there."

"What?"

"Alex wants to focus on what's happening to me, which is all fine and good except for the fact that I don't want to talk about it...not right now. I want to focus on something else—anything else."

"Okay...We haven't talked about Craig Sutton or what he is to you."

Charlie smirked. "I don't want to talk about that either. But, honestly, I don't know how I feel. I keep pushing him away, and he keeps coming back. He asked me to give us a real chance and I want to, but..."

"How's the sex?"

"Mama!" Charlie was red to the roots of her hair, but it was too dark for her mother to see that. She giggled.

Savannah bumped Charlie's shoulder with her own. "That good, huh? Give him another chance, honey."

"It's hard...Mackenzie is already attached to him, and if it doesn't work out, I don't want her hurt." Or myself.

"I know the perfect person for you to speak with."

"Who?"

"Your father."

Charlie paused; she hadn't thought of that. "You're right, I guess."

"Of course I am."

"Fletcher will come back, Mama."

"I'm not as sure of that as you seem to be. There were a few things I didn't tell you the other day when we talked."

"About Fletcher?" Charlie asked and sat back while her mother opened Fletcher's Pandora's box.

Chapter Sixteen

The next morning Charlie made breakfast for her sisters; they were going to have the kind of meeting they'd had many times as children. Fletcher always called them their old-fashioned pow-wows, but Fletcher wasn't here and that was the problem.

"How are you feeling?" Charlie asked Casey while she finished setting the food on the table.

"You mean other than the fact that my little sister is gone and we ruined Jasper? Oh, I'm fucking peachy."

Alexandra rolled her eyes. "Must you always be so vulgar?"

"Yes." Casey snorted. "I must."

"Come on, guys."

"You're the ones who need to calm down," Alex said with a sniff.

"Oh really? This coming from the spokeswoman for the—"

Charlie cleared her throat. "I have something to say."

"Go ahead."

Alex sighed. "Please."

"Last night Mama told me about these horrible nightmares Fletch used to have. Pops would have to sleep in her room sometimes."

"What are you talking about? She never mentioned having nightmares to me," Casey said.

Alex gave a ladylike snort. "Of course, she didn't; I mean, imagine the ridicule."

"That's not fair—"

"The truth isn't always fair."

Charlie growled. "Will you two stop so I can finish? Thank you," she said once they'd acquiesced. "It all started after…well, after everything that happened with Uncle—"

Casey held up a hand. "We got it."

Charlie nodded. They had all promised to let go of that particular piece of the past. "Anyway, all the things we went through brought Fletcher's repressed memories of her birth mother to the surface. Fletcher's birth mother treated her horribly."

"You think!" Casey shifted in her chair. "She branded her, for heaven's sake."

"Yes, well, she also left her in soiled diapers and locked her a closet for hours on end—"

"She always hated closets," Casey murmured.

Alex fiddled with her bracelet. "Why are you telling us this?"

"Mama thought it was important enough to tell me, so I figure it's important enough to tell you."

"What else did Ma say?" Casey asked.

Charlie rubbed her temples. "Other things…"

"Spit it out, Charlie."

A knock came at the door, and Charlie's mouth snapped shut.

Noah walked in. "Good morning, ladies. Sorry to interrupt what I'm sure was stimulating conversation."

"Good morning, Noah, or should I say Sheriff Reed?" Charlie asked through her guilt.

"I am officially interim sheriff, but Noah's fine,"

he said and took a seat.

"What brings you here, *Sheriff?*" Casey asked.

"Bad news. Someone vandalized the diner again last night. Spray-painted every available surface; these are the pictures we took."

He spread the photos out across the table, and Charlie swallowed as words like "whore," "sinner," and "bastard child" stared back at her.

"They didn't get inside. Mildred scared them off."

"No one was hurt, though, right?" Charlie asked.

Noah shook his head.

"That's something, at least. I'm starting to get a mite pissed off about all of this."

"Good, Charlie," Noah said. "But it should also scare you."

Casey gave him a withering look. "If you haven't already figured it out, you should learn right quick the McKays don't scare easy."

"Yes, I'm well aware, but *you* need to be aware that this person is targeting Charlie specifically—not all of you."

"But whoever it is did work with the people after us last time. And he or she's probably an expert at forging documents."

Noah narrowed his silver eyes. "What are you talking about?"

"Didn't Fletcher...no, I guess she wouldn't have." Charlie told Noah about her father's FBI friend and what they'd discovered.

"Damn. I haven't had a chance to go over Jasper's files yet."

Alex smoothed a hand over the table. "How is Jasper?"

"I don't know," Noah said. "Word's out around town about why Jasper's stepping down, and Fletcher leaving town…Accusations run amuck."

"A good few are coming your way, I'd imagine."

"Yes, Mrs. Keller, but I'm not inclined to care. I, for one, am glad your sister is—"

"Let's get back to the case at hand," Charlie said before the conversation could get worse. Or before Casey assaulted an officer. "We know a partial fingerprint was found on one of the letters sent to Mackenzie's school." She had to take a moment to calm the boil in her blood—no one messed with her baby!

"I'm sorry, whose print?"

"When Rick was killed, someone cut off his finger, and it was his print they found on the letter. Fletcher said whoever murdered him has to be the one coming after me. To her way of thinking, if we solved his case, we would solve mine too. So that's where I think we should start." Aside from Mack, most of the Rick-related things in her life were bad.

"Fletcher knew all this?" Noah barked out.

"We believe it was her looking into Rick's case initially that brought about the events of last year," said Alex.

"Oh, yes, how can I forget."

Charlie got up from the table and pointed at the photos. "Are we sure the vandalism is related? I mean, I'm sorry, Noah, but Marylou used these exact words against me the other day."

"Why the hell are you dating that bitch anyway?" Casey wanted to know.

"First of all, I doubt Marylou would do something this juvenile. And the other is none of your business."

"Marylou is *the* poster girl for juvenile pettiness," Alex drawled. "And if you haven't figured that out by now, then you're not as smart as I've given you credit for."

"It wasn't her. Can we get back to the case at hand?"

Casey stood. "I've got to get to the garage." She hugged her sisters and gave Noah a one-finger salute before she left.

"I guess this can wait. I need to go look over Jasper's files anyway," Noah said and made his exit.

"What are you going to do? Go check on your house?" Alex asked.

Charlie took a moment to top off both their coffees. "Pops has already hired a crew to rebuild my house, so I don't have to worry over that."

"Our father has excellent connections," Alex said with a pleased smile.

Charlie snorted. "Yeah, he said it should be ready in a few months. He said money talks, especially this time of year." Thank goodness she'd had insurance. Of course, she had had to dig into the inheritance Granny Vaughn and the Judge left her. Pops had argued with her at first, but if it helped speed things along, then it was worth it to Charlie. She told her sister as much.

"I think it's a wise investment. Besides, we still have the farmhouse in Virginia if money ever becomes an issue," Alex said.

Charlie shrugged. "I need to call the diner to make sure they don't need me to come in. No one signed up for dealing with—"

"Oh, please...Between Mildred, Tiny, and Dad, I'm sure the vandalism is already long gone."

"You're probably right, but I'll call anyway. I think I'll go to Fletcher's cabin too, see if she left anything."

Charlie pulled her jacket on as Alexandra stared out the window. "If it's all the same to you, I think I'll stay here."

"I understand, honey." Charlie kissed her sister's cheek and headed for her vehicle.

****

Charlie stood back as the door to Fletcher's bunker opened. She entered the room and hit the light switch. Other than piles of papers, Fletcher's desk was empty. Charlie flipped through a stack of letters on top of the pile and opened the one addressed to her.

Dear Charlie,

Copies of all the information I've gathered are on my desk in the bunker. I'm positive if you find Rick's killer, you'll find whoever's after you. I know I left abruptly, but I couldn't stay. I'd lose my mind if I did or, worse, hurt Alexandra. I know she's suspicious by nature—hell, we all are—but she went too fucking far this time!

Don't worry about me. I've made some money on the side. I'm not sure when I'll be back, or even if I will. In my safe (to the right of my desk in the bunker) is something for Mack. The combination is the same as getting into the bunker. There's something in there for Bullfrog too; make sure he gets it.

I love you. It may not seem like it right now, but I do. You're one of the best people I know; don't change. And get pissed off a little more; it's hilarious when you do. Take care of the parents. And this may be asking a lot, but could you watch out for Jasper? This hurt him so much, but the man doesn't hold a grudge. Talk to him. Be his friend. He doesn't have anyone else he likes.

Always,

Fletcher

"Oh, Fletcher." She refolded the letter, went to the safe, and entered the combination. She found an envelope for her daughter and one for Jebb. Grabbing the backpack from the cot, Charlie put the papers inside along with the letters to her parents, sisters, and Jasper.

****

Charlie took her time driving to her parents' home the next morning. She still had a lot of papers to go over. She'd spent most of yesterday cleaning Fletcher's cabin. She didn't know why she'd had to clean the entire place, but she did, then fell asleep on the couch.

She missed her daughter. Casey said Mack had been ecstatic to be going on vacation with Uncle Jake, but Charlie wished it was safe for her baby to be here. She pulled out her cell phone and called her brother-in-law. She hung up smiling. Ryan had agreed to help go through all of Fletcher's files with her later.

Pulling into the driveway, Charlie parked between her parents' vehicles. Dawn was hovering on the horizon, but Pops always got up before the cows. She found them at the kitchen table finishing what Charlie assumed was their first cup of coffee. She set the pack on the table and told them about Fletcher's bunker; she unzipped the backpack and handed her parents their letters. She sat down while they read them.

"Emmit?" Savannah said when he rushed away from the table. She folded her letter and wiped a tear from her cheek. She smiled at Charlie. "I feel better now."

"Can I ask what she wrote to you?"

"She said she'd let me know what she was doing and where she was when she got there."

"She left something for Jebb and Mack. I haven't opened Mack's envelope yet." Charlie ducked her head. "I thought we could open them together." At her mother's smile, she handed over Jebb's envelope and opened Mackenzie's.

"Oh, goodness," Savannah whispered.

"What?" Charlie couldn't believe what her sister had set up for Mack. They exchanged envelopes and the same thing was written on Jebb's pages.

Pops came back into the kitchen. "What has she done now?"

"She set up trust funds for Jebb and Mack." Charlie was stunned.

"Oh, that's not so bad."

"No, Emmit, you don't understand. Look," Savannah said and pointed to the sum. His eyes narrowed.

"Dad, where did Fletcher get that kind of money? I mean, I could understand a couple thousand, but this is a quarter of a million dollars each."

"I can read, Charlie." Emmit shook his head and handed her his crumpled letter.

Charlie waited while her mother scooted beside her to read along.

Dear Pops (or since you're pissed I should say Dad),

By now I'm gone, and you're wondering where the hell I got the money to just up and leave. I'll tell you in a sec. First, I know we haven't been seeing eye to eye lately, but I wanted to tell you I love you. How could I not? You gave me the first home I'd ever known and loved me. Really loved me. I don't know anyone I respect and admire as much as I do you. I know you're angry and confused, but I couldn't stay, Dad. I might have hurt Alex if Charlie hadn't been there. And that scared the shit out of me.

As for my financial situation. I took a job a while back. I won't go into the details, but I was paid well and then I did what I do and quadrupled my sum. If you check the bottom panel of the closet in the attic, you'll find some emergency money. Use it to help Charlie get back on her feet faster. I know you're upset and wondering what in the hell I did to make that kind of money. If you must know, ask Noah Reed. That scumbag is who I took the job with.

You'll always be the first man I ever loved.
Fletcher

"I don't think I want to know," Savannah said.

Charlie shook her head. "I'm with you there."

"She knows I'll ask Noah." Emmit reached into his pockets and pulled out two thick wads of cash. "It was where she said it was. Emergency money, my ass. But she did want you to have it, Charlie."

"But, I—"

"It's yours." Pops pushed the money at Charlie, then grabbed his keys. "I have to take a letter to the old sheriff, then go talk to the new one."

Charlie and Savannah stared at the door until after it shut, then both looked at the emergency money Fletcher had left.

"Should we count it?" Charlie asked worrying her lower lip. She didn't know if she wanted to take it. What the heck had Fletcher done?

"I guess," her mother said, and they started counting.

"That's enough to help things along on the rebuild." Charlie shook her head, then made a decision. "I have a few errands to run, Mama. I'll talk to you later."

****

Craig knocked on the door and waited. His nose was swollen and hurt like hell, but he ignored it and knocked again. He had a lot of things he needed to do today, but this was a priority.

"I'm coming, I'm coming, hold your horses," said the voice on the other side of the door before it opened. "Decided to be invited in this time, did ya?" Jasper asked.

Craig gave his best aw-shucks shrug.

Jasper shook his head and moved to let him in. "Come on then."

He waited until the other man had shut the door, then followed him to the kitchen.

Jasper pointed to the table. "Have a seat. I'd imagine you drink coffee."

"I do, thank you." He moved a pile of papers out of the way and sat.

"Why is a bar man out so early in the morning?"

"I'm having a soft opening tomorrow, so I have a lot of things to finish up today."

Jasper handed him a mug of coffee, then took the seat across from him. "What the hell's a soft opening?"

"It's like a test run. So I can get a better idea of what works and what doesn't."

Jasper fiddled with the handle of his mug. "I see."

"And I'll be able to get a look at my clientele,

which will help me make a better assessment of what they like."

"Folks like it simple 'round here," Jasper said. "No fuss, no muss."

Craig sipped his coffee. "That's what I figured."

"Tended bar myself years ago."

"Really?" That was surprising.

Jasper nodded. "Yep, Shmittie, the man you bought the bar from, needed a barkeep, and I needed the extra money for my wife's engagement ring."

"Oh, I—"

"Well? What is it?"

Craig shifted in his chair. "Sorry?"

"Why are you here, boy?"

"I wanted to apol—"

Jasper harrumphed. "I told you I wasn't gonna press charges."

"I know, and I appreciate it, but you deserve an apology in person."

He swept a hand over the table. "I understand."

"Understand what?"

"You were trying to help them. Trust me, I understand. Never do anything like normal folks." Jasper shook his head. "Those girls have been giving me fits for damn near twenty years!"

Craig didn't know if laughing was appropriate, so he sipped his coffee to hide his smile. "I see."

"No, you don't, boy…but you will."

Well, that was cryptic. Craig eyed the other man for a moment, then asked, "What do you make of this person coming after—"

"Let me stop you right there! You've apologized, and I've accepted your apology, but I'm not ready to be telling you my thoughts. Trust is earned, boy. And if you're thinking we're gonna have us one of them bromances Fletch keeps telling me are popular, you can think again; I don't need none of that!" Jasper said standing up.

Craig used his sleeve to wipe the coffee that had come out of his nose and stood. He didn't complain when Jasper ushered him toward the door.

"I appreciate you stopping by."

Craig stepped outside. "Thanks for the coffee." He turned when another vehicle pulled into the driveway. It was Emmit. Craig hoped it wasn't bad news.

"What now?" Jasper grumbled.

"Stop by the bar tomorrow if you get a chance," Craig said to Jasper, then nodded to Emmit as they crossed paths. The other man did not look happy.

****

Charlie checked in with the construction crew working on her house, then called the sheriff's station to see if Noah was in. She was told the interim sheriff had gone home, so she headed in the direction of his house. She had a few things she wanted to discuss with him and he only lived fifteen minutes from McKay property.

The estate came into view, and a wide grin split Charlie's face. She loved it here, and had spent many nights with her sisters in what had once been their grandparents' home. Judge J. T. Vaughn had built this house out of his own imagination. It was elegant yet rugged at the same time, just as he had been. All of them had loved this house, and when their father sold it to Noah, they all cried a bit. Charlie had always assumed that was the real reason behind Fletcher's hatred of Noah, but maybe not.

She breathed a sigh of relief that Marylou's bimbo-mobile wasn't in the driveway. The last thing she needed was another encounter with that vicious creature. She locked her vehicle and headed up to the front entrance.

She rang the doorbell, then rang it a second time when no one answered. Noah's truck was in the driveway. Charlie knocked on the door, jumping when it screeched open.

"Oh, shoot," she whispered. "I've seen this movie." She took out her cell phone and called the sheriff's office again. She told them there was something suspicious going on, and she would have waited outside like they asked her to if someone hadn't moaned from inside. "Tell them to send an ambulance," she said and hung up before they could instruct her to stay put.

It took her only a second to find Noah lying facedown in the den with a knife sticking out of his back—a big one.

"Oh, God." She rushed over to him, sending up a silent prayer. Though his pulse was weak, he was still alive. Charlie sat back on her haunches and took in the scene. "Yep, I've seen this movie." She took Noah's hand in hers and squeezed it. He mumbled something, and she leaned closer, but she was sure she was mistaken, sure she'd misunderstood the name he'd whispered.

Chapter Seventeen

Charlie stood out of sight when Craig rushed off the elevator. She let Alexandra handle the situation while her father paced restlessly in front of her.

"He's going to be fine," Alex assured Craig. "The knife missed his spinal cord by two inches. And luckily, or I should use the term the surgeon did, 'miraculously,' nothing vital was hit. He'll be as good as new in a week or so."

"That long?" Craig asked. His eyes tried to find Charlie's, but she glanced away. She knew he was hurting; she wanted to run to him, and give him comfort—to hold him. But the intensity of those feelings scared her, so she stayed where she was.

"That was the doctor's estimate, but he doesn't know Noah or how bullheaded the man can be," Alex said, bringing a small smile to Craig's face. "I offered to give blood, but I'm not a match. I thought maybe you—"

"Got it!" Craig rolled up his sleeve and rushed to the nurse's desk.

"Is he going to give blood?" Charlie asked, looking down at her hands. She'd washed them at least twenty times since arriving at the hospital, but they still felt stained.

Alex sighed. "Yes. Now, let's take a seat. You too, Dad."

Pops grunted and continued to pace.

Jasper sat down beside her. "Tell me again what happened."

"I told you twice already." Charlie rubbed her temples and explained again.

"Seems cut and dried to me," Alex said.

"Nothing is ever that simple with you people," Jasper mumbled.

Alex shrugged, then stood and went over to where their mother was convincing their father to sit down. Charlie wondered if Jasper could or would ever forgive them for their suspicions and the price he'd paid for them.

"Charlie girl?"

"What? Sorry, Jasper, I got lost in my thoughts."

"It's okay. Now, you're sure Noah didn't say anything?"

Charlie bit her lip.

Jasper harrumphed. "He did...well, spit it out."

"He did mumble...something, but what he said and what I heard may not be the same."

"Okay. What do you think he said?" Jasper asked, his fingers reaching up to fiddle with the badge that was no longer there. It was one of Jasper's many habits; only this one she had helped him lose.

She shook her head. "I thought he said 'Fletcher,' but that couldn't be right." Fletcher was gone, and everyone knew it. Besides, her sister didn't stab people in the back; she didn't have to.

Jasper was about to say something when the doctor came in, Craig right behind him. Craig kept rubbing the back of his neck. Oh, this did not bode well.

"Sheriff Reed has slipped into a coma," the doctor

said and raised his hands to quiet the commotion from Charlie's family. "Let me finish! We don't understand what went wrong; he seemed to be coming out of the anesthesia just fine. With this new development, it could be hours or days before he comes out of it."

"Well, that's convenient," Charlie mumbled, then shook off the bad feeling settling over her. She needed to get out of here, do something. She grabbed her purse and told everyone she'd see them later. Craig was deep in conversation with Alex and the doctor, and Charlie was grateful because she didn't know what she would have said to him anyway. She wasn't nearly as surprised as she probably should have been when Jasper followed her onto the elevator.

"If what you heard Noah say is accurate, then we need to find out why." He pressed the button to the lobby.

"Jasper, why are you helping us? After what we—"

The old man let out a weighted sigh. "I can understand how Alexandra came to the conclusions she did."

She stared. "But still."

"Mrs. Hart and I couldn't have our own children, as you know, and you girls are the closest thing we had to it. 'Sides, you're only half the reason I'm gonna help."

The other half was because Fletcher was his best friend, but neither said so.

"Do you think whoever stabbed Noah is the same person who's coming after me and my family?" Charlie asked as the elevator doors slid open. She stopped in her tracks; she'd forgotten she had ridden with Noah in the ambulance.

But Jasper hadn't. "This way," he said, pointing to his vehicle. Once inside his ancient battered truck—she hadn't even known he had a truck—he slipped on a tattered baseball cap and finally answered her question. "First of all, you need to get it through your head that whoever is doing this is singling you out, not your family. You!"

Charlie swallowed and made herself busy with buckling her seatbelt.

"Noah getting stabbed how and when he did is too much of a coincidence. He may have stumbled onto something, and it may have to do with Fletch." Jasper started the engine and pulled out of the parking lot.

"Hence his saying her name." Charlie needed her sister's brain; unfortunately, it was still connected to Fletch's body. "We need someone who thinks like Fletch, and I know just who we can use."

****

Charlie and Jasper walked into to Fletcher's cabin to find Jebbediah lounging against the cushions of Fletcher's couch. He put down his book and jumped to his feet.

A slight blush tinged his cheeks. "Hey, guys?"

"You're lucky I'm not going to tell Mama or Pops you skipped school," Charlie said, brushing past her brother. She and Jasper had gone to the school, then her parents' house looking for Jebb, only to turn up empty-handed. Jasper suggested they try Fletcher's cabin, and sure enough here was Jebb.

"I didn't want to go today," Jebb mumbled.

"I understand, honey." She gave him a hug; she wasn't surprised when he squeezed the heck out of her. Letting him go, she stepped back and looked at him; he was growing up so fast.

"I'll put on the coffee," Jasper said and patted Jebb on the shoulder before heading into the kitchenette.

"Okay," Charlie said, taken aback. Preparing the coffee was her task. She shook her head and turned back to her brother when he asked why they were looking for him. "We need your help." She began clearing off the coffee table and unloading Fletcher's files when a luxury SUV pulled up in front of the cabin. She smiled when Ryan came in.

He shrugged out of his wool coat. "I brought my eyes with me."

"Jasper and I think this is all connected," Charlie explained. "Noah said Fletcher's name before the paramedics came."

Ryan nodded. "Okay, but let's not jump to any conclusions."

"Good advice," Jasper said. He handed a cup of coffee to Jebb.

"Thanks!" Jebb grinned. "So…what do you guys need me for?"

"Remember the other day when I said your mind works like Fletcher's…" she began, then said, "Wait, do you still have the tracking app—?"

"She…ah…found it."

Ryan gave a gentlemanly snort. "That couldn't have been pretty."

"No," Jebb said blushing again.

"Well, you're still the only person who thinks like Fletcher, so that's why we're here," she said.

The cocky grin returned to Jebb's face, and he took a seat on the couch.

Ryan sat down next to Jebb and pointed to the

coffee table. "Are these all of her files?"

"All that she left," Charlie said. She sipped her coffee, surprised to discover Jasper made a darn good brew. Seeing the older man in a sweatshirt and jeans threw her a bit; when they were younger, they had joked that Sheriff Hart slept and showered in his uniform. Guilt swelled in her chest, but Jasper sipped his coffee, picked up a stack of papers, and started to read. They all followed suit.

Two and a half hours and two pots of coffee later, they still didn't know anything new. Casey had texted Ryan to come home, so they'd all called it a night. Jebb had walked out to the cabin, so Jasper offered him a ride. Once they'd dropped him off, she and Jasper were alone again in his old truck.

"You haven't said much, Jasper. What are you thinking?" she asked as they headed toward Noah's house so she could get her vehicle.

"I'm trying to work out where Fletcher mighta been headed."

"Did Pops give you her letter?"

"Yes, but that ain't what I meant. I was talking about her investigation."

"Oh, Jebb didn't seem to know either." And that had bummed her out. She'd thought for sure he'd come up with something. But none of them had.

"She had a pretty good list of suspects though. 'Course, Mr. Thomas was crossed off the list after we found Rick's print on one of the notes sent to the preschool. He was a good suspect for Rick's murder, but even Ian Thomas can't send letters from six feet under."

Charlie snorted. "Yeah, and Marylou has an

ironclad alibi. She and her mother were in New Orleans at the time."

"Not that they couldn't have hired someone."

"No, Marylou seeks her own revenge, believe me." If she knew anything, she knew that.

"Didn't see her crying in the waiting room of the hospital though, now did yah?"

"My guess is Marylou was in town causing a scene. She'll go to the hospital when there's a large enough audience." It wasn't the nicest assumption, but it was probably true.

"Well, the attempted murder of an officer is like building a bonfire in town square—everyone notices. The authorities won't rest until they find whoever did this to Noah; I know that for sure."

She couldn't agree more. She nodded and thanked Jasper for everything and got into her vintage SUV. Deciding she needed to hear her daughter's voice, Charlie pulled out her cell phone.

****

"All I'm saying is you're using Fletcher as an excuse to avoid your own situation," Alex said. "Like you always do."

"I do not always use Fletcher to avoid my own situations," Charlie grumbled. She'd returned to Alex's after picking up her SUV and talking to Mack on the short ride over. Mackenzie was happy and having the "bestest time" with Uncle Jake.

"I'm not talking about Fletcher," Alex said. "It just happens to be her this time! I'm talking about the fact that you involve yourself in everyone else's problems so you don't have to face your own. You've always done it, Charlie. Don't deny it."

"You're wrong! Just because *I* care about what happens to my family doesn't mean I use them!" Charlie pointed to where Casey was sitting. "Tell her."

"You know I don't want to get in the middle of this crap! *I* should be having sex with my husband right now, but nooo. Alex called with a Charlie emergency, which means you're the reason I'm missing my private time. And with that in mind, it makes it a whole hell of a lot easier saying that Alex is right."

"See, even Casey noticed."

Charlie threw her hands up in the air. "I don't know what you're talking about."

"Then you're fooling yourself. Damn it, Charlie, sit down and listen to me!" Alex said practically pushing Charlie into a chair.

"Fine."

"You wrap yourself up in other people's lives—their issues—so you don't have to deal with yours. I mean, think about it. You're always so hell bent on us not interfering in *your* life and what do you do—"

"I do not interfere in your life," Charlie hissed.

"She doesn't interfere in my life," Casey said. "I think maybe *you're* the one using all this as an excuse, Alex."

Alex glared at Casey. "And what excuse would that be?"

"You don't want to draw attention to the fact that you, Alexandra McKay, fucked up. You think about that, Miss Priss!"

"Don't you mean 'we'?" Alex countered.

"These are the consequences of inciting a riot, Alex. Yours backfired, and now the captain must go down with the ship and all that crap. You two do whatever the hell it is you do; I'm going home to collect on my private time," Casey said.

The door slammed shut, and Charlie turned to Alex not knowing what to say.

Alexandra stood and went to the sink. "Is that what you think too?"

What could she say? She shook her head and pulled the letter Fletcher left for Alex out of her bag. "This is for you; it's from Fletch."

Alex took the letter, read it quickly, then shoved it in a drawer. "That's that, then."

"What did it say?"

"Our sister's typical two-word greeting," Alex said, pouring herself a shot of whiskey. She poured another, laughing when Charlie snatched it and drank it. "Did she leave a note for everyone?"

"Yes. She also left Mackenzie and Jebb some money." She explained to Alexandra about the cash and what they'd found in the attic. "That's why I wanted to talk to Noah. She said she had worked a job for him, and I wanted to know what kind of job she did to make that kind of—"

"I think you proved my point," Alex began, and rubbed her hand down Charlie's back. "You went over to talk to Noah about Fletcher when you should have gone to talk about what's happening to *you*."

She huffed. "Okay, I'll admit it! I do worry about other people's problems more often than my own, but this time it's connected. Don't give me the flipping pitying look, Alexandra. Somehow Fletcher's connected to all this. Noah said her name..." Charlie filled her sister in on all the details, and what she, Jasper, Jebb, and Ryan had been up to that afternoon.

The back door opened, and Craig walked in. "Did you still want to do dinner?"

"Craig, I'm sorry. I completely forgot. Just let me go change," Alex said hurrying out of the room.

Charlie glanced at her watch. "It's almost nine."

"Yeah, we're having a late dinner at the bar." Craig leaned against the sink.

"Is the bar finished?"

"Yep, I'm having a soft opening tomorrow night."

"That was fast."

"I thought about waiting until Noah wakes up, but he'd be pissed if I put anything on hold because of him."

"I get it," Charlie said, looking at the ceiling. Alex could take a while. "Look—"

"No, *you* look," he began and planted his feet. "I understand you have a lot of shit going on in your life right now—I do—but I don't like being fucked with. If you're not going to give us a real chance, tell me now."

"We had sex." Really great, mind-blowing, foot-burning, orgasmic sex. "But that's all that's between us, Craig. That...and Alexandra. I'm sorry if you thought any different." *Liar, liar, pants on fire!* She grabbed her jacket. She didn't need any more complications in her life.

"What about that kiss? What the hell was that then?"

"That was a moment of comfort for both of us. I'm going. Congratulations on your bar." She stopped at the door when he took her shoulder. He didn't turn her to face him, and she was thankful.

"Maybe it's not Alexandra who's the cold one after all...perhaps, you're a better actress than anyone could possibly imagine."

"Perhaps, you're right," Charlie said and walked out.

Chapter Eighteen

Craig squeezed his eyes tight and swore under his breath. He was a bastard. He hadn't meant it—not one word. Turning, he found his sister staring daggers at him. Shit.

"What have you done?"

"Jesus, Alexandra, you can't be mad at me," Craig said, sitting down. Dinner late or otherwise wasn't going to happen.

Alex took the seat next to him. "Yes, I can! Charlie isn't acting or pretending—she is who she is."

"Yeah, well, you could have fooled me." Not to mention his fucking heart.

"Don't tell me you're upset."

"Is that so hard to believe? Look, you don't know me well enough yet, but the fact is I can count the women I've slept with on two hands and still have a finger or two left—including Charlie. My father drilled two things into me."

Alex raised an eyebrow. "I'm all ears."

"One, you don't fuck with people's money, and two…you don't fuck with people's emotions. I don't do either. I've had real feelings for every woman I've ever been with." Okay, at least one of them was the kind of feeling you got after a bottle of booze, but Alex didn't need to know that.

"And you think Charlie does? Rick is the only

other man Charlie's slept with."

"I figured that." Was it supposed to make him feel better? Because he sure as hell still felt shitty. "It's still no excuse for her to toy with me."

"Charlie isn't the type of person to hurt someone intentionally."

"Maybe not, but she hasn't had a problem fucking with my emotions." He spotted a bottle of whiskey on the counter and brought it to the table. Taking a swig from the bottle, Craig eyed his sister. "Just spit it out."

"What?"

"Whatever it is that's eating at you. I'm your brother and you may not believe me, but you can trust me." He handed the whiskey across the table and she took a sip. "With anything."

"Fletcher left because she was afraid she'd hurt me."

"Do you think she was just blowing off steam?" 'Course, the little beast had held a knife to his throat and broken his damn nose, which he refused to get reset. Noah's doctor had offered, but Craig told him it was a memento of something he should remember: never cross Fletcher McKay…and get caught.

"She wrote letters to all of us. You can read mine." She went to the drawer and then handed the letter to Craig.

"Oh" was all he could say. It was a fuck you, but it took up the entire page.

"Yes, 'oh.' If she doesn't come back, it will be my fault. She knows it, and I know it." Alex shook her head. "Everyone knows it."

"I'm sure your family won't hold it against you."

"Don't be so sure." She crossed her arms over her

chest. "Casey does."

"I've noticed you two don't get along."

Alex eyed him. "We bicker, but we love each other—it's just our way. There was a time when we were all the other had…And I know Casey well enough to know that it's easier for her to put the blame on me than to think she had a hand in hurting Fletcher, but I resent it all the same."

"I get it. They seem pretty close," he said. He took another swig from the bottle; the liquor burned, but it was the good kind of burn.

"They're best friends like Charlie and me. Even though Charlie and Casey are sisters by blood."

"They are?" Now *this* he didn't know.

"Yes."

"That still doesn't explain Casey and Fletcher's relationship." Fletcher had conveniently left a hell of a lot out of their conversation. Not that he blamed her.

"We sort of paired off when Charlie was adopted."

"And before that?" She had been alone, and it killed him.

"I had Granny Vaughn." Alexandra's entire face lit up. "Or the Widow Madison as she called herself then."

"Ahh, the infamous Widow!"

She laughed. "Yes! Let me assure you she lived up to her title. She was a real southern lady, and she taught me everything I know. As you heard the other night, this used to be her house; she left it to whoever of us got married first. Of course, I didn't think any of us would ever actually marry, and my sisters didn't have a problem with me opening the B and B. I never knew Jasper pulled strings; I guess I decided not to question my good fortune when things went my way."

"That's understandable—"

"But stupid," she said. "I know better."

"Never look a gift horse in the mouth, as they say."

"Still not a valid excuse, but what's done is done. When Casey *did* get married, she and Ryan gave me the deed."

"That surprises you?"

She shrugged. "It wasn't a good business deal for them, but I can't complain."

"That's good then." Craig was happy she'd had someone before Charlie came along. He owed a lot of his sister's happiness to the other woman, but he didn't want to think about it.

Alex gave him the once-over. "You've fallen in love with Charlie, haven't you?"

"I love Mackenzie. And Charlie's the type of woman I always wanted to settle down with." Or at least he'd thought she was. Craig frowned. "I can't really explain how I feel."

"Emotions are messy."

Craig nodded. "That they are. So, it looks like dinner's off." Craig smiled when Alex laughed. He'd always loved her laugh, when it wasn't for show.

She snorted and toasted him with the whiskey bottle. "I don't cook."

****

Craig stood behind his bar and looked out over the crowd. His soft opening had turned grand indeed. The DJ had Tim McGraw cranking out of the speakers, and the people of Blue Creek were dancing.

Pouring four more beers for his waitress, Cindy, Craig grinned. Cindy Owens was the cousin of Jimmy Mae, who helped manage the diner. She'd told him waiting on people was in her blood, and from the tips she'd stuffed in her pocket, she wasn't kidding. His other waitress was an older woman named Lily Warren. She was the grandniece of...Craig couldn't remember who, but she was quick with her service and her smiles. Both women were wonderful; even his bartender was nothing to laugh at. The man's name was Slim. His brother had worked for Shmittie, and his father before that; it was a family tradition, and Craig couldn't be happier with the flair bartending.

Seeing a familiar face, Craig grabbed himself and his friend a bottle of beer and told Slim he was taking a break.

"Looks like you're a hit," Ryan said after he took a sip of the beer Craig brought him.

"Seems that way," Craig shouted across the bar. It was loud, but that was a good thing. "What brings you here?"

"I wanted to come and have a look around...*and* Casey said she didn't want me hovering over her. But I know what she's up to."

"Oh?" Craig sipped his beer and kept his eyes on the crowd.

"Yeah, the sisters are having a meeting. They always have them, but now that Fletch is gone, Casey's not looking forward to it."

"I heard they're close."

"I'm not even that close to my *twin* brother, if that gives you any idea."

"It's different for sisters, I guess. Alexandra and Charlie seem pretty tight too," Craig said, shrugging like it wasn't a big deal.

Ryan nodded. "They paired off and stayed that

way. Of course, when Casey left, Fletcher found her partner in Jasper—of all people. Casey's jealous of that."

"Heard that too. You really love her, don't you?" It wasn't a question; Craig could see the other man's adoration of his wife in his green eyes. Must be nice.

"I don't think I could live without her, and I wouldn't want to."

"Do you get along with Emmit?"

"Pretty well. First time I met him, he held his shotgun to my head." Ryan laughed.

"Hate when that happens," Craig said grinning. He told Ryan about Fletcher holding a gun to *his* head.

"Don't feel bad. She kicked my brother's ass in three seconds flat, and Jake's a big guy."

"You're identical, right?" Craig asked, killing his beer.

"Yes, but he puts in more time at the gym than I do. My wife says Jake looks like I would after a two-month binge."

Craig laughed. "I'd like to see that. Now, what do you think's going on with this person coming after Charlie?"

"Whoever it is hasn't made a move since Noah was stabbed. And we're pretty sure his attack is linked to all this mess. Somehow Fletcher has the key, but she must not know it." Ryan's brow pinched.

"How's that?" Craig asked after the crowd stopped yelling at the next song the DJ played. The man was damn good. Craig had asked him to play for the soft opening because he was looking for a band, but maybe he could hire the guy on a more permanent basis. He'd bought the jukebox too, but a live band or friendly DJ was more personable.

"If Fletcher knew who was doing all this, or knew the connection, she wouldn't have left without telling someone."

"So we have to assume she didn't know."

"Yes. We've been all through her files and nothing clicked."

"And Charlie thought Noah might know something; that's why she went to see him."

Ryan nodded. "Now he's in a coma, so we're up the proverbial creek."

"I can get into Noah's house." Craig grinned. "I designed the security system."

Ryan toasted Craig with his beer. "I'm in."

****

Charlie sat in the attic of her parents' home twiddling her thumbs while her sisters argued about the Fletcher situation. She'd stop them in a minute. They'd been holding meetings in this attic for almost twenty years. She'd always been safe here, happy.

"That's enough." She rolled her eyes when her sisters continued. "Mama and Pops are gonna hear you and come up here." So what if they were adults? Pops wasn't in the most giving of moods lately. Luckily, her threat had done the trick.

"Let's get down to business then," Casey said, taking a seat in the recliner while Charlie and Alex sat on the couch.

"I still want to go to the bar and see how Craig is doing," Alex said.

Charlie nibbled her lip.

"Why didn't you say so? We can go now," Casey said. But no one spoke. "What aren't you telling me?"

"Charlie and Craig aren't speaking."

"What happened?" Casey grinned. "I thought I was bad at the relationship thing, but you really suck, Charlie...Go figure."

Charlie giggled. "You might be right. Craig thinks I'm acting—"

"You treat the man like a pair of shoes, Charlie; one day you want to wear them and the next you don't. What kind of reaction did you expect?"

"Whose side are you on anyway, Alex?"

"In this case, Craig's. You're in the wrong."

Charlie was speechless.

Casey wasn't. "How the hell is she in the wrong?"

"She hurt him."

Charlie gasped. "I did not!"

"Yes, you did. He told me."

"He told you?" Charlie said.

Casey smirked. "Wait till I tell Ryan that I'm not the one with all the emotional hang-ups."

"It's not always about you, Casey," Alex said. "But yes, Charlie, he told me."

"What'd he say?" It was high school all over again, and Charlie had detested high school.

"He said he doesn't fuck with people's emotions and thinks others should offer the same courtesy."

"I didn't do anything to his emotions."

"Honey." Alex patted her hand. "You're hot one minute and cold the next."

"Yeah, that confuses the menfolk," Casey added. "Do you care about him? That's the real question?"

"When I see him, I want him, and I'm not talking PG-13 here either."

"Do you trust him?" Casey asked. "Would you

trust him with Mack?"

"He loves Mack," Charlie said, and Alex confirmed. So, he'd admitted that at least. But did she trust him? "As far as trust goes, I don't know. Rick destroyed my faith in most of the male gender…OhmyGod."

Casey sat up straighter. "What is it?"

Charlie massaged her temples. "She didn't go to his funeral."

"Who didn't go to whose funeral?"

"Daemon's. Fletcher didn't go to Daemon's funeral."

Alex threw up her hands. "And here we go thinking about other people's problems."

"Shut up, Alexandra," Casey said and pointed to Charlie. "Go on."

"Why wouldn't Fletcher go to his funeral? If she was as in love with him as she claimed, why not go? It doesn't make sense."

"Maybe Fletch doesn't like funerals," Casey said.

Alex frowned. "She's always gone when it's been someone she cares about."

"Exactly, so why didn't she go?" She was on to something; Charlie could feel it. She yelled for her brother, smiling when he stood from where he'd been sitting on the steps eavesdropping. "What do you know about Daemon and Fletcher?" she asked once the others had stopped yelling at him.

"Nothing you guys don't. She and Pops had some knock-down drag-out arguments though."

Casey's brow pinched. "What about?"

"About Daemon," Jebb said, rocking back on his heels. "Pops told her he didn't like what she was doing.

I don't know what he meant by that."

"Maybe he didn't like that fact she was sleeping with him," Charlie said more to herself than anyone.

Alex didn't do a good job of stifling her gasp. "She slept with him?"

"Guess Fletch isn't a virgin anymore," Casey mumbled.

Jebb turned bright red. "I don't want to talk about this," he said but stayed put.

"Let's not," Charlie suggested. "But can you think of anything else having to do with Daemon?"

"She did come up here to use the phone late at night, but I don't think she was talking to him."

"Why not?" Alex prodded.

"Because you don't call the guy you're supposed to love 'scumbag,' do you?"

Charlie stood. "She called him a scumbag?"

"That's what I said."

"What, Charlie? What are you thinking?" Alex asked.

"In the letter Fletcher wrote to Pops, she called Noah a scumbag. Something about 'the scumbag knows'...I don't remember." Charlie slipped on her shoes.

"Okay, so she calls Noah a scumbag. Where are we going?" Casey asked after she finished tying her boots.

Alex rolled her eyes. "She was obviously talking to Noah on the phone."

"I know that. Guess we're gonna do a little B and E." Casey rubbed her hands together.

"Not necessarily." Charlie laughed when Casey pouted. "Noah's house is officially a crime scene, and we happen to know the man who's acting as temporary sheriff."

"Congrats, Charlie."

"On what, Jebb?"

Jebb grinned. "You just thought like Fletcher J. McKay!"

Chapter Nineteen

Jasper flicked on the light in Noah's house. "You girls wanna tell me what we're looking for?"

"We're trying to find out why Fletcher would be calling *Noah Reed* in the middle of the night," Charlie said.

Jasper scratched his jaw. "She wouldn't. At least, I don't think she would."

Charlie explained to him what Jebb had heard and about the letter.

"Hell, seems she was."

"So...where should we start?" Casey asked.

"I'll take the bedroom."

" 'Course you do, Alex."

"Shut up, Casey," Alex said and headed up the stairs.

Casey pointed to the den. "I'll check in here."

"How 'bout we take a look in his office, Charlie," Jasper suggested.

"Sounds like a good place to start." She followed him into Noah's massive office. After opening a few of his desk drawers, she said, "The man's got to be the most organized person I've ever met." Charlie shook her head. Noah had everything in its place, and he'd color coded it. Weird.

Jasper thumbed through the file he pulled out. "Yep, but it makes it easier on us."

"Did the investigating officers go through any of these?" Charlie asked.

"No, I don't believe so. They took his laptop, but not any of the hard files."

Charlie bit her lip. "You're not going to get in trouble for helping us, are you?"

Jasper shrugged. "Some may call it compromising an investigation, but I call it using all the resources at hand. And I'm in charge…temporarily."

Guilt swamped her again. She was about to apologize, but Alex rushed into the office with Casey behind her.

"I think I've found something!" Alex said.

"What?" Charlie and Jasper said in unison.

Alex held up a thick manila envelope. "It was inside a false statue."

"How the hell did you know there was a false statue?"

Alex glared at Casey. "It was one of Granddaddy's pieces that Noah bought."

"Good work," Jasper said and took the file before anyone could say anything more. He took a moment to flip through it.

"What is it?" Casey asked. "Alex?"

Alex narrowed her eyes. "I only glanced at it, but I saw Fletcher's name."

Casey snatched the file out of Jasper's hands.

"Dagnabbit! I wasn't done looking at that."

"Well, doesn't this give you the warm and fuzzies," Casey said and shoved the papers at Charlie.

Oh, jeez. "That answers the money question."

"What?" Alex took the file again and looked up at Jasper. "Did you know about this?"

Jasper rocked back on his heels. "Not the whole of it."

"I want to know which one of us is gonna tell Pops."

"How about we tell him together?" Charlie suggested.

"I left my phone in Jasper's truck," Alex said. "I'll call our parents and have them meet us at the B and B. I don't have any guests at the moment, so it's probably for the best."

"Why her place?" Jasper asked.

"Because," Charlie began, "when Pops finds out, he might flip his lid. And if he's at Alex's, he can't go into his work shed and brood for hours on end."

Jasper hooted. "He'd do that?"

"Hell yeah! Emmit McKay has a black belt in brooding," Casey said. "I'm gonna call Ryan and have him bring me some food; I'm starving."

"I'll cook something at Alex's," Charlie offered.

"Great, but I'm calling Ryan anyway."

"Need him, do you?" Charlie asked, tickled by the prospect.

Casey turned beet red. "Ha! Like I'd ever admit *that*!"

"I reckon we'll have to wait to find out why Fletch was calling Noah in the middle of the night and if it has anything to do with what's been happening to you."

"Just until tomorrow, Jasper," Charlie said and headed for the door. She ignored the here-we-go-again look her sisters sent her way. This was important; the other questions would keep.

****

"Alexandra, you got us here. Talk," Pops said.

"I reckon I should do the talking," Jasper said. "We found out what Noah hired Fletcher to do."

"Now, Dad, don't get upset. Promise?" Charlie added for good measure.

"I hate it when people ask me that; it usually means I'm going to—"

"Be royally pissed," Casey finished for him from her perch on Ryan's lap. "I know, Pops, just promise anyway. You too, Ma."

"Me? Fine, I promise." She snorted. "When do *I* get pissy? I have a perfectly good husband who does that for me, thank you very much."

Jasper grinned. "She's got you there, McKay!"

"Fine," Pops said shifting in his seat. "I promise."

"Wonderful! Jasper, go ahead." Charlie gave him a smile to help him along.

"From what I understand, Noah's a very wealthy man…"

"We don't need to know about the man's finances."

"Dad, let him finish."

"Thank you, Alexandra. As I was saying, Noah is a—"

"Noah's worth millions."

Charlie's stomach dropped at the sight of Craig standing in the doorway.

"Who the hell invited you?" Casey asked. She looked down at her husband. "Why are you squirming…oh, you—"

"He *is* Noah's cousin," Ryan said in a rush. "He has a stake in this too, Casey, and he might be able to help us out here."

Charlie bit her lip to keep from laughing when

Ryan mumbled that he was in deep shit. From the look on Casey's face, he would probably be sleeping at the B and B tonight.

Alex brought in another chair. "Here, Craig, have a seat."

"Now that we're all settled, can I finish?" Jasper asked.

"Wasn't Noah's father an FBI agent like you, Pops? I didn't think they made a lot of money," Charlie said, trying not to make eye contact with Craig, who was staring at her.

"Uncle John was an agent," Craig said. "But Aunt Jude's family was old money—we're talking railroads. She was a wealthy but deeply troubled woman."

"Was?" Savannah asked.

"She died years ago." He paused. "It was right after we graduated from college; Noah was devastated."

Pops said, "I knew Noah's father. John and I were on a few cases together, but I never met his wife."

"Aunt Jude left most of her estate to Noah, and there was a lot. Other than a few extravagances, Noah lives his life using as little of his inheritance as possible."

"I heard John died on the job a few years ago," Pops put in.

Charlie rubbed her arms. "Noah's an orphan."

"In a way, yes, but he has me," Craig said.

Jasper cleared his throat. "Now that we have Noah's business laid out, can we get to the facts at hand?"

"Sorry," Charlie said. She couldn't stop herself from looking at Craig; his accusations the other night had hurt her, but if Alex was right then she'd hurt him more. Which was something Charlie hadn't thought she was capable of. She was the one who got hurt, not the other way around. She didn't know what to feel when Craig turned his gaze away from her.

"All right," Jasper went on. "Apparently, when Noah first came to Blue Creek, he heard about Fletcher's reputation for tracking; he hired her to find someone named"—Jasper leafed through the papers— "Judith R. Bastion."

"What?" Craig snatched the folder out of Jasper's hand. "That's his mother's name. This can't be right," he said, reading the file.

"This just gets crazier and crazier," Casey said. "She must have faked her own death, 'cause Fletch found her."

"But, my God, why?" Craig looked up from the paper and rubbed his neck. "After everything Noah went through—"

Jasper perked up. "What everything?"

"They tried to get her death listed as suspicious. They questioned Noah for hours," Craig said.

The entire room stilled.

"You neglected to tell us her death was suspicious or that Noah was a suspect," Alex said.

"Aunt Jude—or someone else apparently—was on her yacht when it blew up. There wasn't much to go on; all the police had were her dental records and the fact that Noah didn't have an alibi. They didn't have enough evidence to charge him or stop Noah from receiving his inheritance."

Savannah massaged her temples. "Why does this sound familiar?"

"Which part?" Pops asked.

"Something about switching dental records and bodies? Ohmygoodness."

"What?" everyone but Jasper asked.

"There was this episode of an old show about a wife dying in a car accident; all the police could get to identify her were the dental records. But it turned out to be the maid's body. The wife had switched dental records so she could run off with her lover—or some such thing," Savannah explained.

"Sounds like what happened to Jake a while back. Someone framed him for arson so they could collect the insurance," Ryan said.

Casey shifted on his lap. "So that's what happened!"

Savannah shrugged. "Maybe they watched the same show."

"What the hell are you talking about?" Craig asked.

Charlie's eyes widened when her mother giggled, actually giggled.

"Fletcher probably figured it out right away...It was an episode of *Murder She Wrote*," Savannah said, and this time it was Charlie's turn to laugh.

Alex crossed her arms over her chest. "That makes sense, then."

"Okay," Craig said. "I'm the only one who doesn't get it. I mean, I heard it was her favorite show, but come on."

"Did you ever watch the show, son?" Emmit asked Craig.

"I probably caught a few episodes."

"Do you remember the name of the main character?"

Craig paused, then looked around the table with a

smile when it finally sank in. "No, shit!"

"Fletcher's always telling me we need to befriend a local doc," Jasper said shaking his head. Savannah laughed.

"That's my girl," Emmit said, then looked down at his hands.

Charlie cleared her throat. "Fletcher, being Fletcher, probably let her imagination run wild and guessed Noah's mother could have faked her own death."

"Then it was only a matter of tracking her down," Jasper said. "And we know she found her."

"But what happened to cause Noah and Fletcher to hate each other?" Savannah asked. "Wouldn't he be happy, or relieved, that Fletcher found his mother?"

"Here's where it gets sticky," Jasper said. "Turns out Judith was alive, well, and living under an assumed name in some sort of doomsday cult. Fletcher found her and reported back, but Noah decided to leave his mother where she was."

"Which had to have pissed Fletcher off," Casey said.

"That's all there is to it?" Pops asked. "I mean other than leaving the woman in a cult, it's not so bad."

"I ain't done, McKay. Says in Noah's file his mother died a few weeks after Fletcher found her. And herein lies the sticky part: Fletcher was there when Judith died."

"That doesn't mean anything," Savannah hissed.

"I know it don't, but something had to have gone down, 'cause Noah wrote a hefty check to Fletcher for 'services rendered,' " Jasper said.

"What does that mean?" Ryan asked.

"Maybe he killed his mother and somehow made Fletcher an accomplice. It would explain why she hates him so much," Casey offered.

"It couldn't have been Noah," Craig said. "I know my cousin, and trust me, he wouldn't have been able to harm a hair on his mother's head. And he wouldn't have left her in a cult unless she didn't want to leave. Noah would never have done anything to make her unhappy."

"Fletcher wouldn't have killed her, if that's what you're suggesting," Savannah said.

"Ma, no one thinks she murdered the woman," Casey said.

"Emmit, what do you think?"

"I don't rightly know, Savannah. I don't believe she murdered anyone, but we don't have all the facts either. If she didn't tell us or Jasper, then who the hell would she tell?"

"Assuming she told anyone," Craig put in.

"All I can think is she would have been nineteen and still in school," Charlie said. "I was already pregnant with Mackenzie, and Alex was taking night classes." And Casey was gone.

"Jasper, you're her only friend outside this family. Are you sure she didn't say anything? Hint anything?" Ryan asked.

"I would have remembered something like this. Noah's the only other person who knows the truth, and the boy ain't talking right now."

"At least we have a better idea of why they hate each other. That's something," Charlie said. "And it makes their talking on the phone late at night even more suspicious." Charlie then explained to her parents about the late-night phone calls Jebb had overheard.

"Is there anything else?" Pops asked. When no one spoke up, he took Savannah's hand and headed for the door. "Let us know if and when there is."

"I need to be getting along myself," Jasper said. "I'll talk to you girls in the morning."

"We should get home too," Ryan said, and Casey agreed.

Craig rubbed his jaw. "We still don't know the connection between Fletcher leaving and Noah getting stabbed."

"I'll try going through her files again," Charlie said before she left. "Have a good night."

Chapter Twenty

Craig stared at the back door.

"Aren't you going after her?" Alex asked.

"You think it would do any good?"

"You'll never know if you don't try."

He nodded, kissed her cheek, and was out the door.

"Charlie! Wait a second," he called out, jogging toward where Charlie had parked. He stopped in front of the driver's side door, enjoying the way the moonlight made her blonde hair shimmer.

"What now?"

"I'm sorry about what I said the other night; I was an asshole. And I was...hurt." Honesty was the best policy, or at least it was in this instance.

"Why?"

"Why? Because, Charlie, I have feelings for you, and you keep shoving them back in my face. One minute you're hot in my arms, and the next you're telling me to go to hell. I'm not Rick Randle!" His voice came out harsher than he'd meant it to, but that couldn't be helped.

"Rick was the devil himself, and...and I know you're not like him."

"You could have fooled me," Craig said. "Look, I had to hide the truth from you about Alexandra, okay? And I *am* sorry, but I had to put feelers out and establish a relationship with her. I know you can understand that. But I wouldn't lie to you to be malicious. I wouldn't be able to live with that."

Charlie nodded, a tear slipping down her cheek.

"I think I might be falling in love with you," he whispered, bending down to kiss her. The words felt so right—so true! He *was* in love with her. How? He didn't know. She'd hurt him, but he'd hurt her too. Craig had never understood why people made love seem easy when it had claws and could rip you up. But then again, it could give you this sense of wholeness. With Charlie he had that. His body hardened when she returned his kiss.

Charlie slipped her tongue into his mouth, and Craig groaned. He bent down to deepen the kiss, and she stood on her tiptoes to meet him. Her lips were as soft as he remembered. There was no doubt she was the one for him.

"Come upstairs with me?" Craig asked breaking the kiss. He rubbed a finger over her bottom lip and waited.

"I want to," Charlie said. He swept her up in his arms and carried her upstairs before she could change her mind.

Once he got her in the apartment, Craig kissed her hard, and she nibbled on his bottom lip. Man, she drove him wild. He'd dreamt of having her again. Hell, he hadn't been able to stop thinking about her when he was awake.

"Wait. Wait," he said pulling back. Putting some space between them he asked, "Is this just sex to you? I know it's a harsh question—and damn, I hate to kill the mood—but I need to know. Does this mean something to you? Do I?" Her big brown eyes stared holes deep enough to reach his soul. He'd laid himself bare, left himself wide open. "Charlie?"

"I...yes...this does mean something to me too."

He grinned. "I'm glad. But I need to know you're willing to give me—us—a chance? I need your word."

Charlie closed her eyes for a second. "Y-yes," she whispered and relief washed over him.

Craig walked over to her, took her face in his hands, and kissed her tenderly. She wrapped her arms around his waist and kissed him back. It was promise more than passion, but the kiss took them deeper.

Charlie pulled away.

Craig blinked. "What?"

"Maybe it's—I'm so confused. I'm sorry, Craig. I want you. I do. It's just...just..."

"Just what? Explain it to me please." Before it killed him.

"I don't think you're like Rick," she told him again. "I *know* you're not, but that doesn't make this any easier. I'm a mother and that comes with a lot of responsibility. It's not only me I have to think about."

He ran his fingers through his hair. "I love Mack. How could you not know that?"

She smiled. "I know you do."

"I'm not using you to get Mack. This isn't a fucking movie, and I'm sure as hell not Tom Cruise. I love Mack, but I'm falling *in* love with you. You, Charlie McKay, and honestly, I wish I wasn't! My life would be a whole hell of a lot easier."

Her brow puckered. "But you still want to try?"

"Are you looking for confirmation or wondering if I'm crazy?" he asked, partly joking. "Yes, damn it, I want to try. What's between us is special." Craig went to the kitchen and grabbed a beer because he needed to do something.

"We hardly know each other."

"I know all I need to know."

Charlie crossed her arms over her chest.

Craig sighed. "You're a loving person, Charlie, all the way around. And I know that's not what I said the other night, but I was pissed and being a dick. You do what you can for everyone. I feel good when I'm around you—when we're not arguing, that is. You're a great mother, sister, friend, and the best lover I've ever had."

Her eyes widened, and she sat down on the couch. "I don't know what to say. I'm not perfect—"

"I'm aware of that." He took a seat on the coffee table in front of her and set down the beer. "That's another thing I love about you; you're human. With us, it's not a slap-you-in-the-face kind of chemistry, it's just there waiting…deep, under the surface." He had already taken the leap. His heart clenched when she stood and headed for the exit.

"You've overwhelmed me, truth be told. This might be more than I can handle—too risky," she said leaning against the door.

"I didn't ask you up here to watch you leave," he said huskily.

She shivered. His pulse quickened with the knowledge that he'd turned her on.

Craig boxed her in, turned her around, and pressed her into the door with the front of his body. She gasped, and her breaths became short pants. "Is this what you want?" he asked, reaching around her to unbutton her jeans. When she didn't answer, he slid his hands up grabbing the hem of her sweater as he went. He pushed his erection against her back and pulled her sweater over her head, but still she said nothing. Craig unfastened her bra and let it drop with her shirt. Reaching back around her, he held her breasts in his hands and squeezed. He bit her shoulder, enjoying her whimper, and asked, "Is this what you want?"

Charlie nodded.

"Then by all means, allow me to accommodate you." He pulled away and removed his shirt. He pressed his bare chest against her back, then maneuvered her arms above her head. With one hand shackling her wrists, he used his other to pull her jeans and panties down to her knees. Goose bumps rose on her flesh, and he took a moment to get himself under control.

"I'm going to take you, here and now, Charlie. Hard and fast," he murmured, pulling his jeans to his thighs and releasing himself.

She panted. "Yes, please."

Craig nibbled on her arched neck. "Do you like that?" He did it again after she nodded. "Good girl." He bent his knees and moved his free hand around her hips. He slid his fingertips between her thighs and used a knuckle to rub roughly against her most sensitive spot.

Charlie moaned and pressed herself against his hand. "Harder."

Craig let go of her wrists and used that hand to brace against the door. With his free hand he slipped first one, then two fingers inside her, letting his thumb take over for his knuckle. "Move against me," he prompted. He was still nestled against her backside, and he squeezed his eyes shut to keep himself sane when she rode his hand.

Charlie cried out as she climaxed, her hips continued to move. Removing his fingers, he grabbed a condom from his back pocket, sheathed himself, and pressed Charlie harder against the door.

"I think you're ready now," he whispered, then pushed deep inside of her.

Charlie sucked in a sharp breath.

"You feel so good," he murmured, trying not to lose control. He began to thrust, and Charlie slid her palms against the door, bracing herself. He continued to move, but something was missing. He pulled away. "I can't do this."

She spun around, face flushed. "What?"

It was all he could do to keep himself sane looking at her naked body. He shucked off his boots and pants. "I can't do this not looking at you."

"Oh" was all she got out before he lifted her off her feet and out of the clothes that pooled around her ankles. She wrapped her legs around his waist, her arms around his neck, and then leaned in to kiss him.

Their tongues tangled, and he thrust into her once again. Craig held her hips while he moved inside of her, but somehow it still wasn't enough. Locking his arms around her back to keep her in place, he knelt down to the floor and asked her to straddle his thighs.

"Like this?" Charlie whispered.

Craig nodded.

Taking her hips in his hands, he showed her how to move against him. Sweat dripped down his face as she rode him, hard and fast. He squeezed his eyes tight, stars dancing behind his lids, as he climaxed so hard, he thought he might pass out—or die.

But Charlie wasn't done. She kept moving against him, reaching down between their bodies and using her fingers to give herself another release. The sexiest thing he'd ever heard was his name on her lips before she collapsed on top of him.

He used his waning strength to pull Charlie up for another kiss. She sighed and kissed him deeply. She let go of his lips and stared into his eyes. He wasn't sure what emotion played across her irises, but it was gone before she leaned down and kissed him again.

"Don't," he said when she made to get off him. Running away again? He brought up his hand and wiped away a stray tear. "Did I hurt you?" God, he hadn't even thought. Hadn't even been thinking.

"Goodness, no. It was amazing. How did you know I...you know?"

"I visited you at Alexandra's after your concussion, and you told me about this dream you had about us...Are you mad?"

"How can I be?" She blushed. "I don't think I would've been able to actually say it out loud."

"You're amazing, did you know that?" Craig grinned.

She returned his smile and rolled her eyes. "Thank you, I think."

"Will you stay with me tonight?" His heart waited for her to answer and started beating again when she nodded. Charlie rolled off him and headed for the bedroom, Craig hot on her heels.

Once they'd both used the bathroom and were under the covers, he pulled her into his arms.

****

Craig woke up for the second time that morning to

find himself alone. When he'd woken the first time, Charlie had been using her sweet mouth on him. He stirred at the memory. She'd said she was a novice at giving head, but Craig had to disagree. He'd climaxed so fast he was almost embarrassed.

Getting out of bed, he went to take a piss. He rubbed his abdomen with his free hand and hoped Charlie hadn't left. Finishing his business, he went in search. He smelled coffee and smiled. There she was wearing one of his shirts and drinking from his favorite mug.

"I was scared you'd snuck out," he said and poured himself a cup of joe.

Charlie started coughing. "You're naked."

Craig grinned and bent down to kiss her silky lips. "Don't go anywhere," he said and went to put on some sweatpants. When he came back, he asked, "What's all this?"

"I thought I'd make us breakfast," she said as she gathered ingredients.

"Sounds great! I'll get the paper."

She laughed.

"What?"

"I thought only my parents still got the newspaper?"

"Are you calling me old?"

She made a production of batting her eyelashes. "Wouldn't dream of it."

He smiled all the way to the door, but when he opened it, he got a shock. Emmit McKay handed him the paper. "Ah, Charlie?"

"Yes?"

"Your father's here, honey." A pan clattered to the

floor, and Craig winced. He let Emmit past him and shut the door. "Charlie's making breakfast; are you hungry?"

Charlie's eyes widened as they came into the kitchen. "Daddy, are you hungry?" she asked, her face bright red. "I'm an adult, Dad."

"I can see that, Charlie. And yes, I'm starving. I figured I'd find you two together, but thinking it and seeing it are different things entirely." He took a seat at the kitchen table and said, "I'd appreciate it if you both put some more clothes on."

"I'm sorry," Charlie told Craig when they went to the bedroom.

"Don't worry about it, honey. We're both adults. And yeah, this is uncomfortable, but he should get used to seeing us together. Right?"

Charlie smiled. "Right. I'll make breakfast, and we'll find out why he's here in the first place."

"Good." She'd just agreed that they were officially seeing each other. Right?

Chapter Twenty-One

"All right, Pops. Spill," Charlie said after they'd finished eating in silence. She refilled all their mugs and sat down.

Pops sighed. "I went to Alexandra's looking for you, but she said you were here—had that cat-who-ate-the-canary look on her face too."

"I just bet she did," Charlie said, rolling her eyes. "Why were you looking for me? Oh, no. Has something else happened?"

Craig put his hand on her thigh and gave it a squeeze.

"No, no, I needed to tell you something I didn't wanted to say in front of your sisters...or your mother."

"You're keeping something from Mama?"

"No, I discussed it with her when we got home last night."

"How'd that go?" Craig asked.

Pops rubbed his neck. "I slept in the attic, if that tells you anything."

Charlie frowned. "What on earth is it?"

"This Daemon Randle-Fletcher thing; your sister and I were having words about it."

Charlie's brow puckered. "*Words?*"

"You've always seen right through me, Charlie...Okay, we had some knock-down drag-outs about it."

"I may have heard something about that," Charlie admitted. She sipped her coffee and took Craig's strong hand in hers.

"She was sleeping with him," Emmit said, incredulous.

"Umm. Yeah, I know," Charlie said. "She's an adult too."

"I know, but she...she was investigating the man."

Craig flinched. "You can't be serious!"

Charlie shook her head; this couldn't be right. "What are you talking about, Dad?"

"She was investigating Daemon Randle. One minute he was on her scumbag radar, and the next she's sleeping with him. Jasper didn't know anything about it either. She was investigating on the side—she told me."

"But she told me he'd asked her to marry him!"

"I know, Charlie. I asked her what the hell was going on, and she said she'd stopped investigating him and started seeing him." Pops shook his head. "She said maybe *they'd* been mistaken. I assumed by 'they' she meant Jasper. After what you said last night, I have to assume it was Noah, but—and I've been thinking about this all night—why would she work with a man she hates? I thought maybe you could think of something, because I sure as hell can't come up with anything."

"Why are you asking me? Why not ask Casey?"

Pops snorted. "I *did* ask Casey; she's as in the dark as the rest of us."

"You guys didn't find any other files when you went to Noah's last night, did you?" Craig asked.

"No, we stopped searching when Alex found—"
The chair wobbled when Charlie stood up. "Alexandra!"

"What about her?" Craig asked.

"Why that little…" She headed out the door, with Craig and her father right behind her. The moment she stepped inside Alex's kitchen she shouted, "Alexandra McKay, get your butt down here!"

"What in the world are you hollering about?" Alex asked, coming into the kitchen. "Good morning," she said when Craig and Pops came in.

Charlie ignored them and started searching drawers. "Where is it?"

"Where's what? If you break something, I'll be mad at you."

"If anyone gets to be mad at anyone, then it's me being mad at you. Where's the other file, Alexandra? I know you found more than one."

"I—"

"Don't lie; you knew I'd want to tell Pops and Mama about Fletcher and wouldn't even think about there being more. You used it to cover up something," Charlie said, waving her hand in the air. "And I want to know what."

"Is that true? I hate to say it, but if anyone's good at keeping secrets…"

Alex's cheeks turned pink. "Though true, your statement isn't entirely fair, Dad."

Craig stepped forward. "Is there something you want to tell us?"

Alex sighed and went to pull something out of the oven. Charlie would have laughed if she hadn't been furious.

"Here," Alex said and held out a folder.

Charlie snatched it from her. "What does it say?"

"I haven't had a chance to read it yet."

Charlie smirked. Yeah, right.

"Alexandra, I'm getting sick and tired of having to navigate the secrets you keep," Pops said and took a seat at the table.

Alex stared at their father for a moment, then went to pour him a cup of coffee. Charlie couldn't help but feel a bit guilty for getting Alex in trouble, but her sister had to stop keeping secrets that affected them all. Shaking her head, Charlie read through the file.

"All this contains is Daemon's schedule and useless stuff like that." Charlie dropped the folder on the kitchen table, and her father picked it up, and began thumbing through it.

"The fact that Noah has Daemon's information at all confirms that he was looking into him," Pops said.

Charlie shifted from foot to foot. "But we don't know if he was looking into him because Fletcher asked—"

"Or because I asked him?" Craig said.

"Why would you—"

"We asked Craig to ask Noah, Dad," Charlie said and explained their reasoning.

Pops rubbed a hand over his jaw. "That makes sense."

"The only way to find out for sure is to ask Fletcher or Noah. And neither of those two options are available at the moment," Craig said.

Charlie turned to Alex and pointed to the folder on the table. "Why'd you try to hide this?"

"Force of habit."

"Might be time to break that habit, sweetheart," Craig said.

"I suppose."

"I need to go to the store," Pops said, standing. "I left your mother in charge, and she's probably giving stuff away. You"—he pointed to Alex—"no more secrets. And you, I'm watching you," he said, pointing to Craig. He kissed Charlie's forehead. "Behave."

"I need to go check on Mildred," Charlie said after Pops closed the door.

"I'm going to see Noah, and then I have to get ready to open the bar."

"How did that go?" Alex asked.

"We did great business last night. I was actually surprised. Come tonight if you get a chance," Craig said, kissing Alex's cheek and leaving.

"I'm mad at you, Alexandra," Charlie huffed. "You can't keep hiding things from me."

Her sister stared at her nails. "Sorry."

"I'm choosing to believe you are. I'll see you later, okay?"

"All right," Alex said, returning Charlie's hug.

Craig was waiting for her on the bottom step of his apartment.

"Sorry I didn't ask about the bar." She hadn't even thought about it. How caring was that?

"You had a lot on your mind. Besides, you weren't exactly speaking to me."

"I'm glad the soft opening was a success."

"Me too. You wanna come upstairs and take a shower?"

She started up the steps. "You wouldn't mind?"

"No," he began, his slow smile sending a delicious shiver up her spine. "Not at all."

****

Charlie walked into the diner and wanted to burst

into tears. She'd missed the place more than she'd let herself believe.

People stopped her to say hello and tell her they were keeping their eyes and ears open for any trouble. By the time she got to where Mildred was serving people at the counter, her eyes were damp.

"Hello, boss lady," Mildred said. The older woman had a barrette holding back the bangs of her shoulder-length gray hair, and a white apron covering her hot-pink McKay's Diner T-shirt. She smiled and handed Charlie a cup of coffee. "I didn't expect you today."

"I needed to see the place, Mildred. I missed it." She took a sip from the mug and winced; it was stronger than she usually made it.

"I wanted to talk to you about that," Mildred said with a twinkle in her eye. "I was thinking maybe after you come back to work, I could come in—oh, I don't know, once or twice a week and help out."

"Oh, Mildred, really? I was thinking about hiring a couple more people anyway. I'd love it if you'd stay." Charlie smiled. Mildred didn't want to give up the gossip, but she'd be a welcome addition. They would both win.

"Wonderful. Now…" Mildred leaned in to Charlie. "Have you heard from your little sister? Or is she really gone?"

"She's really, really gone, Mildred."

The older woman's face fell. "That's a shame," she mumbled.

"It is," Charlie agreed and pushed through the swinging doors.

Tiny was in his usual uniform: McKay's T-shirt, sleeves rolled up over his bulging biceps showcasing his tattoos, jeans, and one of the colorful aprons Julia had made for him. He glanced at her while he cleaned the grill, but he didn't say anything.

Charlie swallowed. "Good morning, Tiny."

He grunted.

She straightened her shoulders and planted her feet. "I know you're upset with me, but I'm not sure why?"

He grunted again.

"Tiny?"

The big man took a deep breath. "Sheriff Hart stopped by to see Julia yesterday."

She blinked.

"Julia wasn't home."

She knew the answer to her question but asked anyway. "Did *you* talk to him?"

Tiny crossed his massive arms over his chest. "I did."

Uh oh. "We didn't—"

"What? Mean it? Mean to ruin a good man who's done nothing but try to help the people of this town?"

"We only—"

"What? Wanted answers? You thought it was okay to break into a man's home to steal them?"

"I—"

"Shame on you," Tiny said pointing a spatula at her. "Shame on all of you. Do you have any idea what you've done?"

Tears gathered in the corners of Charlie's eyes. "Yes, I do. Fletcher—"

"Yes, your very own sister driven away by your deeds. Where have we heard this story before?"

"There's no excuse. We made a horrible mistake."

The big man nodded. "That you did, shug. That

you did."

She hung her head and reached for the door.

Tiny sighed. "Jasper only wanted to talk about you girls."

Her brow puckered. "What?"

"Mm-hmm. He's worried about all of you." Tiny gave her a side glance. "Shows the character of the man. He's already forgiven y'all. Ya know, he cares so much about your family, he's putting *you* before his pride."

She stared at Tiny, not knowing what to say.

"When people are afraid, they'll believe almost anything if it abates their fear or gives them hope. But as history has shown, not much good comes from that. And that's what you girls did. Grabbed on to something—anything—to find hope in a desperate situation."

"You're absolutely right, Tiny. I'll find a way to make it right with Jasper." If it was the last thing she did.

Tiny gave her a hug. "I know you will, shug." He kissed the top of her head and let her go.

Charlie smiled and again reached for the door.

"Oh, and Julia wants you to bring that boy over for supper one night soon."

Her face turned eight shades of red. "You mean Craig?"

Tiny's gold tooth flashed. "That's the one."

"Okay," she said and rushed out the door before her nerves got the better of her. She poured herself a cup of coffee to go, then went outside and sat on a bench between the diner and the hardware store. She thought over all the things that had gone on—Jasper,

Craig, her sisters—and what Tiny had said. Half an hour later, she still didn't have any answers, but she thought she should stop in to check on her parents—or at least her mother; she'd seen enough of her father this morning.

"Hi, sweetheart," her mother said when Charlie came into the hardware store.

"Hi, Mama!"

"I heard your father caught you in a compromising position—"

"Oh, whatever!" Charlie laughed. "Both Craig and I were dressed. He even ate breakfast with us."

Her mother smirked. "I know. How is *that* going?"

"He said he loves me." He'd been half asleep when he said it, but he said it.

Savannah cocked her head to the side. "How do *you* feel?"

"I…" Love him too? Charlie sighed. "It's not only me I have to worry about."

"Have you talked to Mack?"

"Yes, I called her on my way to the diner this morning. She's having a good time, but she wants to come home. 'Course, we don't exactly have a house, but I want her here too."

"Your father said the construction's coming along. And when I drove by this morning, it looked like they were making progress."

"I drove by too. Actually, I stopped and talked to the crew. Pops added a few things to the house— wonderful additions—but he should have asked me." With the extra money from Fletcher, her house would be even better than before. How did she feel both grateful and guilty at the same time?

Savannah smirked. "He's in the back if you want to have it out with him."

"I think I will," she said and headed in the direction of her father.

"And remember what I said about your father being a good person to talk to about your other situation," her mother called out.

Charlie slipped in the back door without being detected. She smiled, thinking how handsome her father was. She waited for him to notice her and turn off the sander before she spoke. "I stopped by the construction site."

"Did you?" He wiped his hands on his apron, then sipped from a glass of ice tea. "What'd you think?"

"The additions are beautiful, but I wish you'd asked me first," she said, hopping up on the counter in front of him.

He paused for a second. "I'll try to remember that next time. Where's your friend?"

"Craig? He went to see Noah, and then he was going to the bar."

"Heard he's done a damn fine job fixing up the place."

"I haven't seen it yet...Dad, can I ask you something?" Charlie pulled a hair off the sleeve of her sweater.

"It's, uh, not about sex is it?"

Charlie's entire face heated. "Um, no."

"Good. Don't look at me like that, Charlie."

"I just—"

"Casey does, you know, talk to me about it," he sputtered and his cheeks got ruddy. "Not that I mind. You girls can talk to me about anything, but Casey

239

doesn't always filter."

Charlie bit her lip. Oh, Casey, really! "I see. Well, rest easy because that's not why I'm here."

He relaxed. "Okay."

"What did you do when you realized you loved Mama?"

He laughed. "You mean other than panic? I had a talk with you girls, remember?"

"How could I forget? We interrupted you before you could even pop the question." That had been one of the happiest moments of her life.

"You girls always had the strangest timing. Still do."

"What I meant was, how did you deal with loving someone and being a single parent?"

"Oh…" Pops took another sip from his tea glass, then set it on the work bench. "You love him?"

"I think so." She shifted on the counter. "I keep fighting myself on this, but yes, I do."

"And Mack?"

"She adores him, and they get along like two peas in a pod."

"How does *he* feel about Mack?"

"He loves her."

"Then, sweetheart, what's the problem? Wait, you don't know if he loves you."

"No, he does, but he doesn't know how I feel."

"You know what it is?"

She shook her head.

Pops took a seat next to her on the counter and put an arm around her. "You're scared of getting hurt again. You want to trust him, love him, but your past is choking you. You feel like he's the one you could spend your life with, but you'd felt that before and look what happened. It was the same way for me. I could trust Savannah—with you girls, with my demons, and my heart, but my past experience crippled me. It took a lot for me to come to grips with the fact that what Gracie and I had wasn't love; what I have with your mother…that's love."

She thought about that for a moment. "Gracie and Rick were practically the same; no matter what the disguise, evil is still evil."

"Being with someone like that messes you up."

"How do you mean?"

"I had a real hard time letting your mother into our lives."

"You did?" Charlie didn't remember it that way, not really.

Pops nodded. "She put up with a lot from me. Sometimes I was a downright bastard."

"What?" She couldn't see it.

"Yeah, I'm not proud of it. Hell, it took me a while to even realize I was doing it. I pushed her away so many times, ran hot and cold. Sometimes I was an all-out ass."

"People have been accusing me of some of those very things," Charlie admitted.

Pops dropped his arm from around her shoulders and turned to face her fully. "It's a defense mechanism. Our past relationships were so deceitful, caused us so much pain, that we have a hard time believing the next person's sincere. We've got to be certain they're in it for the long haul. It's not fair to them. You know, I honestly don't think your mother and I would have ended up together if she hadn't loved you girls so much—"

"You were that bad?"

"I was," he said. "It was like, the more I loved her and wanted her to stay, the more I pushed her away."

"Because you were scared."

He paused, then said, "From the first time she had dinner with us, she fit, and it scared the hell out of me."

"Like a missing ingredient?" A little dash of pepper was all you needed.

"Yeah, a piece was missing from our lives, and I didn't even know. That first night I was already thinking of all the things that could go wrong, all the pain. But Savannah saw past my foul moods enough to fall in love with me, and she loves the hell out of you girls. It's rare, Charlie."

"Love like that?"

"Well, yes, but I mean it's rare to find someone—a virtual stranger—who genuinely loves your children as much as you do. Who sees the good, even in the bad—like you do—and loves them anyway. It's a rare gift."

She had that gift with Craig. Tears stung her eyes; it made perfect sense. She hopped off the counter and kissed her father's cheek. "Thanks, Dad."

"Glad I could help," he mumbled.

Charlie stepped back. "Then why the long face?"

Pops sighed. "I've just lost another daughter to another man."

She smiled. "I feel the same way Fletcher does."

"How do you mean?" His brow bunched.

"You'll always be the first man I ever loved," she said, then closed him inside his workshop. She ran into her mother.

"Had a good talk, did you?"

"Yes, Mama. You were right; he's the one person who can relate to my situation."

"I figured as much."

Charlie gave her mother a big hug.

"What's this for?"

"For not giving up on him."

Chapter Twenty-Two

Craig was behind the bar when he spotted her. Charlie was wearing a sexy pink dress, and she had her hair pulled up with a few curls framing her sweet face. Craig hardened against the zipper of his jeans. She was a knockout.

She took a seat at the corner of the bar and waved at him.

"Hey, beautiful," he said.

After a slight blush, she winked. "Hi, handsome."

Craig leaned across the counter to kiss her. Their lips met and held for a minute or two. He stilled when she reached across the bar and wiped the gloss from his mouth.

"You could have left it there."

Charlie laughed.

"I'm glad you came by." He looked away so he wouldn't drown in her big brown eyes. He poured her a glass of wine. People were staring at them, but he ignored it. If Charlie was comfortable, then so was he. "What do you think of the place?"

"It's fantastic, Craig. Everyone says so! I was in town today, and everywhere I went, it seemed like people were talking about it."

"Thanks." Her praise meant a lot to him. Craig went to tell Slim he was taking ten and came back to Charlie with a beer in his hand. He sat down next to her and inhaled the sweet scent of her shampoo. "I talked to Mack this afternoon."

She choked on her wine. "You did?"

"Yeah, she wanted to call and check on me. Is that a problem for you?"

Charlie shook her head.

"Good. She said she's ready to come home, and asked me if I'd ask you, but I told her you knew best."

"Thanks for having my back," she said with a smile. "It's hard telling her no, especially when I miss her like crazy and want her home."

"How much longer are you planning on her being away?"

"I don't want to risk bringing her home too soon. Especially since we don't know whether or not Noah's stabbing is connected. I was thinking I'd go visit her though."

"That's a good idea."

"You could come with me if you want."

"I'd love to go, but I can't leave the bar." Damn it. This was a big step for Charlie, asking him to go with her.

She touched his face. "I understand. I know you want to go, and the knowing is almost as good as a yes would've been."

"I can't tell you what it means that you asked." Craig sighed and sipped his beer. His brows rose when Slim brought him the phone. A slow smile spread across his face as the caller told him the news. "Thank you," he said and hung up the phone.

"Good news?"

"Yeah, Noah's awake; he's not all there yet, but he's up. The doctor said they found evidence that the

IV had been tampered with. Someone was feeding drugs through the line to induce the coma." Craig shook his head.

"Can someone do that?"

"Apparently, the doctor ran every test he could think of to explain the coma, and it showed up in a tox screen, or something. At least we'll be able to get some answers so…" He celebrated by planting a kiss on Charlie's lips.

"Tell them." She smiled, then pointed to the crowd. "This is a small town and everyone knows Noah. Trust me; tell them."

He hopped onto the bar and yelled for everyone to listen. "Noah Reed has come out of his coma and is in stable condition," he announced, and everyone cheered. "Slim, a round of drinks on the house."

"Was that wise?" Charlie asked when he got back down.

"Sure. I'll bill my cousin," Craig said, grinning. "I need to get back to filling drinks."

"I'm going to call my sisters and Jasper," Charlie said pulling out her phone. "Do you need a hand?"

"It's your night off, and I don't want you to get all mussed up. Besides, you look too good, and there are too many single men here."

Charlie snorted. "The word around town is I'm taken."

"Is it now? *Well*, in that case, you got yourself a deal." He sealed it with a kiss.

****

By the time the bar had emptied of all but the two of them, Charlie had a new appreciation for Alexandra. How in the heck did her sister walk around in heels all day?

Craig looked up from wiping the bar. "Feet hurt?"

"Everything hurts," she said but smiled. "Running a bar is a lot more chaotic than running a diner. It might have to do with the fact that alcohol is involved, but still."

"I can see that." Craig moved from behind the bar and picked a slow song on the jukebox. "Let's dance." He held out a hand and pulled her in his arms.

"I don't think I've ever danced with anyone I was seeing."

"Not even in high school?"

She shook her head. "Marylou tripped me the day before prom; I twisted my ankle and couldn't go."

"I'm sorry."

"I'm not." This was well worth the wait. She loved being in his arms—loved being around him, period. It didn't scare her too much now. Her father was right; it was a gift. A precious gift, and she was going to take it and everything that came with it, without reservation. When the song ended, Craig took her face in his hands and kissed her.

"I love you, Charlie."

She looked into his eyes and took a deep breath. "I love you too."

Someone screamed.

Craig pushed Charlie behind him. "I'm getting really sick and tired of the interruptions! Is that you, Fletcher? You're ruining a pivotal fucking moment here; the woman I love finally admits she loves me back, and you're fucking it up!"

A little laugh—probably hysteria—slipped from Charlie's lips. It was too dark to see anything more than a small shadow holding a big gun; she didn't think it was her sister. Fletcher preferred a knife—what a thought!

Craig started to navigate them slowly to the door.

"Do I look like that psycho?" the woman said, coming into the light.

Craig turned his head and whispered, "I don't recognize her."

Charlie peeked around him, and her eyes about popped out of her head. "Da...Dana?" she sputtered. Holy moly! "What in the world are you doing?"

"Charlie," Craig hissed. "Stay behind me."

"Oh, don't worry. Charlie McKay is incapable of taking responsibility for her actions," Dana Randle said, waving her gun around.

Charlie stared at the woman; Dana looked like she was going to church with not a hair out of place and her blue dress perfectly creased. She'd actually felt sorry for the woman. Of all the...Charlie took a step forward so she was standing next to Craig. "Here I am."

"What is it you want?" Craig put out his arm to stop Charlie from going any farther. "What did Charlie do to you?"

"She ruined everything; that's what she did! Everything we'd worked so damn hard for. And you know, we'd put that behind us and moved on, but then the McKays can't leave well enough alone, can they? Well, tit for tat; you wanted to dig up our secrets, so it's only fair we dug up some of yours."

Charlie gasped. "You—"

Craig glared at her, then turned back to Dana. "Who is this 'we' you keep mentioning?"

She ignored him and directed her aim at Charlie.

"If it wasn't for you and that horrible sister of yours, my brothers would both be alive."

"Rick died in a robbery," Charlie said, though thanks to Fletcher's files she knew better.

"Yes, I know. We'd worked so hard to get all of the Thomases' money, and then he had to go and get *you* pregnant. Stupid, stupid man. He gave up any rights to the child and everything would have been fine, but no! Rick found out how much you people were worth and got greedy," Dana said, disgust on her face but her hand steady. "If he had only stuck to the plan…We couldn't let him admit to the world he was the father of Charlie McKay's bastard."

"My daughter is no one's bastard, you bitch." Charlie was stopped by Craig's arm. He shook his head. Was she supposed to listen to this? And why did he keep looking at the bar? Her cell phone!

"Oh, give me a break. If he'd admitted to being the father, we would have lost everything. The Thomases would have countersued."

"But Daemon helped the Thomases get most of their money back," Charlie pointed out and Dana laughed. It was one of those chilling laughs you heard on late-night horror movies.

"*We* bought their property and then sold it to the contractors, tripled what we'd put down. Daemon was a genius."

"I thought Rick was the mastermind," Craig said, taking baby steps toward the bar. He whispered to Charlie to keep Dana talking.

"Don't get me wrong, Rick was devious, but nothing like Daemon." Her tone was wistful.

"But Daemon killed himself," Charlie said.

"You know *very well* he didn't."

Charlie's eyes widened. "You bugged my house."

"No." Dana rocked back on her heels. "Not me."

"Daemon did it before he died?" How long had they been spying on her?

"My brother was an amazing man, and he had big plans for us. Once he got rid of that horrid wife of his, we would've been free to go to the next level. But he had to go and get involved with that sister of yours—a cop, of all things! I knew she was up to something. Everyone knew Fletcher McKay was pure as the driven snow. If Daemon hadn't been so *sure* he could conquer her, he'd still be alive."

"You killed him," Charlie accused. "And Rick." And dug Rick up. Disgusting.

"Not me. Daemon said you're only as strong as your weakest link." She shrugged. "Unfortunately, Rick had become ours. It was brilliant though, and no one would have been the wiser if Fletcher had kept her nose out of it."

Charlie shook her head. "You could have gotten away—"

"She brainwashed him, like you did Rick. She'll pay for it too. Who do you think killed him?" Dana asked, cocking the hammer of her gun and pointing at Craig.

Charlie shoved Craig out of the way and dropped her cell phone when a bullet grazed her arm. Her ears rang and her hand trembled as she covered her wound.

Craig reached out, but Dana aimed at him again. "Step away from her...now. There's a good boy."

Craig's eyes met hers, and Charlie nodded. Dana directed him to take a seat on top of the bar, and he did as he was told.

Charlie bit her lip; she would not become hysterical. Would not! Her arm stung, but she would take that any day rather than have Craig shot. Or killed. She had to get Dana to focus on her. She refused to lose this chance—this gift—with Craig. "Fletcher didn't kill your brother."

"I don't believe you, nor did I believe the new sheriff when he tried to hand me the same garbage. Of course, Noah's always been more brawn than brain."

"You—"

"If he'd stayed in a coma, I could have waited until your daughter came home—no loose ends—but now I have to improvise."

"You won't touch a hair on my daughter's head!" Charlie lunged. Hot pain pierced her thigh, smoke stung her nose, and the ringing in her ears was louder than before. She'd made a mistake.

"You stay, or I'll kill her now," Dana told Craig when he started to jump down.

****

Craig's gut twisted; Charlie had been hit this time. Damn it! He scooted back on the bar as Dana waved her gun in the air. Something dug into his butt cheek, repeatedly. Who in the hell was hiding behind the bar? Not taking his eyes off the woman as she paced around her prey, he slowly put his hand behind his back and a small handgun was placed in his open palm. Before he could even react, the front door swung open and his sister waltzed in. What the hell was she doing? This wasn't a fucking tea party.

"Stop right there, Alexandra," Dana hissed. "Move over to where your sister is. Good girl. You shouldn't

251

have come; you're the only one who's not like them, but you've sealed your own fate."

"I have to disagree with you, Dana. I'm quite like my sisters," Alex said, taking off her scarf to tie it around Charlie's leg.

Dana shrugged. "You know what? I don't really care."

"Why're you trying to kill Charlie anyway?" Alex asked. Craig caught her eye, and she mouthed that they were not alone. He swallowed hard and tried to appear unthreatening while Dana continued to rant.

She motioned to Charlie with the barrel of the gun. "If she'd kept her hands off my brother, Rick would still be alive and I'd be soaking up the sun on an island somewhere. But no! Daemon always said revenge was always best with age—served cold. But once Fletcher started looking into things again, it was only a matter of time. I couldn't have that, could I?"

"Did your parents know about this?" Charlie asked.

Craig didn't know whether to laugh or shake his head. Who but Charlie would be thinking of Dana's parents at a time like this?

"If they'd listened to me, they would have been spared."

"Really? Your parents too?" Craig was sickened by the thought.

"But they moved to Florida," Charlie said.

"Yes, they reside at the bottom of the Gulf." Dana raised her gun. "Now, who goes first? I think it should be you." She pointed her gun at Craig.

"I wouldn't do it, sweetheart," Craig said, when she turned the gun back toward his sister and Charlie. Two of the people he loved most in the world.

"Good thing you're not me, isn't it?"

He shrugged. "Yeah." He shot her in the arm holding the gun. But it wasn't enough to stop her. She swung toward him and fired her weapon; Craig dodged the bullet and shot her again. This time in the heart.

Dana looked down at the blood seeping from her chest, then back to Craig.

He shook his head.

It took a moment for Dana to crumple to the floor, but Craig was there to knock the gun from her slack hand when she did, just as Jasper and the deputies came barreling in. "Could have used you a minute ago."

Jasper took in the scene. "We've got an ambulance on the way," he said, then started giving orders to the deputies.

Craig squatted down next to his girl. "How are you holding up, honey?"

"Well, I've been shot and I'm bleeding, but other than that I'm wonderful." She half smiled when he laughed. "Are you okay?"

"I'm good." He kissed her forehead.

Jasper hovered over the fallen woman. "Still can't believe it was Dana Randle."

"How the hell did you put two and two together anyway?" Craig asked, adding more pressure on Charlie's wound. He wished he could have spared her this.

"Noah told us, then we put out an APB on Dana's car, and someone spotted it out here." Jasper shrugged and stepped out of the way when the paramedics came through.

"Easy, honey," Craig said when the paramedics put Charlie on the gurney. He turned to Alex. "Are you all right?"

"Yes, but that's about to change," Alex said and motioned to where Casey was barreling through the door.

"Alexandra, retribution is a bitch. Remember that." Casey walked with Charlie as the EMTs rolled her out the door. "Can you believe she cuffed me to the truck? Like I couldn't pick the lock. 'Course my husband helped her so I wouldn't come in here. The nerve of the man!"

Craig laughed. He couldn't help it.

Chapter Twenty-Three

A few days later, Charlie was finally able to leave the hospital. The bullet hadn't gone all the way through her thigh and had to be surgically removed. When the doctors asked if she wanted to keep the darn thing, she declined. She could walk fine and the pain was minimal, so Charlie let herself enjoy being safe and at home. Her temporary home, at least.

"Do you need anything, sweetheart?" Craig asked for the hundredth time.

"No, thanks, I'm good. Seriously, Craig, I'm fine."

He crossed his arms over his chest.

"Hovering must run in your family, because Alexandra does the same thing. Not that I don't appreciate it. I do," she said when he looked sheepish. He'd come to the hospital each day, and some nights he hadn't left. If she didn't already know she loved him, she would be hard-pressed to doubt it now.

Craig grinned. "It's because I love you that—"

"That what?"

"It's because I love you," he began as someone put a key in the front door and unlocked it, "that I asked Casey to come over and not my sister."

"I'm here," Casey said. "You can leave now."

She glanced between Casey and Craig. "You gave her a key?"

Casey laughed. "It took a bit of convincing, but he

saw things my way."

"I—"

"How are you feeling?" Casey took a seat next to Charlie on the couch. "You look a whole hell of a lot better."

"I'm fine." Charlie shifted when Craig picked up his keys. "Where are you going?" He bent down and kissed her and her cheeks flamed.

Craig stepped back and winked. "I'm going to see Noah again. The last couple times I've kept our visits light, but I think he's well enough now to answer some questions."

"All right, but don't be too hard on him, okay?" She ignored Casey, who was making a production of rolling her eyes. "And take him the soup I made." He did as she asked, and she smiled. He was an obedient man.

"I'll see you later, sweetheart. Bye, Casey."

"Later," Casey said, then turned to Charlie as the door closed behind him. "So, what's up?"

"Not much. I've only been out of the hospital for twenty-four hours." And Craig had given her one hot homecoming, but she'd keep that to herself.

"Pops said you're gonna stay here with 'that man.' His words not mine." Casey laughed. "You gotta love him!"

Charlie grinned. Pops never changed. "Well, Craig asked, and until my house is finished, it will do. When Mackenzie comes home, it'll be different. He moved everything out of the office and bought a twin bed and a ton of toys. Go look for yourself." When he'd brought her here yesterday and showed her the room, Charlie had cried. He'd even painted it pink.

"Looks good," Casey said, coming back.

"What's wrong?" Charlie stared at her sister. "Are you crying?"

"It's obvious how much Craig loves you and Mack, and for some reason it causes my hormones to spike, sprout wings, and come out my tear ducts, that's all."

Charlie bit her lip. "I see."

"So when's Mack coming home?"

"In two weeks. Why?" Charlie sensed there was more to this than Casey wanting to change the subject. In fact, Casey was fidgeting...then the answer hit her. "You're going to have to get used to Jake, Casey. The man's Ryan's brother, and he's not going anywhere."

Casey's sigh was heavy, and her eyes narrowed. "I know. I just don't like the way he treats Ryan. It's like he couldn't give a flying f—"

"Jake's not like Ryan; he doesn't wear his heart on his sleeve." She smiled when her sister snorted. Charlie had thought Jake was a bit of a jerk the first time she'd met him too, but if you looked hard enough...

"Yeah, well, Ryan does have a good heart—the best."

"He does."

"Craig seems to have a good heart too," Casey said.

Charlie turned to fully face Casey, who rarely talked about touchy-feely things. "He does, Casey."

Her sister stared at her hands. "And he makes Alexandra smile in a way I haven't seen in years." She pointed a finger at Charlie. "Not that that doesn't make me wary, 'cause it does, for some reason."

"He's her brother—flesh and blood. He's really hers, not by a piece of paper or a name, but by blood. It makes a difference."

"It doesn't make a difference for us."

"Yes, but we're not Alex. She—oh, I don't even know."

"What do you mean? You *always* know everything about everybody. People are drawn to you like wheels on an open road; they tell you shit."

"I'm well aware of that, but maybe it's time I wasn't so involved in other people's lives. I have my own to live." And for the first time in a long time Charlie had let herself dream again—

"Could you maybe do that tomorrow and fill me in today?"

****

Craig took a seat in one of the oversized chairs in Noah's plush den and sipped his water. A few weeks ago, he'd sat in this same spot and, Craig realized with a grin, in the same clothes; the only difference was he had more answers—not all, but most—and he was in love.

"So when do you take your duties as sheriff back?"

"Doctors said next week." Noah shrugged. "So tomorrow."

Craig chuckled. "That's good for you, but bad for Jasper. Any idea what he's going to do?"

"I think he's planning on taking a vacation. He's been sheriff for over thirty years; the man deserves a little R and R." He sighed. "What is it, Craig? I know you want to ask something, so for the love of Christ ask."

His good humor faded and he asked, "Why didn't you tell me your mother faked her own death? And what happened to her after you found her? And why the *hell* didn't you ever tell me about it?"

"I figured you found the file when it wasn't where I'd left it."

Craig shrugged. No need for Noah to know exactly what went down.

Noah stood and stared out the window. "I didn't tell you because within twenty-four hours of Fletcher, Dad, and I getting Mother out of the cult, she was dead."

Craig swallowed. "How?"

"She slit her wrists in the hotel bathroom."

"God, Noah, I'm sorry." What the hell could he say?

Noah shrugged and poured himself a scotch from the sideboard. "Dad called in favors so everything was swept under the proverbial rug. But in the end, he couldn't live with knowing she would rather be dead then be with us again. Then he made his own choices, and just like that, both my parents were dead."

Craig rubbed his hands over his face. "Noah…" He didn't know what to say. The FBI had covered up Uncle John's suicide by saying he'd died on the job. Technically he had, but they all knew Noah's father had jumped in front of that bullet.

"I've come to grips with it." He sipped from his glass.

"Then what happened with Fletcher?"

Noah sat back down. "I had offered her an obscene amount of money to find my mother, but after everything that happened, she wouldn't take it…not at first."

Craig didn't think he wanted to know, but he asked anyway. "What did you do?"

"You have to understand...I needed her to take the money—not wanted, needed! I had to get closure; all loose ends *had* to be tied...but she wouldn't take the damn money. Finally, I told her it was the least she could do. After all, if it weren't for her, both of my parents would be alive."

"You can't believe that!"

He swirled the liquor in the glass. "No, I don't. But she hated me for guilting her into taking the money, and I resented her for the same reason. Thus our war began. Turns out we excel at hating each other."

Craig could only stare at his cousin.

"Next question?"

"Okay." Craig sat back, then said, "Fletcher was working with you investigating Daemon Randle. Why? And why didn't you tell me when I asked you to look into him?"

"She brought the case to *me*—don't ask why, I don't have an answer. All I do know is she suspected Daemon of murdering Rick, but she couldn't prove it. I looked into it as she asked but couldn't see the connection."

"She was right though. Dana said Daemon had murdered their brother." Craig wouldn't ever forget all the venom the woman had spewed.

"Jasper told me," Noah said. "Had a visit from Mr. McKay too. And I'll tell you what I never wanted to tell them: she was using herself to get into his twisted world. We didn't have proof he'd killed Rick, but we knew he was dirty, tangled up in a web of God knows what."

"Then why would she—"

"She said he'd figured out what she was doing, so

she needed to flip the script. She told Randle she'd been investigating him but stopped because she'd fallen in love with him, that what he'd done didn't matter to her. The son of a bitch *really* got off on that; it made him feel powerful or some shit."

"So Fletcher didn't love him?" Craig sat up straighter. "But Charlie said she'd had a major breakdown at her house."

"She knew the place was bugged. But she didn't know who—if anyone—was listening; she didn't want to give anything away. She had to make it seem like she thought Daemon was innocent of all wrongdoing. She was damn convincing."

"She slept with him!"

"You don't need to remind me...Fletcher's a dedicated individual."

"She was a virgin." How was he going to tell Charlie this? Craig winced when Noah spit his scotch all over the place.

"Oh, that's fucking wonderful." Noah wiped his face with his sleeve. "The things I said to—never mind. Christ."

Craig could imagine what his cousin had said, none of it good. But what was bugging him was why, why would she do it? He voiced this to his cousin.

"Who the hell knows?"

"Do you think he killed himself?"

"Fletcher claimed he didn't. I saw the crime scene, and it was a textbook case. That's why I let Dana Randle in here. She wanted to talk about her brother's murder. She was well aware Fletcher had been investigating Daemon; then she fucking stabbed me."

"She must have been *very* convincing—Fletcher, I

mean—if he asked her to marry him. And it must have sent Dana into a rage."

"A killing rage to be accurate. As far as Fletcher's concerned, we won't know any of the gory details until she tells someone. I'm pretty sure it won't be me. And as far as not telling you the truth when you asked me to look into Daemon, I honestly didn't know what the hell to say. You wanted Fletcher to know the truth about him, but she knew more than anyone."

Craig stood and turned to go. "Thanks for being honest with me."

"Hey, Craig?"

"Yeah?"

"The gun, the one you used to kill Dana Randle, where'd you get it?"

"You know, Noah, I've wondered the same thing," Craig said and waved before he shut the door.

****

"Fletcher!" Charlie guessed later that night. Craig had come home and had an early dinner with her and Alex. Then he told them what he'd learned at Noah's, and they all agreed it wasn't to leave the family.

"You think?" Craig asked.

"Someone called Jasper to let him know where Dana Randle's car was. They called Jasper, not 9-1-1. And if anyone could get into a place without anyone being the wiser, it would be Fletcher," Alexandra said.

"I swear she was at the hospital too. I thought I'd dreamed it up." Charlie smiled. Fletcher wouldn't have left them to fend for themselves. No, she would always fight the good fight.

Alex studied her manicure. "You never mentioned it."

"I thought I'd dreamed it." She couldn't soothe Alex, so she turned to Craig. "Where else did you go today?"

"I stopped by your dad's store to get some wood to repair the damage at the bar."

"I'm so sorry you had to close this week. Just when you'd opened it too." Charlie smiled when he kissed her and said not to worry. She would try not to, but she wasn't promising anything.

Chapter Twenty-Four

Charlie held her daughter as tight as she could. The minute Jake had pulled up, Charlie opened the door to reach for her. Her hair had grown, and Charlie was sure she was a little taller, tanner too. She looked beautiful.

"Mama, you squeezing me," Mack said through a giggle. "I'm so 'cited to be home I can't think right, but if you don't let go, I think I'ma gonna have an accident."

"I'm sorry, baby. I'm just so glad to see you!" Charlie kissed her again.

"I'm Jake. You must be Craig." Jake Keller stuck out his hand.

Craig shook it and grinned. "You *do* look like Ryan—after he's been on a binge."

Jake wore his long hair in a manbun and torn jeans with a leather jacket instead of Armani, but there was no denying he was Ryan's twin.

Jake laughed. "I get that a lot. Shit," he mumbled. "Mind if I use your bathroom?"

"Help yourself," Charlie said, turning to wave at Casey as she pulled up and parked. She smiled at Jake's hasty retreat up the stairs.

Craig held out his arms to Mack and grinned when she jumped into his embrace. "Hi there, sweets."

"Pepper!" Mack shouted and gave Craig a big kiss. Charlie's heart melted at the sight.

Casey stood next to her. "That's sweet."

"Yeah." She sniffed. Craig whispered in Mackenzie's ear and more tears sprang up in Charlie's eyes when her daughter broke into a fit of giggles. She went to the back of Jake's truck and started pulling out Mack's things. That's when she saw it—Mack's treasure box.

"Mackenzie, where did you get this?" Charlie asked when her daughter headed her way only to stop in her little tracks. "Where, honey? Mama thought it was destroyed in the fire."

"Where's Uncle Jake?" Mack asked, looking around, then staring at her shoes.

"Mackenzie?" Charlie asked.

"Auntie Fletcher went back into the fire for it. She brought it to me; she was with me for most of my trip."

"Really?" Charlie looked at Casey, who seemed as clueless as she was.

"Uh-huh! She came, and then left, and then came back again. We had lots and lots of fun. We spun in the teacups 'til we got sick!"

"Jacob Keller, get your ass down here!" Casey screeched. "Sorry, Mack."

"It's okay, Auntie Casey. You can put money in the no-profanny jar next time."

"What's going on?" Craig asked, putting his arm around Charlie's shoulder as Jake came back down the stairs.

"Jake's gonna tell us," Casey said while pulling out her cell. "If Ryan knew about this, he's gonna be spending an awful lot of time here with Alex!"

"Ryan doesn't know a damn thing!" Jake said. "Fletch came to stay with us to fill me in on what was going on. But more than that, she wanted to spend some time with Mack."

"Was she here when—?"

"Yeah, she said she helped out where she could, and then she came to spend the rest of the time with her niece."

"Why'd she go to you?" Casey asked after hanging up on Ryan.

"What can I say? We're friends. I like the kid, and she trusts me." Jake crossed his arms over his chest.

"Did she say where she was going?" Charlie asked. She stepped back as Craig lifted Mack up in his arms again, and more vehicles pulled into the parking area. She wasn't really surprised to see Ryan or her parents.

"Nope."

"She said she wanted to spend time with me 'cause she had to be staying somewhere else for a while," Mack said from her perch in Craig's arms.

"Charlie, why don't we get Mack settled in, and then we can all meet back at Alex's," Craig suggested.

"All right. Everyone go to Alex's. We'll be there in a few minutes," Charlie said and followed Craig upstairs after her parents had hugged their granddaughter.

Once Mackenzie had stopped jumping up and down after seeing her room, Charlie began to unpack her small bags. She listened to her daughter chatter on and on about her trip. She'd be talking about this for weeks, but Charlie didn't mind.

"Charlie?"

"Yeah?" She stopped what she was doing when Craig came in and sat on the bed.

"Come sit with me a minute." Craig patted the

mattress next to him and waited for her to sit. Once she sat down, Craig slipped off the bed and onto his knees.

"Ohmygod," Charlie screeched. He couldn't be…

"Charlie McKay, I love you and your daughter with all of who I am. I've asked Mackenzie and your parents if it would be all right with them if I asked you to marry me and they said yes. And I know it seems too soon, but…I know a good thing when I see it," he said with a sheepish grin. "So, Charlie, will you marry me?"

A million thoughts crashed into Charlie's brain. "I can't."

"Mama!" Mack cried.

Craig sat down hard. "You're saying no…I hadn't thought—"

"No! No, Craig, no…I mean—damn it."

Mack gasped. "Mama, you said a bad word."

"I know, Mack, sorry." Charlie dropped into Craig's lap and took his face into her hands; his cheeks were wet. "I meant I can't have a wedding with Fletcher gone; but I love you with all that I am, and yes, I *will* marry you." She smiled when he fastened his mouth onto hers. She kissed him back with gusto until Mack's giggles had her pulling away.

"Give me heart failure, why don't you!" Craig grinned, then straightened, his expression serious. "There's one more thing I need to ask."

Charlie's heart dipped. "Okay?"

"I'd like to adopt Mackenzie and make her ours."

Mack gulped air and tears filled her eyes. "You wanna be my daddy?"

"Yes, sweets, I want to be your daddy. What do you say, Charlie?"

"Yes, of course," she whispered and hugged him

hard. Mack's small arms came around them. They were going to be a family.

"Waits a minute," Mack shouted and jumped up on the bed. "Mama needs a ring."

"Oops. Sorry," Craig said and reached into his pocket. He pulled out a diamond ring set in white gold in the shape of a heart.

"Oh, Craig, it's beautiful. But it's extravagant, and you just opened your business."

"Well, honey, I did sell a profitable security firm," he said, slipping the ring on her finger.

"Oh!" She was staring at the diamond. He nudged her, and she looked up at him.

"And remember when I said Aunt Jude had left most of her estate to Noah? She left me a lot too."

"The money doesn't matter, I—"

"I know it doesn't, but I know you'll worry about it, and me. I wanted to ease your mind."

It amazed her how well he knew her. Giddiness welled up inside her, and she snagged Mack's hand. "Let's go tell everyone."

They were all in Alexandra's kitchen. Charlie cleared her throat and was about to make her announcement when Mack yelled, "We getting married!"

Everyone stopped talking for two seconds, then erupted. Charlie was bombarded by the females of her family while Craig got slaps on the back and shook hands.

"I might have a small complaint," Alex said, getting glares from both Casey and Jake.

Craig frowned. "What is it, Alexandra?"

Charlie sighed.

"No one else sees a problem here? My sister is marrying my brother," she said, deadpan.

No one spoke until Charlie broke into a fit of giggles. "I just can't see it," Charlie said, hugging her future husband.

"What?"

"Alexandra McKay on Jerry Springer...Can you imagine?" Charlie laughed along with everyone else while Alex turned pale.

Epilogue

"Well, I did it," Charlie said, closing the apartment door behind her. She couldn't wait for their house to be finished. If Craig and her father would only stop adding things here and there, then they'd probably be home by now. Not that she was complaining.

Craig looked up from his seat on the couch. "How'd she take it?"

Charlie sighed. "About as well as you can imagine. I told Alexandra that she had to make things right with Fletcher and bring her home, not just for her own sake but for the family's too. Not to mention Casey is driving everyone bananas—who knew what a buffer Fletcher was for Casey's temper!"

Craig smirked, but they both knew he wouldn't comment on the latter.

"I told Alexandra I would not have a wedding without Fletcher, and if she didn't bring her back within two months, we were going to go to the justice of the peace by ourselves and be done with it."

"You don't think that was too harsh, do you?" he asked, getting up and following her into the kitchen.

"No, she needed a little kick in the pants. Besides, I know Alex, and she'll find Fletcher. She wants to be maid of honor so bad, she can taste it."

He shook his head.

"Is Mack asleep already?"

"She's spending the night with your parents."

Charlie laughed. "I told you Savannah McKay gets what she wants."

"She's tricky. I didn't even realize what I was agreeing to until Mack was jumping up and down talking about a sleepover."

Charlie snorted. "That sounds like my mother. Why don't I go change, then we can watch a movie?"

"Sounds like a plan to me."

She kissed his cheek and headed in to the other room. "Let's make some popcorn too!"

"What do you want to watch?" Craig asked when she came back from changing into her PJs.

"*Annie*," she said grinning at him.

Craig would never admit it, but he kinda liked the movie; he groaned appropriately though. Once the popcorn was ready, he took his place next to her on the couch. "Hey, Charlie."

"Yeah?" She turned to him with the remote in her hand.

"I want to show you something." He took off his sweater and turned around.

Her fingers caressed the swollen red patch of skin on his back. "Oh, Craig," she whispered. "I don't know what to say…You got the other half of my heart."

He turned back around and lifted her in his lap. "I only thought it was right, you know? You have my heart, and I have yours. Together we make a whole and all that shit." He kissed her wet cheeks.

"This is the nicest thing you could ever do for me. When did you think of it?"

"The first time I saw yours." When she gave him a "yeah right" look, he continued. "No, really. I thought if I ever loved someone enough to get half their heart permanently placed on my body, I would. And I love you more than enough." He smiled when she kissed him. Then groaned when she bit his lip. "What about the movie?" he asked when she got up and headed for their bedroom.

"Who needs a movie when we can make our own happy ending?"

A word about the author...

W. L. Brooks likes to write like she reads—with a bit of mystery, romance, suspense, and, to keep it interesting, the occasional dash of the paranormal. Living in Western North Carolina, she is currently working on her next novel.

www.ingramcontent.com/pod-product-compliance
Lightning Source LLC
Chambersburg PA
CBHW051536260626
47170CB00003B/954